Magic in the Snow

Ryan Jo Summers

MAGIC IN THE SNOW
Copyright © 2020 by Ryan Jo Summers

ISBN: 978-1-68046-997-4

Published by Satin Romance
An Imprint of Melange Books, LLC
White Bear Lake, MN 55110
www.satinromance.com

Published in the United States of America.

Cover Design by Caroline Andrus

Dedicated to my Lord, Jesus Christ, for allowing me to continue down this incredible journey.

Dedicated to Susan Hogle; sister, friend, and literary conspirator.

Dedicated with sincere appreciation to my fans who accommodate my dreams by reading my books.

C edar Falls looked the same as when Dawson Patrick left it. She stopped her truck and looked down Main Street. It was a perfect Hallmark Christmas scene, or a Thomas Kincaid painting come to life. She shook her head, not quite able to believe she was back in Maine.

She shivered against the cold air coming in off the Atlantic, silently cursed it under her breath, and looked at the snowy street view before her. Assorted shops lined the snow-covered sidewalks of Main Street, their business signs swinging in the wind. Most were old houses converted to stores. She suspected many still housed apartments above for rent or for the shopkeepers. Some were white Colonial clapboard, several elegant Victorian with turrets, others were brick, and a few were Tudor. Most harkened back to the 1800's era when the town settled. All were decorated with merrily twinkling lights to match the blinking ones on each black lamppost dotting the length of the street. Red ribbon bows fluttered in the crisp wind.

She exhaled a deep sigh. *Hallmark.*

The things you do for family.

She rolled the window down a few inches and let the cool

ocean air in to circulate throughout the SUV. She inhaled the salt-tinged scent and sighed again.

She looked at her three suitcases in the back, one bought specially before she left Roanoke, Virginia and filled with thrift store chunky sweaters, flannel shirts, corduroy pants, and extra gloves, scarves, boots and gloves. Plus one colorful case full of gently used, new things for her son, Adam. She thought she was done with needing a heavy winter wardrobe when she left Maine seven years ago. Apparently not.

Traffic was light as she eased through town, and then picked up speed on the other side. Her destination was her dad's place, her old home, about five miles out of Cedar Falls. She glanced in the backseat and she smiled at Adam.

"How are you doing, buddy?" she asked her son.

He bobbed his blond head and smiled back at her, showing off his dimples. He hugged Bear-Bear tight. Her heart melted at the sight of his trusting face. He'd been so patient and well-behaved during their nine-hundred-mile trip.

Peter has no idea what he walked out on.

Dawson turned her attention back to the road, as her mind traveled two different paths of thought. The scenes before her were familiar. This used to be her way home. She drove by her old school, a three-story, L-shaped brick building that housed K through twelve. Automatically she made the turns to reach her destination. No GPS needed here in Cedar Falls. She glanced back at Adam again.

His position was as it had been for most of their journey, sitting straight in his car seat and watching intently out the window. How much of what he saw did he understand? Peter swore Adam processed next to nothing of what he experienced. Dawson disagreed. She had so much proof that her son had a decent understanding of life for his age.

Peter was an idiot. In so many ways.

She turned on the wipers to brush away the thin layer of snow that fell on the windshield.

"Look at the snow, Adam. See the snow falling?"

"Snow."

She smiled back at him. "That's right, sweetie. Snow. Good job."

Then she saw her destination; a rusty, dented mailbox. 1135 Patrick. It leaned haphazardly to the left, as if it had been hit a few times. Well, she did bump into it once when she was seventeen and late getting home that one night, but her dad had propped it back up. Now it bore witness to more recent attacks than just hers. Her fingers curled around the wheel and her heart rate sped up.

"Snow," Adam repeated, almost making her jump.

"Yes. Snow. We're here now. This is where I lived when I was young." She pointed through the windshield at the pale yellow, two-story farmhouse. She tried to make her voice upbeat, but the sight of her old home closed off her throat. Her brother had not been exaggerating.

Josh was an anesthesiologist with Doctors Without Borders. He'd come home to visit Dad during one of his rare breaks. It had been his first visit home in several years and he was shocked. Right before he left again, he called Dawson and outlined his concerns.

For Dawson, the timing proved to be...convenient. It did not take her long to wrap up her business in town and pack for Adam and herself and hit the road. Since they had nowhere else to go, returning to Cedar Falls seemed...fortuitous.

Josh promised to provide some money if she could chip in too and together, they could get their dad squared away. So she agreed and budgeted some of her savings to the dad cause. Since Peter absolved himself from Adam, he was freed from any child support. And because he had the better lawyer, and she had the wimpy lawyer, he was also freed from any alimony. Dawson left with her savings and her retirement from her job. Period.

Adam kicked the seat, jarring her back to the present.

"Well, buddy, we're here now, so we're going to make this work. Right?" *Because there was no going back, and she couldn't think of anywhere else to go.*

She inhaled a deep breath and slowly let it out. Rinse and repeat. She took another breath and let it out. She could do this. She went around the car and helped Adam out of his car seat. Once free, he held Bear-Bear in one chubby hand and clutched her hand with his other. She held him tight, hoping he didn't pick up on her nervousness.

They mounted two steps. The door opened and Dawson's pulse skipped. "Hi, Dad."

Her father leaned in the doorway, a disbelieving expression on his weathered face.

"It's me. Dawson. I've come at Josh's request." She thought it best to preface her visit with a stamp of suggestion from the golden child.

"Who's that?" He stabbed a bony finger to her side.

"This is your grandson, Adam Lloyd Patrick."

"Lloyd?" Her dad tilted his head to one side.

"Yes, he's named after you." *One more thing that ticked Peter off.*

He looked beyond her to the car. "Patrick. Your husband's all right with using your maiden name for the child?"

"He isn't 'the child', Dad. His name is Adam." She tried to keep the edge from her voice, but she'd had her fill of people talking about Adam as if he wasn't there. "Please use his name."

"Where's your husband?"

Her dad ignored her request and looked closer at her truck, as if he expected a man to climb out. Dawson exhaled. "Peter and I are divorced. It's just Adam and me." *So recently divorced, the ink is barely dry on our decree.* She watched his lips thin and eyes

4

narrow. Dad didn't believe in divorce. Well, neither did Dawson, but sometimes divorce wasn't a two-way decision like marriage was. Beside her, Adam shifted and tried to pull away from her. The weariness of almost twenty hours on the road with a toddler sapped her energy.

"Look, Dad, I'm here because Josh asked me to come. He is concerned about the house and you. But if you can't offer your daughter and grandson some basic hospitality, say so and we'll go." *Somewhere.*

He scrubbed his chin. "Of course, come on in. How old did you say little Lloyd was?"

"Adam, and he's almost three." She led him up the steps, steering him around the rotted boards. "Let's go see Grandpa, little man," she said cheerfully. Shy, Adam clung as close to her leg as he could. She could see in his face he wanted to explore but he kept glancing at her dad. He did tend to be wary of all strangers and she insisted it was a normal by-product of his age.

"The house has seen better years," her dad said as he led them past the entrance, down the short hall that opened to the kitchen and dining room. Dawson felt her jaw drop as they walked along. This was her childhood home? Her mom would be appalled at the peeling wallpaper, chipped paint, creaky boards and more. Better years? What an understatement. Now she understood part of her brother's concern.

She stopped in the kitchen and released Adam's hand. She turned in a circle and looked at the cabinet doors hanging crooked, the dripping faucet and missing sections of flooring. She placed her hands on her hips and faced her dad.

"I can fix this. Give me a little time, and I will fix this."

Her dad shrugged. "If you're so sure, get your things and bring them in."

It wasn't an open-arms, engraved invitation to stay, but she would take it. She gave him a nod. "I'll put Adam in my old room, and I can take the spare bedroom if that's okay."

Again, her dad shrugged. She began to wonder if some of Josh's other concerns might be correct too. Well, in time she would get a much better idea of what was going on. Right now, she had a temporary place to stay, enough repair work to keep her busy indefinitely and hopefully Adam might get to know his grandfather. The only problem was, she knew nothing about home repair.

Early the next morning Dawson cooked breakfast from the meager supplies her dad had on hand. She had found a can of concentrated orange juice in the freezer and had that floating in hot water while the coffee slowly perked. She made two lists as she buttered toast and scrambled eggs. One was labeled *groceries* and the other she called *house*. The grocery list was going much easier than the house one. So far, she'd identified no less than seven different types of repairs, and she was clueless where to even start. Back home she'd march her list into the local building center and the helpful people there would fill her cart with everything she'd need and recommend professionals for things she felt were beyond her. Cedar Falls didn't even have a local hardware store. According to dad, the nearest one was the next town over.

"Eat up, little man, we have another road trip ahead of us." She forked scrambled eggs onto Adam's plate.

"Bear-Bear?"

"Sure, we can bring Bear-Bear."

"The boy doesn't talk much, does he?"

Her dad took a seat at the table and she grimaced. "Adam, Dad. Please refer to my son as Adam. And yes, he talks when he wants to." She handed over a coffee cup now that it was done perking. Next, she went to check the status of the thawing juice.

After pouring glasses for herself and Adam, she handed the pitcher to her dad and took a seat for herself. She passed over the plate of buttered toast and the jar of jelly.

"And what did you and Josh discuss when he was here?"

Her dad thoughtfully chewed and swallowed. Dawson took the moment to breathe in the scents of warm yeasty bread and coffee.

"We talked about the Panthers. They're going to have a great season. And the Warriors have been playing well."

Sports. She felt her jaw tighten. "Didn't you two talk about anything besides sports? Like the condition of the house? The lack of groceries?"

"We decided it might be a dry summer."

"Oh for Pete's—" She squeezed her eyes shut and pinched two fingers over the bridge of her nose. Either her dad or her brother was off their rocker and she wasn't sure which one.

"Dad?" Adam looked up, his eyes lighting up hopefully.

Dawson's heart crushed. "No, sweetheart. Daddy's not here." She reached over and smoothed his hair. She wanted to pull him into a hug.

"Go see?"

She blinked back the tears. "Maybe later."

She knew he'd never bother making the trip to come see his son. He had glossed over visitation during the court hearings. The very fact he allowed her to have Adam's last name revert to her maiden name without argument told her all she needed to know. He was absolving Adam from his life. And she would be damned if she ever let that fact break her little boy's heart.

She turned back to her dad. "Adam and I will go into town and see what I can find for the house and pick up some food. Is there anything special you'd like?"

"Nope. This was good." He stood up and walked into the living room. Exhaling a heavy sigh, she scooped up their dirty plates and cups. "Baby, you just stay there for me. Once I wash up these dishes, we'll grab Bear-Bear and get going." She gave him that big hug and kissed his head. She loved running her fingers through his silky-soft blond hair. Thank goodness he had her hair, blue eyes, and mostly her facial features. The fewer reminders of Peter he gave her, the better. He smiled as she placed a piece of paper and some crayons in front of him.

Twenty minutes later she and Adam were on their way to town. Fortunately, he'd forgotten about hearing what seemed like his daddy's name. Thank goodness. But it was more proof of his intelligence. She added magnets to her shopping list to secure his artwork to the fridge. She reached town and studied the meager offerings. Two grocery stores, one a local mom and pop and the other a regional chain. She'd find a better selection and maybe better prices at the chain store, but she always liked supporting local-owned shops. And there was not one hardware store. Darn.

On the other hand, she felt a shadow of relief because she still had no clue what she needed to do or get. Her brother owed her big time for taking on this project—while he talked about sports and weather.

"Looks like we're heading out of town, buddy. We'll get the groceries on the way back."

She passed a sign and her foot eased off the gas. *Chapter Twenty-Five Bookstore.* Clever name. An idea formed in her mind. If the bookstore had home improvement books, she could better figure out what she needed before heading over to the hardware store. At least she would be forearmed. And she'd feel less stupid.

"Change of plans, Adam." She pulled the truck over to the curb and threw it into park. "Gloves and hat, sweetie. It's cold out."

Dawson and Adam walked along the shoveled sidewalk to the bookstore. A light dusting of snow still covered the brick pathway. They stopped at each storefront to admire the unique Christmas displays. Twinkling lights, perfectly decorated little trees, wrapped gifts in pretty paper, white or gold angels, and more filled the windows. Dawson laughed along with Adam, taking delight in his merriment. Christmas was for the children. Watching his blue eyes light up like the Christmas trees, she wished she could freeze time.

"Cold," he finally said, and wrapped his arms around his middle.

She hastened to the bookstore and ushered him in. "It'll be warm in here, buddy."

Immediately the smell of old and new books enveloped her, as did the warm air. She glanced around for the holiday decorations. The only thing she saw was a spindly tree standing in the corner, with four gold balls hanging from its sparse branches. She blinked twice. Was it a joke? That tree made Charlie Brown's tree look the National Christmas tree in D.C. Confused, she looked around for the staff.

"Can I help you?"

The baritone voice directed her attention to the old wooden counter stacked high with books. Behind the counter stood a man, one that many women probably wanted to find under their own Christmas tree. He towered over her by several inches, and his broad shoulders gave the impression of firm muscles beneath the checkered flannel. His smile was cautious but friendly. Gold, wire-framed glasses framed brown eyes crinkled at the corners. Dark brown hair curled near his ears and eyes. The early morning scruff on his chin only added to the rugged appeal. *Yum.*

"Um, yes, I wondered if you had some books."

He looked around. "Yes, I have a few. Can you be more specific?"

Heat filled her face. Oh, for Pete's sake! He hadn't even grinned at her faux pas. "Home repair," she blurted. "I have a home that needs repair."

"All right." He stepped around the counter and she took one long moment to appreciate his long legs and how well those worn jeans clung to them. Muscular. He led her to a row of books and gestured to a shelf. "Home repair." His gaze flickered to Adam where he clung to her leg. "Is your little buddy going to help fix up the house too?"

She grinned at his reference to little buddy. "He might. This is Adam. I'm Dawson."

He knelt and extended his hand to Adam. "Hi, Adam. I'm Samuel."

Adam tightened his grip on Dawson. "Don't take it personal, but he's shy with new people. It normally takes him a while to warm up."

Samuel stood up. "No worries. So—Dawson—here are the home repair books I have on hand."

She was a little disappointed he didn't offer to take her hand. She'd bet his grip was strong and warm. But he made an effort to connect with Adam and that was pure gold in her eyes. She brushed her hair aside and scanned the titles. "Building a patio, installing a fishpond, and putting in a shed." She looked up at Samuel. Her heart skipped a little. He was good looking. She cleared her throat. "I hate to sound picky, but these aren't quite what I had in mind."

"What did you have in mind?"

She exhaled. "Plumbing, basic electricity and wiring, repairing drywall, carpentry and cabinets. That sort of repair."

His mouth formed an O of surprise as she named her list.

"That is some serious repair. And you're going to do all that?" He arched one brown eyebrow, his tone almost a dare.

Dawson lifted her chin a little higher and squared her shoulders. "Yes, I intend to. Now, that's why I need the books. Do you have them or not?"

He scrubbed his scruffy chin, like her dad did. "Not on hand, but I can probably order them. Come back to the counter and I'll see what I can find."

He led them back to the counter. "Come on around." He patted the wooden top and stepped to a computer on a lower desk attached to the counter. He moved the mouse and the screen flickered to life.

She watched as he scrolled around and then pointed to the display.

"Okay, here are some repair titles. Look and see if they would work for you."

She settled into the chair he offered and lifted Adam onto her lap. "Yes, these are more like it." She pointed out specific titles that offered descriptions suited to her needs. As her finger trailed the monitor and he took down titles and information he needed, their hands brushed. Startled, Dawson looked into his brown eyes and her breath paused. He looked just as affected. He turned away first and cleared his throat. Well, he just made his point loud and clear. She waved to the screen.

"Can you get these?"

"I can order them." He fluttered the list he'd created. "They should be here in about two days."

Two days. She was at a standstill for two days? She chewed her lip as she considered the options. She hated to go to a repair store and have no idea where to start. The books would tell her what she needed and how to figure how many of each item. In the long run, they would save her time and money. She just had to wait two days.

"Okay, go ahead and please order them. I really need them as soon as they come in."

"Yeah, it sounds like you have some important ventures planned. Electricity? Carpentry?" He flashed her a smile. It did wonderful things for his looks. "Is this a side job of yours?"

"No. It's…complicated."

He nodded. "I get it. If you leave me your number, I can call you once the shipment arrives." He passed the paper with the list to her. "That way you won't waste any time."

She wrote her cell phone number down. "I appreciate that." She handed the list back. "Tell me, what is the deal with your sad little Christmas tree?" She inclined her head toward the pitiful sapling.

He looked taken aback. "What do you mean?"

"It is the most pathetic holiday tree I've ever seen."

"It does the job. It adds the Christmas cheer required by the town's good citizens."

Dawson thought about the lovely lights and festive decorations and stately, full trees she and Adam had seen. She looked back at Samuel's dejected evergreen. It was almost comical. She took a couple steps closer, aware he was following. "Don't you want somewhere to put presents?"

She watched his lips thin and wondered what was wrong with an innocent question.

"I don't plan on giving anyone presents and I don't expect anyone to give me gifts."

Her breath hitched. "Samuel, that is quite possibly the saddest thing I've ever heard. Don't you even want an ugly sweater?"

"No." He held his palm out to her. "Let me stop you right there, all right? I know this town lives and breathes all things Christmas and embraces the holiday with an open-armed spirit that sometimes doesn't know when to quit. I put up that tree and a handful of decorations to avoid a citizen mutiny, but I do not share the sentiments of the rest of the good people of this town. I guess you need to know that since you're now a part of Cedar Falls."

She worked his speech around her mind, looking for the logic and reason. Finally, she gave up. "Well, Samuel, everyone is entitled to their views. Please do let me know when the books are in." She took Adam's hand and guided him toward the front door. She paused as she held the door open for Adam and looked back over her shoulder at Samuel as he stood behind his counter. The barest twitch of a grin threatened to betray her. "Merry Christmas," she called just before she shut the door.

Dawson and Adam walked hand and hand along the snow swept brick sidewalk. Adam giggled at the sights in each window. They entered the grocery store and immediately the strands of "Jingle Bells" came through the overhead speakers. Dawson placed Adam in the seat of the firetruck Kiddie-Kart and took out her shopping list.

She looked at it and sighed. It was exhaustive as her dad didn't have much on hand. Yet another tidbit her brother failed to mention. Some things he extolled as if they were life and death, while others he omitted completely. Maybe it was a guy thing. She lifted a shoulder in a shrug. Maybe he was afraid she wouldn't come if he'd been completely honest with her. Like she had so many other appealing options.

"Cookies?"

Adam's question jolted her back to the moment. He scooted forward in his seat as if willing the Kiddie-Kart to move.

"I'm sorry, sweetheart. Yes, we can find you some organic oatmeal raisin cookies. How does that sound?"

As she pushed Adam and added things in the cart, and the overheard songs changed from "Jingle Bells" to "We Wish You a Merry Christmas", and on to "Winter Wonderland", she thought about Samuel's firm comment regarding an expectation of no gifts and his lack of holiday spirit. What could have happened to make him dislike such a nice holiday?

"Dawson Patrick? Is that you?"

Hearing her name, she turned to the woman to her left. She took a few seconds to study her eager face.

"Wendy? Oh wow, it's you!"

She and Wendy Albright had been best friends since third grade when Wendy's family moved to town and lasting until Dawson left town. They moved their carts and hugged.

"It's so good to see you, how have you been?" Dawson asked.

"I'm good. How long have you been in town? And who is this handsome man?" Wendy knelt to introduce herself to Adam.

Dawson smiled at how Adam took Wendy's hand. She explained she and Wendy were friends and then explained to Wendy a little about her situation and Adam.

"Well, honey, I'm glad to see you back in Cedar Falls. You plan on staying?"

Dawson brushed her hair away and blew out a breath. "Long enough to get Dad and his house squared away." She explained about needing some books on the subject.

"Have you checked with Samuel Johnson at the bookstore?"

She nodded. "Yep, we just came from there, where I placed an order with him."

Wendy gripped her wrist, reminding Dawson of when they were teen-agers. "He is so hot on the outside, but so cold on the inside." She clucked her tongue. "What a waste of a prime piece of male."

Dawson agreed on most of Wendy's assessment. "What made him so chilled? How long has he been in town?"

"Let's see. He moved in about three, four years ago. He's always been the quiet loner, you know. He's happy just holed up with his books. But he's friendly enough when he needs to be."

Just friendly enough if her experience was anything to go by.

14

"No one seems to know much about him. He bought the old Cedar Falls Books and gave it a new name and then stuck his head inside his shell."

How odd. How mysterious. "Tell me about yourself, Wendy. What's new? Are you married? Kids?"

Wendy's cheeks blushed. "I've been a newlywed for about six years now. Remember Warren Anderson? He's my knight in shining armor. Together we have three kids, ages two, four and five. Warren is home with them now so I can have some quality mommy time here." She giggled and motioned to her shopping cart, already half filled with assorted goods.

Dawson shared a laugh, fully understanding. Beside her, Adam began fussing at the long delay. Wendy was ultra-quick to pick up on it. Again, she grabbed Dawson's arm.

"Honey, it was so great seeing you. We've got to get together soon. I'm in the phone book. Take care and don't let your daddy run all over you."

They hugged once more, and Dawson promised to look her up and give her a call soon. Walking away, she caught herself humming. Finally, something had gone right since she arrived in town. And, unless she was mistaken, Wendy could help shed a few rays of light on the mysterious bookstore owner. And it was refreshing to realize she was back in a town that still utilized a phone book.

Samuel closed the shop and turned off the lights. All day his thoughts returned to the blonde beauty who powered into his life. She blew in like a candy-coated snowstorm, dressed in an oversized sweater and knee-high boots, her hair piled up in a messy bun full of flyaways, and that adorable pint-sized munchkin with the wide eyes hugging her leg.

There was something in her pale blue eyes that hinted at sorrow, but she kept an upbeat candor when she assured him she could wire a house and rebuild walls. *He* probably couldn't do that stuff. She impressed him on many levels, the least of his list might be the tender way she dealt with her son—Adam. There was something about the little boy that tugged at an unseen and long-buried string deep inside his heart.

Just before he went to his upstairs apartment, he glanced over to the tree he put up each year. Once the town citizens realized that was the best he was willing to do, no one mentioned it again —until her. He tilted his head to the left. Maybe it did have a certain pathetic look to it. Or maybe it was just fine. It had been fine for years—until her.

He blew out a tired breath and trudged up the steps. It would be interesting once Miss Hurricane's books came in.

Dawson hugged Adam's sleepy head to her shoulder as the credits rolled on the Grinch movie. They've watched the movie twice so far, and Adam was a big fan.

"Max," he said, his voice muffled by her sweater.

"Umm hum. Maybe someday we can get a dog, sweetie. You can call it Max if you want." She longed for the day she would leave her dad's home, and she and Adam could settle someplace nice. She'd rent a small house, with a yard and a fence. She'd get a job and find a good day care for Adam. And she'd adopt a dog. A wistful sigh escaped her. Until she could get to work on the house, she was pretty much stuck here in Cedar Falls. Of course it wasn't like she knew where else to go. Maybe she could throw a dart at a map on the wall.

"As long as it's somewhere warmer." She turned the television to a cartoon channel and set the remote aside. "Baby, I need to go bring some firewood in, I'll only be a few minutes. Stay right here for me."

She slowly withdrew, noticing he was already engrossed in the singing...er...whatever those colorful things were on the screen. Adam was easily amused, swaying to the catchy beat of the music.

She wrapped a scarf around her neck, grabbed her coat, gloves and boots and headed out to the woodpile. Darn, she needed to split some first. Why hadn't Josh split the wood while he was here, talking about sports and weather? Her gloves weren't thick enough to fend off all the splinters and last time she split wood; she'd still ended up pulling splinters out of her palms.

"That darn Joshua." Muttering, she picked up the mallet and wedge and balanced them over a round chunk of wood. Slam. The log broke neatly into three sections. If nothing else, splitting wood was good for stress relief and probably some therapeutic benefits. "Like imaging certain undesirable faces." She giggled as she swung the mallet down on the wedge again.

Minutes later, with a large bit of wood tucked under her arm, she rushed back in the house. Was Adam still good with the cartoon? Would her dad ever help watch Adam so she could split wood and handle the repairs once she started on them? So far, he took meals with her and Adam, and might watch a TV show, but preferred his own space. He liked to sit in the rocker in the living room, the family room, or stay ensconced in his bedroom.

She dropped the wood with a thud as her cell phone rang. She tripped over the logs and snatched it off the table.

"Is this Dawson Patrick?"

The blunt, rough voice could only belong to one be-speckled, anti-Christmas, handsome man. Her heart fluttered at the quick baritone.

"Yes."

"Your books came in today."

She smiled. Great. Now she could really get some work done. "Thanks." She copied his curt speech. "We'll be in this morning."

"Okay. Bye."

She stared at the phone in her hand and shook her head. The man took abrupt to a whole new level. She moved over to the fireplace and fed a few logs into the fire, poking the embers to life. Heat lifted out into the room.

"Dad, Adam and I are running into town. Do you need anything?"

His voice drifted into the living room like a ghostly specter. "I'm not so old I can't drive myself in if I need to."

"I was only offering," she muttered under her breath, huffing into the fire. Her bangs fluttered against her forehead. Soon she'd need a haircut, as she hadn't taken time during the whirlwind divorce. Her dad closed his bedroom door and her heart sighed. "Come on, sweetie. Let's go shopping."

Adam pulled away from the dancing...things, and eagerly dressed.

"We can see more Christmas decorations."

"Ginch?"

She smiled and could not help but think of Samuel Johnson. "Yep, we'll probably see one of those too."

"Yes!"

At least her little man showed some enthusiasm over something. First, she wanted to change sweaters. On their way out, she cast one lingering look at the dishes she'd left soaking before she joined Adam with his show. Maybe while they were out the dish fairy might stop by. Hopefully, she'd bring a bunch of her friends. They could wave their magic wands and not only wash the dishes but fix each item on her list.

She helped Adam into his car seat. And if the fairies fixed the house, would her dad allow her to stay on until she came up with a better plan? She blew out another heavy breath, feeling weights settle down upon her shoulders.

"Magic."

"What's that, baby?"

Adam pointed out to the lazily tumbling snowflakes she hadn't noticed. "Magic."

His tone wasn't questioning. He seemed confident in his short statement. She studied the large flakes. "Sort of. They're snowflakes. They're frozen water like rain drops. Except these are cold. They look the same but supposedly no two are ever alike."

"Magic," Adam cheerfully affirmed as he pressed his palm to the windowpane.

Dawson's heart melted at the wonder in her son's eyes. "Yes, they sure are. You are so smart."

They arrived in town and she parked two blocks from the bookstore. "Take my hand." Together they walked the snowy brick path winding along the storefronts. City workers balanced a huge evergreen as they secured it to its base on the city square. They paused to watch, and Adam laughed at the utility trucks. Doubtlessly workers would string lights and decorate it with baubles.

She'd read in the paper how Santa was arriving Saturday to light the tree and the shop keepers were offering cocoa and caroling and games for the kids and there was even supposed to be a sleigh ride. The fire department was going to hose down part of the park and let it freeze for a small skating rink. Dawson glanced at Adam. Saturday they were coming back to town. He would have a front row seat to see Santa. Maybe she could get her dad to come too.

She remembered when she and Josh were younger, Mom and Dad always brought them to see the tree lighting, drink cocoa, meet Santa, sit on his knee to read her wish-list. How many times had she fibbed about how good a girl she'd been all year?

She glanced at Adam, his gaze riveted to the city workers and their big truck. Her heart constricted. Would he boldly approach Santa and speak? Could the child who saw magic in snowflakes have the potential to grow into complete sentences?

"I sure hope so, baby." She gave his gloved hand a squeeze. "But if not, that's okay too." Adam gave her a mystified glance and began catching snowflakes on his tongue, giggling when he caught one.

"Okay, let's go get our books. Grandpa has a long list for us."

Some stores had music playing and it filtered through the doorways, each shop offering a different song. Chimes of *Little Drummer Boy* and *Angels We Have Heard on High* made her want to stop and linger. It felt like she'd just stepped back in time to an old Christmas card. But she was on a mission today and couldn't linger.

"Here we are, Chapter Twenty-Five." She guided Adam into the space and immediately noticed the lack of holiday cheer. It smelled clean, and lacked any clutter, but it might have been June for the absence of holiday cheer. Her gaze drifted to the motley tree and the pitiful gold globes that drooped on their branches. It was just so wrong.

"Morning."

Samuel's neutral greeting snapped her attention back to the counter where he seemed to magically pop up from. She smiled at the thought and moved her hand through her hair, suddenly self-conscious.

"Hi. So you're ready to put me to work."

He blinked, a startled gaze passing over his face. "Huh?"

Still with the one-word sentences. Talking to him wasn't

much different than talking to Adam, or her dad. "The books. Now I'll have to read them and get to work on my dad's house."

"Oh." He gave her a slow nod and slid a stack of books toward her.

Dawson brought her wallet out. She hated to charge them but right now she didn't have too many other choices. Instead of taking her card, Samuel came around the counter and knelt by Adam.

"Hey, buddy. I have something you might like." He held out his hand with a shiny red and blue racecar in his palm.

Adam's eyes lit up and he reached for the car. Halfway, he stopped and looked up at Dawson. Her throat clogged with love for her son and gratitude for Samuel. She nodded and cleared her throat.

"Yes, sweetie. You may play with it."

Adam wasted no time in taking the car. He dropped to the floor and began making car sounds as he pushed it around.

"That was very kind of you."

Samuel shrugged. "I used to keep a box of cars and dolls out here for the little kids."

Interesting. A man who can hold only one and two-word conversations with her can speak a whole sentence. And he likes kids enough to keep toys out for them. Yet he dismisses Christmas as unimportant. Samuel Johnson was an enigma, but right now, Dawson wanted to hug him.

"Why don't we keep the car here for Adam to play with the next time we come in?"

His dark eyes flashed with surprise at her suggestion. "You plan to come back?"

She didn't need any more repair books. And she sure didn't need to be charging luxuries like romance novels or mysteries on her credit card. She blew out a sigh. "Sure, why not?" Now that Samuel was speaking full sentences, she regressed to short replies.

He smiled, a slow twist of his lips that reached his eyes and twirled her tummy. At her feet, Adam roared and chugged, playing for all he was worth. She'd have to search dad's house and see if they had saved any of Joshua's old toys. She'd only brought a few stuffed toys on their trip and now she regretted not packing more for him. Samuel's smile made her heart stammer. Then she realized she still held her card. "Oh, um, how much? For the books?"

Samuel named a price and she handed the card over. Their fingers brushed and he quickly looked away as he made the transaction and slid the receipt over for her to sign.

"Is that your ugly sweater?"

She took her card and receipt, jolts of electricity zapping through her fingertips.

"Um, no, this is my tacky sweater." She'd taken some tacks from her dad's garage and stitched them onto a thrift store sweater, spelling out the word NOEL. Suddenly she felt ultra-conscious of his hooded stare and she questioned the sanity of her impulsive shirt. Samuel turned to the register, his head bent.

"Stay away from magnets."

"What's your favorite Christmas movie?" she asked impulsively.

"My what?"

She stepped closer to him. "Your go-to Christmas movie. Are you old-fashioned and like Miracle on Thirty-Fourth Street? Classics like It's a Wonderful Life? Feel good with a dependable array of Hallmark movies or do you secretly binge the cartoons like Charlie Brown's Christmas?"

"I do not like Christmas shows."

She shrank a little from his stern admission.

"None at all?"

"None."

"Oh," she inhaled and drew back. "So you're more the Grinch-y type."

"Who?"

He was starting to look frustrated and she edged toward the door. "You know, the green fellow who stole Christmas from everyone else. Remember?"

"I'm sure I don't."

CHAPTER 2

"It's cold in here."

Dawson blew out a breath at her dad's words. "I was thinking we need to get a tree, Dad, a fat fir to go in that corner." She waved to the corner and hoped it distracted his thoughts of being cold. When Mom was alive, she always insisted on having a full tree in the corner of the living room and she trimmed it with all kinds of lovely ornaments, bows, garland, mistletoe, and a big wreath on the front door. Dawson and Josh had caught mom and dad kissing under the mistletoe many times. "I could haul the decorations out of the attic and pick up a tree in town at the lot." She hated the hopefulness in her voice.

"Seems smarter to be concerned about fixing the cold house than worrying about a tree."

Her dad got up from in front of the television show he'd been watching with Adam. She didn't watch to see where he was going, because she'd bet her last dollar he wasn't going out to split that pile of wood outside.

Silently cursing Joshua again, she set aside the tools and book and stood up, dusting herself off. Home repairs were evidently going to have to wait in favor of home heating. Why wasn't the heater kicking on? She'd turned the thermostat up a notch when she came in last time.

Maybe later tonight she could pop some popcorn and show Adam how to string it on a line for garland. Tomorrow she might go into town and buy a blasted tree and her dad could just get over it. She'd do it for Adam and herself. She closed the heavy book and the paper she'd been writing notes on fluttered away. She snatched it back and stuffed it inside the front cover. She walked over to the thermostat on the wall, aware of the chill now.

"It's set at 72." She turned it up one more notch, waited and sighed deeply when the furnace failed to kick on. She turned it down a notch, counted to twenty, and back up to the original setting, then moaned when the furnace remained frustratingly silent.

"What? Why? Come on." She ground her teeth and went over to snatch a book off her stack. She flipped through it. "Heating. Where is heating?" She found the chapter and quickly scanned the contents.

"Change batteries. Circuit breakers. Mounting screws. Only the red and white wires. What? This is sounding more like wiring for a lab monster than a furnace." Well, she could change the batteries, maybe, and see if that worked. She pried the faceplate off to reveal the batteries. Next, she searched the laundry room and under the kitchen sink to find the right size of batteries. She changed them out and decided it was cold enough inside that she needed to bring in more wood before she returned to the furnace issue.

She walked over to Adam and touched her finger to the tip of his nose. It was a game they sometimes played and now his nose felt cool. "Adam, sweetheart, can you stay here like a big boy? Here's a blanket." She dragged her mom's crocheted afghan blanket over and draped it around his shoulders. Wistfully she buried her nose in it and sighed. It had lost her scent a long time ago. "Watch television and I'll be right outside that window." She pointed to the window overlooking the woodpile. "Be my big boy and when I come back in, we can watch the Grinch show."

Adam had fallen in love with the green mean-spirited Grinch tape she'd found in the discount bin at the grocery store. He beamed her a big smile.

"Love Ginch."

She loved his smile. It was so innocent. So pure. "Yes, and I love you." She traced her fingers through his hair and kissed his forehead. "I'll be right back."

She moved to the closet by the door and pulled on boots, gloves, coat, and scarf. "Dad," she called into the house's interior. "I'm going to split wood. Can you keep an eye on Adam?"

Silence greeted her. She waited, heart thumping in time to the tick tock of the Grandfather clock by the mantle. Finally she gave up with a disgusted groan. If she were not here, would he simply sit and freeze, or would he have found some way to get the wood inside?

She stared at the pile and moaned. "Thanks, Josh. We can't have those specialized anesthesiologist hands of yours get roughed up, can we?"

She had a few words for her brother the next time they chatted, whenever it might be. Meanwhile she vented her irritation by splitting more wood until her shoulders stretched and complained. She dropped the tools next to the pile and picked up some logs. She balanced them in her arm and walked around to the front door.

An older blue pickup truck braked to a stop as she turned the corner and she eyed it critically. Since very few knew she was here, it had to be a friend of her dad's. Her caution turned to surprise when Samuel stepped out and slammed the cab door.

"Hi, what are you doing here?"

He looked taken aback by her lack of manners but hastened to take the bundle of wood from her.

"Hello. I'm here...to help you with this."

Without waiting for an invitation, he headed to the front door and waited for her to open it. Wordlessly, still a little stiff with shock, she swung it open for him. He motioned for her to go ahead and she led the way to the fireplace. He neatly deposited the load on the hearth and tossed two logs in the fire, poking it to life.

"Do you have more wood to bring in?" he asked, looking up at her.

"Yes, I just split a bunch more."

His eyes rounded. "You split it?"

Indignation rose within her. "Well, yes. Who else is going to do it?"

He shook his head, got up and walked back outside. She raced to the window and watched him pick up another armload of wood and head back around. She met him at the door.

"Wouldn't it be easier to bring this in through a back door?"

"It would, except the back door is broken and won't open. It's on my list to fix."

He grunted and set the logs down and returned for yet another load. After he brought in a full six loads, filling the hearth and the adjacent wood bin completely to overflowing, he stopped.

"Thank you, that will get us by for a while." She hesitated as he stood in her living room. The heat kicking out from the fire did nothing to cool her own personal furnace. "Can I get you something? Water? Coffee?"

"Water, please."

She returned with a big glass of ice water. She watched as he drained half the glass in one swallow. She reached for it. "I'll refill it."

"Where's your dad?"

"Probably in his room, sleeping." She waved to the bedrooms.

Adam came over and shyly approached Samuel.

"Well, you didn't come all the way out here to load us up with firewood. Though I appreciate that you did. So what brought you here?"

"Adam, actually. I have a book that he might like. It's in the truck." He slipped out while she refilled his glass. He returned and she opened the door. Adam stayed glued to her side, his eyes wide on Samuel.

"Hey, buddy, I thought you might like this."

He took it, inhaling sharply at the cardboard cover. He traced the picture of the whale with a dog on its back. Happily, he sat down and opened to the first page.

"That's kind, Samuel, but I really can't afford to buy...things now." What kind of mother was she that she couldn't even buy her son a book? Shame filled her cheeks.

Samuel shrugged. "Kid's books are pretty cheap. Wholesale that's like a five-dollar book. He will probably get a lot more use out of it than it's worth."

Together they watched him turn another page and inhale at the picture. He fingered the image.

"Can he read yet?"

"Only a few words."

Samuel studied Adam a minute. "He's on the spectrum, isn't he?"

Her heart dropped. "Just barely. But yes. Does it show?" She hated to ask.

"It only shows to those who know what they're looking at. I doubt most people would see it. Don't worry about the book, okay, just let him enjoy it."

She shook her head. "I can...I have five..."

He stepped closer, setting the glass on the coaster. He

wrapped his hands around her wrists, stilling her. "Dawson, let me give it to him..." He swallowed and looked down at the chipped floor for a moment. His gaze returned to hers as he slowly added, "As a gift."

If she wasn't so stunned by his hands on her arms, she might easily forget his firm affirmation that he didn't want nor give gifts. Her jaw slacked as she realized what it cost for him to give her child a present. She had no idea why he scorned gifts, but she suspected the book just cost him much more than five dollars.

"Thank you, Samuel." She licked her lips as his gaze dropped to hers and her pulse leapt. She inhaled his musky and pine scent.

"You're welcome, Dawson." He smiled, inching closer.

Her heart jumped and her eyes closed.

"I thought I heard voices. Good, you got the fire going."

She jumped, hand going to her throat and eyes flying open at her dad's words. He strolled into the room like he was coming back from a walk through the park. She looked over at Samuel, who picked up his water glass again.

"Dad, Samuel stopped by, and he got the heat going."

"Good to see you again, Lloyd," Samuel said, stepping forward to shake her dad's hand.

"Welcome, Samuel. Sit and visit a minute if you've got time."

He looked over at Dawson, then at Adam and back to her dad.

"I do. Thank you."

He settled into one of the easy chairs and Adam climbed into his lap, bringing the new book along. "Ginch. Ginch."

Samuel looked over at Dawson, his eyebrows raised.

"Um, he means Grinch."

Samuel grinned. "Is that the new name the town's people have for me now?"

Heat flooded her face at his humor. "No. I promised Adam

we'd watch the Grinch show when I finished with the wood. He loves that show."

"Ginch." Adam nodded in agreement.

Samuel chuckled. Dimples pinched his cheeks and her heart skipped and her tummy took off. Her insides felt like a carnival ride.

"Um...I need to see what's wrong with the furnace, so excuse me while you two visit." She inched toward the control panel on the wall.

"There's something wrong with the furnace too?" Samuel asked as he spun around to watch her.

She waved at it, startled by the disbelief and concern in his tone. "Probably nothing too serious." At least she hoped not. "I'm working on it." She hefted the book, open to the heating and furnace chapter that read like something a mad scientist wrote it. "See. Working on it."

She stood at the wall unit like a preacher at a pulpit, confident to her small audience but doubtful inside. She glanced at the words that looked like a foreign language and peeked over at Samuel. He'd turned back to her dad and they now engaged in low conversation. Adam sat between them, slowly pouring over the book. How close had they come to kissing? She felt his firm grip on her arms, smelled his warm breath on her face, and saw the dark spark in his eye. If her dad hadn't come shuffling out...

"My son, Joshua, is a doctor with Doctors Without Borders. He's the guy who puts the patients to sleep and keeps them breathing during surgery."

Dawson ground her teeth. You'd think Josh hung the darn moon for the way Dad was always bragging about him. One would think she'd be used to it by now. Apparently not. She finished cleaning the inside of the unit, blowing off about forty years' worth of dust and grime and turned it off again, counting to thirty.

"Joshua has traveled all over the world with his job. He's helped saved countless lives and in some of the most dangerous locations. And Dawson's work is make believe."

Dawson dropped her book and screwdriver. They thudded to the floor. She huffed a breath and turned to the men, keenly aware of Samuel's extremely interested stare.

"Dad, it's not make believe. My work is every bit as real as Josh's."

"What is your work, Dawson? When you're not repairing furnaces and hauling wood?"

She stood tall and proud. "I'm a senior software engineer." Or at least she was. She held her head high.

"Any job that needs to be explained isn't a real job."

She snorted at her dad and turned back to the control panel. Hadn't he just explained what Josh did? She had a real job up until last week. And she would have another one someday. She made a nice six-figure income. She would not let her dad's ignorance belittle her accomplishments. She peeked over at Samuel and he grinned at her, almost as if to say he understood. She hoped so, and her heart fluttered.

"I need to go turn the power off at the circuit breakers, so it's going to get quiet in here." Better to do this step before it got dark. She took her trusty book out to the back yard and pried the rusty breaker box lid up with a squeak of protest. Cobwebs broke away. She studied the breakers, labeled, scratched out and relabeled over the years. "Good grief." Finally she spotted one labeled 'furnace' next to it. "Must be the one." She squeezed her eyes shut and rested her thumb against the tab. "Please don't let me leave Adam an orphan." She inhaled, pursed her lips, and moved her thumb over.

Nothing happened and she eased out a shaky breath. Anxious, she rushed back inside. The men were still where she left them, the television was silent and there was a stillness in the house. The steady ticking of the Grandfather clock seemed deafening in the quiet.

She flipped a couple pages. "Okay, this shouldn't take long." She sounded cheery, but she knew if they resumed another conversation about Josh, she'd scream.

"I realize you have this under control, but can I help?"

Samuel's quiet comment shook her. His warm breath touched the back of her neck, and his hand reached around to take her screwdriver from her grasp. She inhaled softly, and her breath caught as he moved alongside her, his eyes soft as he looked deep into hers. "You hold the book, okay?"

Mutely she nodded, sure that was all she could do. He read a little bit, his lashes alternating between dusting his skin and brushing his lenses. Finished, he carefully studied the panel.

"You changed the batteries. It's nice and clean inside. Let's see if the wires are loose."

"That's exactly what I was going to do next." She barely got the words out without stuttering. He smiled again and her insides turned to jelly. All the way to her toes. He looked away and she took the opportunity to drag a breath into her compressed chest and pinch herself.

"They seem okay."

"Red and white?" She'd read that in the book. It was all she could manage to get out.

"Red, white and everything else."

He sent her a smile, that dimpled his cheeks. Her chest tightened. She was going to faint right at Mr. Swoonworthy's feet.

Samuel drove away from the Patrick house, shaking his head. He could not recall an afternoon filled with more...stuff. Emotions yanked at him like the blowing winds of a tornado. He didn't do gifts, but that had been his intention when the whale and dog books came in. He flipped through the colorful pages and easily envisioned Adam trying to figure out the words and matching them to the pictures.

He figured he'd get roped into another story or two about Lloyd's son, Josh. Old Lloyd told the same stories each time like they were brand new. He just leaned back and listened, knowing they brought the old man pleasure. He hadn't expected the defiance from Dawson when her daddy blew off her occupation. Senior software engineer. He was going to have to look that up. While he disagreed that it wasn't a real job, he wasn't sure what it was.

And Dawson. Oh boy. He could almost choke on the friction between them two. She and her daddy clearly don't get along and he applauded her for hanging around to fix the old house. He had no idea Lloyd was sitting there with no heat and no wood and a broken door and a bunch of other broken things to judge by the books Dawson bought. She planned to fix all that stuff by reading books? He shook his head. She had grit and determination. And now she had plenty of firewood to last a few days and a working furnace. She'd have gotten to the problem eventually, but he'd simply pointed her in the direction.

Just like he almost kissed her shiny lips seconds before Lloyd walked out and caught them. He suddenly felt like a seventeen-year-old. It didn't seem like Lloyd even noticed. Maybe next time he wouldn't stop.

His mind drifted back to another time when he was a different person. One who believed in the magic of Christmas and the purity of the season. He caught glimpses of that in Adam. He saw hope in Dawson. Maybe that was why he came out today with the book. And why he felt good inside about helping Dawson with wood and restoring the furnace. Except he wasn't that person anymore. Chills slid over him as he remembered the reasons why.

But the glow he felt earlier cracked something in him, allowing those long-buried emotions to shine through. Like rays of yellow sunshine lighting the frozen ground. Before he could change his mind, he fished his phone out of his jacket pocket and pulled over to the side of the road.

"Tom? This is Samuel Johnson. Say, you still have that pickup and trailer full of split cordwood? You do. Great. I want it, all of it. Can you deliver it for me? Out to Lloyd Patrick's house. Fantastic. I'll stop by tomorrow morning and give you the money."

He returned his phone to his coat pocket. Another gift. What was wrong with him? He didn't do this...gift stuff. He didn't do...holiday spirit.

Dawson heard an engine's rumble and a slam of its door. Then someone knocked at the front door. Surely Samuel wasn't returning, was he? Her heart skipped and butterflies in her tummy took flight at the thought. Mr. Swoonworthy almost kissed her, and she wished he had. She pushed aside the book on repairing exterior doors and went to the door. She fluffed her hair and plumped her lips. Disappointment took her by surprise.

"Hi. I'm Tom. I have your delivery." The heavily bearded man jerked a thumb over his shoulder.

"Delivery? Of what?"

"Firewood."

Had her dad ordered wood?

"I'm sorry, but are you sure you have the right house?"

Tom nodded. "Lloyd Patrick. Guess you'd be his daughter." At her slow nod, he continued. "Then I'm at the right place. Now, where do you want it?"

Samuel? Another gift from the man who doesn't give presents. "Out here, near the back door." She'd be all set once she got the door working. She was fairly sure the problem was swelling from the cold and she could plane the top rail down a little and chisel a bit around the strike plate. If nothing else, she was learning a whole new vocabulary. She grabbed her jacket and followed Tom outside.

Three hours later Dawson and Adam walked into the Chapter Twenty-Five Bookstore. A gray-haired lady in black yoga pants, scrunchy boots and a bright orange sweatshirt stood at the counter with a few pieces of paper spread before her. Samuel stood behind the counter. He raked a hand through his hair, leaving it messy before splaying both hands on the counter. When he looked up, she was sure it was relief and surprise crossing his face.

"We can wait." She held up a hand. "You're busy."

The woman turned and Dawson read the bold letters on her shirt: *Needful Paws of Cedar Falls* along with an adorable image of a puppy and kitten sitting in a basket.

"I'm not buying anything. I'm trying to convince Samuel to keep a few shelter kittens here to foster temporarily. The local shelter is crowded this time of year. See?"

Dawson released Adam and he raced to take the car Samuel held out to him. He found an open spot on the floor and soon started his imaginary race. Dawson moved to the counter and gazed at the photos of three kittens. "They're cute."

"I can't keep cats here."

"Why not?"

"Because."

Dawson and the other woman shared a glance. Dawson rested a finger on the photos. "Lots of bookstores keep cats full time. They lounge on the shelves, keep customers entertained, are great to bring new customers in, and they keep rodents away."

Samuel groaned. "I don't have rodents."

"They offer many other positive side benefits."

He shook his head. "They could ruin something or get hurt. Or hurt someone."

"They're babies, Samuel. They are incapable of hurting anyone And Paws would be responsible for any damage they do. And supply all their food, litter, and toys."

"I don't have time to take care of some animals."

"I'll do it," Dawson piped up, after listening to Samuel and the persistent lady banter. She raised a hand and met Samuel's shocked expression. "I like cats. I can come in every day and clean their litter box and play with them and make sure they have plenty of food. You won't have to do a thing."

"Every day?"

He looked doubtful. She firmly nodded in defiance to his doubt. "Every day." She glanced at the rescue lady. "But I suspect if others learned you had kittens here, they'll make excuses to stop by and see them. It might even increase sales for you."

"Every day?" Samuel repeated.

She bobbed her head. "Even Sunday. Cute little babies like this need love and attention on Sunday too."

Samuel blew out a heavy breath and looked around. Dawson almost felt sorry for him. He couldn't really say no without coming across as an ogre. She glanced at Adam, fully engrossed in his car. Surely a man who liked kids as Samuel did also had a soft spot for kittens. "Adam would probably like to play with them too?"

His shoulders sagged and he turned back to the rescue lady. He exhaled again. "Three?"

"Yes, we have a litter of three siblings that just turned seven weeks old. They're completely weaned away from their mom." She turned the one page around for him to see all three in one candid shot. "We call them Winking, Blinking, and Nod."

"When can they be here?" Samuel asked.

The rescue lady beamed brighter than a Christmas tree. "I can have their stuff packed up, have their paperwork filled out, and have them here in about two hours."

Again, another exhale. "Fine. We can try it and see how they do." He turned a finger to Dawson. "And I will see you every day to take care of their litter and all that stuff."

"Absolutely. Thank you for giving these little cuties a chance. They'll be much happier here than in a cage in a shelter." She clasped her hands in front of her. "I would be willing to almost bet once people come in and see them, they won't have to go back to the shelter. They'll probably find adopting families here."

"We can certainly hope so. I'll leave a few cards so if someone wants to adopt one, just turn them our way." She grabbed Dawson's hand and wrung it. "I'm Barb Sutton, by the way. Thank you for agreeing to help out."

A few minutes later Barb left, practically singing. Dawson turned to Samuel; her earlier confidence gone. "That was very nice of you to agree to fostering those kittens."

He laughed, dry and humorless. "I don't feel like I agreed to anything."

"You did. You could have said no."

He gave her a dimpled grin. "I did say no. Several times."

"Yes, but you could have stuck with it and not given in."

"Umm. And then I'd really earn my Grinch name."

She smiled and he laughed again, sounding more amused this

time. She joined him because it felt good to laugh with him. He looked good when he laughed.

"Are you going to be here when Barb brings them?"

She wasn't sure she could keep Adam occupied for two hours in the bookstore. "How about we come back in two hours? I want to find a tree and a few other things in town. We can go now and come back before Barb returns with the kittens."

He nodded. "Okay. Sounds good. Thanks."

She bundled Adam back up and they headed out onto the street. The cool air felt invigorating compared to the warmth inside Samuel's store. Mentally, she ran through her list of things. Tree from the corner tree lot. Cranberries and popcorn from the grocery store. While she would love to walk along the brick streets, past the large Victorian homes and stare at the lovely wreaths on each door and elaborate decorations, she knew it was better to drive,

Outside the grocery store some people set up a small table.

"Canned food drive. Sponsored by the Boys and Girls Club." Two young kids called to her. "We're collecting canned foods for the needy."

She smiled at them. "I tell you what, let me buy a few extra things inside and I'll stop by on my way out with them. What do you specifically need?"

The girl handed her a list. "Anything from that list will be appreciated, Ma'am."

"Great. See you in a bit." She hastened into the store and secured Adam into the fire engine cart. "Let's see. I bet most people will provide the canned foods. Let's get a few personal hygiene items too." She read from the list. "Toothpaste, deodorant, shampoo. We can do that too, right kiddo?"

In the end, she found some sales and bought a full two bags of things for the drive. She had Adam help carry some to the collection table. As they went back to the truck, she explained what a food drive was.

"Hungry." Was his takeaway and she smiled. "Yes, and now they won't be hungry because you and I helped with what we could." Community involvement was something she had missed while living in the big cities. Community outreach was limited to streets or neighborhoods. Here, it was encompassing the whole area. Since Samuel had come along and blessed them with ample heat, she felt doubly good at providing some food and supplies.

They drove to the tree lot and Dawson was glad to see they still had a good selection left. Adam marveled at the large white lights stringing from pole to pole. It gave the lot a fairy tale atmosphere and she would love to see it at night.

"Hold my hand, honey, and don't let go." This was not the place to misplace a small child.

Trees were stuck into buckets of snow according to type and size. Scotch Pine and blue spruce seemed most popular but mom always loved a good Balsam fir so that was Dawson's choice and soon she found the traditional aromatic Christmas tree fragrance she loved as a kid. She studied the firs lined up in buckets. Since it was doubtful she'd get help from dad, she better select a shorter tree instead of the six footers of her memories.

"How about this nice four-foot tree?" she asked Adam as she pinched a branch and breathed deeply.

"Kind of short, don't you think?"

Gasping, she whirled on her son. Suddenly Samuel stepped out from behind a plump evergreen, wearing a big smile.

"What are you doing here? And what would you know about Christmas trees?" She challenged him.

He tried to look wounded by placing his hand over his chest. "Hey, I'll have you know my tree is that way by design and purpose."

She snorted. "To help win the town scrooge title."

He smiled and came closer. He knelt to greet Adam and then studied her choice.

"I just wasn't expecting you," she said by way of apology.

He lifted a shoulder in an absent shrug. "I hung a 'Gone to lunch' sign on the door. I figured you would need help wrangling your tree inside, so I have a plan. We still have an hour and a half before the little beasts arrive. Pick your tree, I'd suggest a taller one, and I'll take you and Adam out to lunch. I did put the sign on my door after all." He winked at her. "Then I'll follow you home, help you get the tree inside and up where you want it, and we can still be back to town in time to meet Barb."

She was speechless he could put so many sentences together. "That is the most I've heard you ever say at once," she admitted. She mulled his offers over. "Are you sure we'll have enough time? I was going to go with a shorter, smaller tree so I could handle it myself."

"Yes, but is that the tree you really want?"

She sucked at her bottom lip, aware of the brisk chill in the air and the warmth radiating from Samuel's smile. "No. When Mom was alive and us kids were younger, we always had a big, full fir tree in the living room. Mom really loved Christmas. I think she enjoyed everything about it."

A look passed over his face and she was taken aback by the depth of it. Part sorrow and part faraway memory, she wondered at the thoughts lingering behind his dark eyes. Then suddenly it was gone. He shook himself, almost like a dog waking from a deep sleep. He fixed her with a smile, pinning her to the spot. Would a man who disliked Christmas as much as he claimed really be here now?

"Right, so go pick yourself out a tall fir tree and be quick about it. I can watch Adam. I'll also call Barb and ask her to bring the heathens a little later."

He took Adam's hand and she was glad to see Adam went so readily to his side. He walked over to a row of tall firs and she had no choice but to follow. As she studied them, she cast glances at him and Adam. He made a quick phone call, pocketed his phone, and knelt to interact with Adam by digging through the snow. Soon she found the perfect tree and flagged the lot man down.

Once she paid, the man wrapped the tree in netting and together he and Samuel loaded it to the roof of her SUV and tied it down.

"Okay, Barb has given us an extension until three. Where do you fancy lunch?"

"I haven't had a chance to see what is still around and what might be new, so why don't you pick?"

He assessed Adam and rocked back on his heels. "Do you guys like seafood?"

"Yes."

"I know just the place. I walked here so I'll hitch a lift with you guys if that's okay."

Dawson had always considered herself a relaxed driver, comfortable behind the wheel. But with Samuel riding shotgun, giving directions, she felt jitters she'd not felt since her teens. She gripped the wheel and tried to concentrate on the pop music, but Samuel had a quiet way to fill the vehicle with his essence.

He guided them down Main Street, all bedecked with lights and garland and bows, and east of town.

Dawson cleared her throat once they left town. "I appreciate the wood. That was very thoughtful. How much was it and I'll repay you."

"Don't worry about it. Tom owed me a favor and that's that." He sliced his palms horizontally through the air. "Another half mile up here. About two years ago someone decided to open a seafood restaurant where the Cedar Falls stopped, and the river curved away from town."

She didn't believe that Tom owed him a favor. Even if he did, that wood still cost money. And it made her opinion of Samuel grow. And clearly more conversation on the matter wasn't going to get her anywhere.

They parked in the lot, along with about fifteen other cars. Stepping out, Dawson could hear the rush of the water a little further up the road. "I can't remember the last time I've been to the falls," she replied wistfully. In her teen years, exploring the Cedar River and its waterfalls were her summer must-do and a good escape from life's teen drama.

"Do you hear that sound, Adam? That's lots of water, creating a waterfall." Maybe she could find a picture later for him.

Inside of The Falls Seafood Restaurant, she marveled at the rustic décor, reminiscent of a hunting lodge. The walls were log, the tables covered in green checked cloth, and pictures of moose, bear, and fish were plentiful. "Something sure smells good."

"Could be the special of the day. Or the seafood bisque. That's a great soup."

Within minutes they were seated with menus. Adam lined up his crayons carefully before selecting the light blue one and began filling in the sky on the placemat picture with determined strokes. Dawson watched him fondly. Her son was not stupid.

"So tell me a little about yourself, Dawson. Where's his d-a-d?"

She appreciated him spelling out the word and gave him a smile. "P-e-t-e-r. We're divorced. We disagreed about many things, him included." She nodded her head to Adam and grinned when he exchanged the blue crayon for a green one and startled filling in the trees. "As part of the agreement, he had his name taken off as father on the birth certificate."

Samuel's eyes widened. "How'd he manage that?"

"Good lawyer. And I didn't contest it. Better to have no father listed than one who despises you."

Samuel sucked in a deep breath and dusted off the table.

"I'm sorry if that upsets you."

"What? No. It's true." He glanced at Adam. "And no child support either."

"And no alimony. Clean break. He played his hand well." Irritation laced her tone, but she had a feeling Samuel would understand.

He nodded. The server arrived with their drinks and a basket of bread. Dawson buttered one and passed the small plate to Adam.

"So when did all this happen?"

"One week ago."

"One week?" he blurted. "What did you do? Sign the degree, pack your bags and drive from there to here?"

"Pretty much." She finished buttering a bread slice for her and took a bite. Warm buttery goodness filled her mouth, easing some of the bitterness of their conversation. "Josh called me about three weeks ago, concerned about dad and the house. Our final court date was coming soon so I knew A-d-a-m and I would be leaving soon. Josh and I agreed to pool our money for expenses, and I'd do what repairs I could do. I just had no idea how bad things here really were. Mom would be beside herself."

Samuel took his own bread and bit into it without butter. "And I'm partly to blame. I visited Lloyd a few times, but I've not been up there in the last seven or eight months."

"Don't be too hard on yourself. Things might have been starting before then or didn't begin until afterward. It hardly matters now. I'm only here to clean up what I can."

"And then what?"

"I don't know. A lot depends on d-a-d." She was spared further conversation when the server arrived with their lunches.

43

Once the meal was complete, Samuel launched his next surprise on Dawson. She packed up Adam and his drawing and crayons while he settled the bill.

"You know, it's silly for us to both drive out to your place. I'll just ride along with the tree."

She had to agree with his logic. Suddenly the thought of driving Mr. Swoonworthy seemed very pleasurable. "That does make more sense."

They reached her dad's house and she went inside with Adam while Samuel untied the tree. "Dad, are you around?"

"In the living room."

She rushed in. "Perfect. I bought us a tree. Samuel came here with us to set it up. We're going to put it in here, just like Mom used to do." She didn't wait for his reply and began moving furniture out of the way. She kneed the bigger pieces to make room. "I just need to move your chair a little to the left and we can set the tree between those angled windows. Please watch Adam while I help Samuel." Without awaiting his answer, she rushed outside.

Samuel had the tree off the roof and was standing by it, watching the front door. "Ready?"

"As much as possible."

They grunted and struggled and pushed and finally got it into the living room. "Adam, honey, push that stand over here to us," she panted as they each held a side.

"Thanks, buddy. Now back up so this thing doesn't fall on you."

"Twee."

Samuel shot a grin at Dawson. "Yes, you're right, it sure is."

It took a coordinated effort to get the tree into the stand and secured.

"You're the one who talked me into getting a taller tree," Dawson accused with a laugh as they cut the netting and the tree sprang to full size, knocking Samuel backward.

"Only because it's what you really wanted. And it looks rather good."

"Twee!"

"Yes, it sure is. Now your mom gets to decorate it. Later, we have a date with Barb soon."

"I'll go up in the attic later and get the old decorations down. I've got cranberries and popcorn in the truck. Maybe Adam and I can string garland." She leaned over and hugged Adam. "Let me get the groceries in and we'll be ready to head back to town."

Samuel stopped her, reaching out to touch her arm. She wasn't sure what surprised her more, his touch, the unexpected zaps of electricity rushing through her, or his odd expression of that far-away sorrowful look mixed with uncertainty.

"Tell you what, you get the groceries and I'll go up in the attic. Tell me where to look for the decorations and I'll bring them down."

She looked up at him, her eyes rounded with astonishment.

He splayed his hands out. "I'm just trying to be time conscious." He tapped his wristwatch. "Barb and the heathens."

She checked the time on her own watch. It was already two. Time had flown! "Okay, when we put everything up there, we had six boxes. They should be on the right side of the hatch. There is a pull string for the light immediately to your left on the rafter."

"Left side light, right side decorations. Six boxes. Got it." He saluted her, spun sharply, and headed down the hall to the attic access.

"The tree does look nice, doesn't it, Dad? It smells so good too." She inhaled the woody scent. It remined her of Samuel's aftershave.

She'd noticed he stayed in the room as she and Samuel set it up. He'd moved his chair out of the way and remained quiet during their workout. But then again, once she and Josh were old enough to help, he was never active when Mom set up the tree either.

"I suppose so. What do you plan to do with it after New Year's?"

She couldn't resist. She gave him her brightest smile and slowly inched toward the door. "I'm thinking we'll leave it up all year and just change the decorations to fit the holiday. Paper hearts. Flags. Firecrackers. Pumpkins."

When she returned with the groceries, Samuel already had two boxes down and stacked under the tree.

CHAPTER 3

S amuel rode back to town with Dawson and Adam, his brain filled with so many emotions. He had no idea what was influencing him lately, but it scared him.

Firewood. Fostering cats. Christmas trees. Was he losing his mind?

The pop station Dawson played on the radio changed to another ear-blasting song and he fought back a groan. She would probably fall asleep if she listened to his classic station. He didn't like contemporary pop music. He found it too loud and not having enough meaning or depth. He liked songs with a purpose and some history. And evidently, he was in the minority on this. Dawson started singing to the new song and even Adam chortled and waved his arms almost in time to the music. The kid had some natural rhythm. And his mom had a good voice, albeit wasted on a terrible song.

He closed his eyes. No, he wasn't losing his mind, he was losing his heart. Between Dawson and Adam, they were a mighty force on his resolve. When his ears heard what his mouth has offered lately, he can't believe it. He just knows it feels good to his soul when Dawson gives him that shy, appreciative smile.

He glanced back at Adam. The poor kid's dad had bailed, legally and physically, because he didn't want to deal with an autistic child. What a prick. Adam wasn't even severe. And Dawson was trying to be mom and dad to him. If she stayed in town, she could get some speech therapy and maybe a few other assistance programs started now and Adam would probably be fully functioning, or close to it, when he matured.

Of course, if he mentioned any of this to Dawson, would she want to know how he knew so much about autism? When he asked for confirmation of his suspicion, she paled and got a fight-or-flight look in her eyes. He felt bad then because he hadn't meant to upset her by his question, he just wanted to make sure of what he felt he saw. Now he knew why she was so wary and defensive of the anything negative about Adam. She'd married quite a jerk. While she might not see it now, her divorce could be the best thing for her and Adam.

They arrived back at the store and Adam pulled free of Dawson's hand before he even had the 'out to lunch' sign removed from the door. The boy rushed to where they had left his racecar and quickly started a new game. Samuel made a mental note to look for the other toys he used to have and see if there were other toy cars.

Dawson moved over to the section that housed the puzzles, games, and cards. She stood; hands clasped in front of her. She looked so cute and unsure.

"Now what?"

"Barb should be here in about ten minutes. Where do you suggest we put the wooly creatures?"

She frowned, and he presumed it was his negative name for the kittens, and he had this insane desire to take her into his arms and kiss that frown away. He glanced at the ceiling before he yielded to the temptation. Maybe he needed a mistletoe ball to hang up there somewhere.

"I don't think you're going to put them anywhere. Cats go where cats want to go." She stopped and studied him. "Haven't you ever had a pet?"

"Not one of my very own. I've known people who had a cat or dog or goldfish or whatever." He walked over to the pet section and scanned the titles he had on pets. Finding one with Cats in the title, he withdrew it from the shelf and flipped through the pages.

"Oh…" The more he scanned, the less enthusiastic he was about fostering the kittens. "They can vomit up hairballs?"

"I guess so. Maybe brushing would help."

"I'm pretty sure that falls under your daily care."

"Fine. I'll brush them."

He smiled at her defiant tone and resumed his quick study of the pages. Admittedly, the kittens in the pictures were cute and fluffy, but they were only photos. He also noticed the many pictures of the cats lounging on furniture, counters, bookcases, refrigerators, and every conceivable vertical surface. How high would the heathens Barb was bringing be able to climb?

And he did recall some cats from his youth, not his of course, but around him. They tended to do their own thing as he recalled. The dogs he might be around tended to be more involved with what their humans were doing whereas the cats were aloof. Okay, he could handle aloof. That suited him.

Barb arrived, carrying a plastic carrier. She set it on the counter and Dawson peeked through the grate at the kittens.

"They're even cuter in real life."

Samuel looked over her shoulder at the huddled pile of fur with round eyes like miniature owls. "Do they move?"

Barb scoffed at him. "Of course. Once they warm up to the sights and sounds around, they'll come to life. In the meantime, the rest of their stuff is out in the van."

"Guess that's my cue to go fetch it in."

"I think we can just leave the door off the carrier, and put it over in this quiet corner," Barb said. "Once they feel comfortable, they can come out and still go back in the carrier if they want the security."

Dawson called Adam over to see the kittens. He slid onto her lap.

"Kiben."

"That's close. Kitten. And one day soon they will grow into cats."

"Meow." Adam copied the sound of a cat.

"Very good, young man."

Dawson smiled at Barb's praise. "He's learning."

Samuel set his armload down with a thud. "Where else are you stopping today? I don't want to accidently grab something that isn't theirs."

"Oh, everything in the back is for them."

Samuel's eyes rounded. "Everything? Barb, the whole back of your van is full."

"Yes, I know. Litter, food, bowls, litterbox, scooper, tower, scratching post. There's also a box of toys, brushes, and treats. I don't think I've forgotten anything." Barb rifled through her pockets and produced a handful of cards. "In case any of your customers ask about adopting." She plunked the cards on the counter and Dawson hid her smile.

Samuel sighed. "Where do you suggest we put all their stuff?"

She shrugged, unfazed by his shock. "Dawson and I decided it was best to leave the carrier in a quiet spot. The food and litter should be behind the counter somewhere. And the scratching post and other things could go out on the floor, where they can eventually interact with your customers."

"Here, I'll help." Dawson got up and grabbed her jacket. "We can bring their stuff in together." She elbowed him playfully on her way out the door.

Splitting the workload, they had the stuff inside in only a few minutes.

"This is the last of it," Samuel said, as he cradled what Barb called a tower in his arm and shut her van door. As he walked to the door, a cold snowball slapped him on the back of his head. Snow exploded and slid down the back of his neck. Shivering, he looked around.

"Sorry."

Dawson looked anything but sorry as she stood there, grinning for ear to ear. A glance at her mittens confirmed she just handled snow.

"Really? You're gonna hit me while my hands are full?"

She giggled. "Can you think of a better time?"

He dropped the tower, bent and scooped up a handful of snow, packing it. She did the same, rushing to make another snowball. They took aim and simultaneously let fly. She squealed and darted out of the way. His missed her and hers hit him square in the chest.

"Two for two, Samuel."

"That's because you don't play fair, Dawson."

They reloaded, and this time he waited till she released her ball first. He sidestepped and hers missed him by an inch or two. He let his snowball fly and laughed as it connected with her hip.

"Fink!"

"I've been called worse. What else do you have?"

They tossed another few snowballs each missing or hitting, until they were evenly matched in white circles.

"Now I'm getting cold," she complained.

He smirked. "You're just sore because I'm ahead on direct hits. And remember, you started this."

She headed to the door, and he picked up the cat tower. Just before she reached the door, she bent over, scooped up a handful of snow and flung it at him. It flew into his face. He cried, and she giggled, darting inside.

Barb sat in the chair by the local history section, cradling a furry kitten. She glanced up as they came through the door. "Is it snowing again?"

"Something like that," Samuel muttered. "Where does this go?"

Barb gestured to her chair. Adam stood nearby, fascinated by the kitten she held. Dawson stood, watching her son. She nibbled her lip and Samuel again had the impulse to kiss her and nibble her lip himself. Instead, he deposited the tower and returned to the counter to watch the interaction.

Hours later, after Barb was gone, Dawson and Adam were gone, and the last customer left, extolling him for fostering the rescue's kittens. He turned the sign and closed the bookstore. He began the climb up to his apartment and stopped at the crate. All three kittens played around the outside of the crate. One batted at a belled toy and two wrestled. With a sigh, he sat down on the floor and propped his elbow on the chair. What was he thinking?

It wasn't that he disliked cats. He just had minimal experience with them. However, they made Adam's eyes light up and Dawson giggled as she filled their dishes before she left. She knelt and played with them, encouraging Adam and instructing him on how to gently pet them. Samuel had been taking notes from his post safely behind the counter.

And now the lights were dimmed, and he was alone with the furry beasts.

A gray and black striped tabby slowly worked its way to Samuel. It sat at his knee, watching. Samuel returned the stare. He tentatively reached out, ready to scoop it up like Barb had done so easily, and then hesitated. Barb probably scooped a dozen kittens and puppies a day. Instead, he counted the four neatly marked white feet, the white chest that looked like a bib, and the white splash around its mouth and reaching between its eyes and up the forehead like a blaze.

"You'd think they would have called you Blaze. So who are you?"

The kitten blinked once.

"Does that mean you're Blinking?"

Yes, it was silly sitting on the floor, in the dimmed room, talking to a cat. But he was. He'd heard it said that cats were considered magical and Christmas was a magical time of year. Perhaps the fates were conspiring against him.

The kitten crawled up onto Samuel's arm and blinked again. It meowed once, a thrilling chirp that sounded too loud for such a tiny body. Samuel sat as if electrocuted. He couldn't breathe, talk or even think. Magic indeed filled his senses. Then a tiny rumbling purr filled the air and the kitten rolled over, closing its green eyes.

A feeling Samuel could only describe as enchanted settled around them. He swallowed once. Twice. And gulped for air. He felt like a fish out of water.

"Barb did not warn me how much power a two-pound cat could have." Tentatively he stroked the kitten's head and down its fluffy back. He was acutely aware of how large his hand was compared to how tiny the kitten was. He was also aware of who held the authority in the moment.

"Blinking is a stupid name for you. You should be called George Washington, Titus, or Maximum. Maybe Sampson or Griffin. Anything but Blinking."

The kitten answered by waving his white feet in the air and increasing the frequency of his purr.

"How am I supposed to go upstairs with you attached to me like this?" Despite his gruff question, Samuel stroked the upturned belly, marveling at the soft fur. He placed a fingertip to each front toe, some pink and some black. "What do you suggest I do with you?"

He watched the other two kittens play and wrestle, bat the toys and climb the tower while the gray tabby lay contentedly in his arm, purring loudly. In the stillness, he sensed an innocence and curiosity he'd forgotten existed. It reminded him of Adam. It was youth, untarnished.

"Apparently babies of any species can bring this."

Finally the other two kittens scampered into the carrier and curled into one colorful ball. Blinking rolled out of Samuel's arm and joined the other two.

"Must be bedtime. I'll see you beasts tomorrow."

Samuel slipped away, aware of the warmth on his arm where Blinking had lain. He climbed the stairs to his apartment with the feeling he just left something precious behind.

Dawson filled the popcorn bowl and gathered her supplies. She'd found a large tapestry needle in her mom's old sewing kit and an abandoned box of heavy-duty dental floss in the upstairs bathroom. She hoped it was Josh's. With the popcorn and cranberries, she was ready. She settled on the sofa and patted the spot next to her.

"Come on, Adam. This used to be a special part of our Christmas tradition when I was young. First we take a bite of the popcorn and the cranberry." She giggled at his face when he tasted the tart cranberry. "I know, better for decoration and not so good to eat."

She tied a series of knots at the end of the dental floss and threaded the needle. "You hand me the pieces, and I'll put them on the string."

Dawson hummed while they worked in harmony. She'd stop

to count out the pieces. "One popcorn, two popcorn, three popcorn and four." Then followed by, "One cranberry, two cranberries, three. Great job." Soon Adam counted out the pieces as he handed them over.

She hoped he would remember this Christmas when he was older, and how they sat on the sofa, stringing garland, and listening to carols on the radio. She may not have much for him this year, not even a home of their own, but she could give him pleasant things to remember.

The lights they put on the tree twinkled in multicolored hues. She could halfway close her eyes and they blurred into a dizzying display of light. Next, they would put on the garland and after Adam went to sleep, she would add the old ornaments. Maybe she could take a couple to Samuel to add to his pitiful tree. Maybe they should make a garland for it instead.

Early the next morning, Dawson decided to work a bit on the house before heading into town, and Samuel's store. She did have an extra length of garland to take, as a gift, though he'd specifically said he didn't expect any. Technically this wasn't a gift for him, it was a gift for the tree.

She finished planing the back door, and was satisfied it would open and close now, and still create a nice seal to keep drafts and summer bugs out. Would she be here come summer, in July, when every creepy and winged creature tried to get inside the house? A lot could happen in seven months. She put the stepladder away, deciding she would do better concentrate on now, and not so far ahead.

Next, she took some measurements and notes for a supply list for the leaking toilet upstairs and the one downstairs that seemed to constantly run. The kitchen faucet leaked as well, and she wanted to caulk and grout the bathtub. So she took pictures and sizes too, consulting with the thick plumbing book for everything. Now she had a list to tackle the plumbing issues.

Now that the more critical things were fixed, her plan was to address the long list in a sequence based on type of repair. Plumbing now.

Carpentry, which included repairing the deck, fixing the sticky drawers in the kitchen, fix the loose cabinet knobs and rehang the utility room door. For electrical she had listed repair broken light fixtures and replace a bad burner socket on the stove. Truthfully, she was scared to death to do those. Except she survived the electric panel once. And it would be an exceptionally long time before she forgot Samuel standing behind her, with his warm breath tickling her skin. She could close her eyes and see that smile that set butterflies off inside her. So, she'd think of Samuel and carefully do those other electrical repairs in due time

She also had gutters to look at, windows to repair, drywall to mend, wallpaper seams to fix, and a few other miscellaneous things she wasn't sure where to classify them. What exactly were ceiling stains considered? Cosmetic? Or along with the drywall and wallpaper issues? Either way, they fell further down her priority list.

She studied her list and blew out a long breath. "At this rate, Adam, you'll be graduating high school and I'll still be working on this house."

Adam giggled as she helped him get dressed for their road trip.

"Glad you find it funny." She went to find her dad. "Adam and I are heading over to the hardware store and then we'll stop at Samuel's bookstore on the way back. Would you like anything special for dinner?"

"I can find it if I do."

Her hands curled into fists and she sucked in a calming breath. "Okay. I just thought you might like a change from frozen TV dinners and pot pies. Adam and I may grab dinner in town then." She turned around and snatched her keys and purse. Did he not notice how the house was falling apart? Did he not care? She needed to have a serious talk with Joshua when he surfaced again.

Once they arrived at the hardware center in Higgins, and armed with her list and a helpful employee, Dawson made short work of her list. She was amazed—and proud—at how much she had learned about home repair tools and most importantly, the language. She got all the plumbing supplies and a few tips from the experienced employee and only winced a little at the total.

Hopefully, she and Josh pooled enough money. For what it was costing them to repair their dad's house, he could be a little nicer to her and Adam.

"Ungrateful old grouch."

Once they were finished, she took Adam to look at the department store across the street just so he could enjoy the Christmas decorations. Angels, toy nutcrackers, candles, and plenty of Santa figurines filled the windows and entrance. Adam's eyes shone with youthful delight and awe.

"Magic." He pointed a tiny finger at the angels flying high above the scene.

She let out a wistful sigh. "I sure hope so, buddy. We need some magic this year." She ruffled his baby fine hair. "Okay, sweetie, time to go back to town. Mr. Johnson and his cats are waiting on us."

"I was starting to think you'd never show up."

Dawson stopped short, wincing and wounded by his sharp words. "Don't you start too. I've got enough grumpy attitude at home. Adam and I had to go to Higgins for plumbing supplies first." She planted her hands on her hips. "And besides, Adam has a gift for you."

Samuel had the grace to look apologetic. "I was worried. Sorry."

She silently watched as Adam offered the paper sack to Samuel, his smile bright and innocent. She sat in the chair, legs crossed and arms over her chest and one kitten scampered over to her. She scooped it up and hugged it to her chest.

"Gif."

"Yes, it is." Samuel withdrew the length of garland and looked it over. "Did you make this?"

Adam nodded, and pointed to Dawson, then placed his finger proudly on his chest, and back to Dawson and back to himself once more. "Gif."

"I see. It's very nice. Thank you, Adam."

"Twee." Adam pointed to Samuel's pitiful tree.

He smiled. "Okay, here goes." He draped the four-foot strand around the tree.

"We used yarn for that because the dental floss was running low. But it should last the entire season."

Samuel nodded, watching her scrub the kitten under its chin.

"Which one is this?" she asked.

He shrugged. She returned his shrug and reached into the tote bag she'd carried in. "Adam, take this scrap paper and make those airplanes like we were doing earlier today. I need to get these babies taken care of."

She set him up at the front window. Once he started folding the sheet, she reached for the cat bowls. Kittens clambered at her feet, meowing pitifully.

Samuel watched Adam for a few moments and then went to the counter and withdrew a pair of shears. He walked over to Adam and knelt.

"Did you know there was a way to cut a hole in the paper airplane to make it fly better? I read it somewhere recently."

Dawson peeked over as she cleaned and filled the bowls and then started scooping the litterbox as Samuel folded a piece of paper and cut sections away, explaining as he went. He told Adam all about aerodynamics, velocity, and things no one would expect a three-year-old to understand. Finished, he threw the plane and it sailed smoothly across the room. One of the kittens pounced on it and Adam laughed. Dawson couldn't help but smile.

Samuel repeated the steps and explanations as Dawson took the dirty litter outside to the trash in the back. She found the brush and returned to her chair to watch Adam fly the newly designed paper airplanes, chortling as they landed further and further away. One kitten climbed up and she brushed its soft furry coat.

"You seem distracted today," Samuel pointed out quietly. He threw a plane in her direction and it landed at her feet. She slid it under the chair.

"Oh, just Dad again. What does he expect? That the fairies will just show up, wave their wands, and magically fix and clean everything? And while they're at it, they'll fill the house with food and firewood too?"

He grinned, coming to kneel by her side. "Well, in a way, that's what's happened."

She frowned. "Not much magic involved. No wands either."

"No, just a lot of hard work, patience, determination, and guts."

"You think so?"

He rested a hand on top of hers. "I know so." He looked deep in her eyes.

Startled by the honesty in his voice and the warmth of his touch, she paused. The kitten jumped down. She licked her lips.

Logic told her they were in his store and anyone could walk in, and Adam was sitting just a few feet away. That was logic. His eyes unlocked something else in her. Desire. Desire said to kiss him. Desire was winning.

"Car?"

She jumped, inhaling sharply. Adam stood, pointing to the box Samuel used to hold the race car. "Um…yes, sure, go ahead." She cut a guilty glance at Samuel and her breath hitched at his dimpled grin.

"That was almost the best kiss I had."

"How would you know? We…"

"Samuel! I need some Christmas gifts. I just learned my sister is coming for Christmas with her kids, so I need stuff!"

Samuel gave her a wink and climbed to his feet. "Sure thing, Hyacinth." He walked toward the customer who'd just barreled in like a winter hurricane. "What did you have in mind? Books? Toys? Puzzles? Stationary? Mugs?"

Dawson watched Adam play with the car and Samuel fill Hyacinth's shopping list. She glanced around the store, finally taking the time to really look at the merchandise on display. She saw so much more than just neat rows of books. What she saw also clashed with the bookstore memories of her youth. Only the heavy wood counter remained the same.

She partially listened to Adam as he made car sounds and Hyacinth ramble about her family and their interests as she let her mind wander between the kiss she and Samuel almost shared and the Cedar Falls Bookstore of her past.

The old bookstore sold books, mostly classics, non-fiction, and popular fiction. Thrillers, mysteries, romance and sci-fi lined the old wood shelves. The shopkeeper also stocked a good supply of magazines and newspapers. There used to be lots of cozy reading nooks to gather with friends or sit alone to peruse new titles or the week's news.

Samuel had taken out many of the nooks to bring in different stock. Not only did he carry all the original book genres, he added several more, including an entire travel section with fiction and non-fiction for popular travel geographic locations. He had an arts and crafts section with books and select supplies that covered scrapbooking, origami and more. He had an area devoted to greeting cards, audio books, comic books, calendars, educational toys, and gifts like mugs, bookends, bookmarks and more. How did he keep up with it all?

Everything in the store flowed seamlessly from one section to another and she admired his design even if she did miss the cozy nooks. The gray kitten returned to her lap and she stroked it from its chin to its tail. This gave her an opportunity to watch Samuel through her lowered lashes.

They'd almost kissed! And she was disappointed they hadn't. Anticipation at the heat in his eyes stole over her and made her dizzy with eagerness, and disappointment at their interruption was a cold dousing. His touch felt electric. His laugh sounded musical. His eyes held her prisoner. And she wanted back in his arms.

He rang up Hyacinth's large order and bagged her items, then he carried them out to her car. He came back inside with a young couple in tow.

"We need to surprise the kids with some smaller gifts."

"Absolutely," Samuel brought his hands together in a soft clap. "And what are their ages again?"

Listening to their thoughts, he headed them over to the novelty gift section. Catching her watching, he sent her a wink and a dimpled grin. She shrugged and smiled back. Adm was still playing happily and she was in no hurry to jump into her plumbing projects.

Before the couple could finish their purchases, another

shopper came in wanting audio books for his wife. Another customer came in for some non-fiction best sellers.

Dawson marveled at how easily Samuel went from one customer to another, listening intently to their wants and guiding them to the different sections of the store. He didn't pressure them, which she appreciated, but offered suggestions and left them to make the final choices. Whatever he had done previously must have helped prepare him to be a great business owner. So what had he done before arriving in town?

Finally the excitement ended, and the last customer was served. Adam had climbed into her lap a short time ago with the kitten and now both napped happily. Samuel sat down by Dawson and ran a hand through his hair.

"Is it often like this?"

Samuel blew out a tired breath. "It comes and goes, maybe a little more so today given the time of year, but yes, it tends to go in pockets like that." He nodded toward Adam and the kitten. "That's a cute image."

"Yes, kids and pets just naturally go together if given the chance."

He seemed to be considering her words. "Would you consider adopting one of them?"

"I can't. I don't have a home of my own. There's no telling how long we'll be at my dad's. And then where will I go?" She wiped a tear away. "It's hard enough providing for a child, let alone a pet."

"You're right. Sorry, I wasn't thinking."

She shook her head, sniffing. "It's a good question. Clearly, I like cats. And dogs. It's just a bad time for me. If I had a stable environment, yes, I'd seriously consider this little sweetie here." She stroked the kitten once, and then turned to Adam's blond locks. She turned her gaze up to him. "Why do you ask?"

"No reason. Simply curious."

They sat in silence for a few moments. Finally Dawson broke the quiet. "You've done a lot with the old place. I can't get over how much it's changed."

He raised his eyebrows. "You came here before?"

"Um hum. I read a lot when I was young and spent many a Saturday here, hanging out with friends or squirreled away alone at one of the nooks. Why did you call it Chapter Twenty-Five?"

He flashed her that dimpled grin. "I bought it on my twenty-fifth birthday."

"What a present." Her eyes rounded, then she sucked in a shaky breath. "I do have another question. Will you join Adam and I tomorrow at the town festival? He wants to see Santa and we'll probably get cocoa and maybe a sleigh ride and walk around town and we'll have to stay and see the big tree light up." She watched his face slowly dip into a frown and she drew her lip in, waiting. A muscle in his jaw ticked as his gaze darted to the pitiful tree now draped in cranberry and popcorn. She couldn't help but wonder why he loathed all things Christmas.

"I'm open till noon tomorrow."

She took in a hopeful breath and summoned up a smile. "That's okay. We wouldn't get here until after that anyway. I have to get a few things done at the house if I want to play hooky the rest of the day." Taking advantage of his wavering decision, she hastened to outline her plan.

"And I'll stop in here just before you close to take care of these little guys. How does that sound?"

He looked like she just asked him a question that required a painful answer, but he hadn't said an immediate no. She took heart and waited, her breath coming in short bursts. She licked her lips.

"On one condition."

"Okay, what is it?"

"I want that kiss that was interrupted."

She drew back, surprised.

"In fact, I want it now."

She inclined her head to the child sleeping in her lap and raised her eyes to his, brows lifted. "Now?" she mouthed. Her heart hammered in her chest like a kick drum. His eyes darkened and he nodded.

He leaned over Adam, careful not to touch him. He braced his arms on either side of Dawson's knees. His spice aftershave curled around her. Somewhere along the line, he must have grabbed a peppermint or gum. She smelled fresh mint as his mouth hovered over hers. He pressed his lips to hers, turning slightly. She closed her eyes and heard a moan. Startled, she realized it was her.

Slowly he withdrew, a satisfied smile on his face. He licked his lips and moaned himself. Her chest beat and heat flared up through her cheeks. He could kiss!

"All right. Tomorrow at noon, I am all yours."

Dawson felt giddy as a schoolgirl when she left Samuel's store. Her step was light, her heart sang, and she couldn't stop the big smile on her face. She held Adam's hand and they swung their arms and skipped along the brick path. He pointed to the endless array of decorations and she laughed along with him on the way to their car.

She drove the short distance to the grocery store. She sang along to the carols piping through the overhead radio as she pushed Adam's firetruck buggy. With a carefree air she'd not felt for weeks, she selected staples and meats with abandon, piecing meals together in her head.

"Meatballs and spaghetti. Garlic bread. Sloppy joes and steak fries. Fish and chips. More garlic bread. Meatloaf and mashed potatoes. Shepherd's Pie. That will take care of a few pounds of ground beef. We'll need fried chicken too, and maybe some pork chops for variety. And we need lots of veggies." She was probably spending more than she should, but they would eat well for a while. "You know, honey, we ought to invite Samuel over for a dinner or two. Maybe just a random weeknight and for sure Christmas. I can't imagine the original scrooge has special plans for Christmas." She tapped her chin. "Dad and I haven't talked about dinner, but I suspect he'll grumble along with whatever we decide. So...ham or turkey?"

Adam tilted his head and stuck his arms out, flapping as though he were a bird.

"Okay, turkey it is. Let's see if we can find any left. And how about more cranberries?"

He made a face as though he'd bit into a lemon and she laughed. He chortled along with her. How much he fully understood, she didn't care. He understood enough for her. And she discreetly slipped another bag of cranberries into the cart when they reached the produce section.

She did overspend a bit, but it was Christmas. She envisioned Samuel joining them for a homecooked meal she prepared, and it was worth whatever the grocery bill came to. Finished, ideas filling her mind, she pushed the cart out to the car.

"Dawson! Wait up."

She halted, skidding to a stop on the snowy parking lot and looked around. Wendy and two other women approached her.

"Dawson, you remember Sonya and Talia? We were all in high school."

She searched her memory. Oh, yes. Sonya and Talia were cousins and they'd all hung out at gym class and a few other classes.

"Good to see you all again. This is my son, Adam."

They fussed over him, keeping him laughing. They chatted, catching up in the cool air.

"Do you want to go for coffee?" Talia asked, shivering against the weather. "Someplace kid friendly?"

"The Grinder is good for kids," Wendy said. "It's just over on the next street.

"Perfect. I've got time. Let me stow these groceries and we'll join you there."

Her day was just getting better and better. "I know you might not understand school yet, sweetie, but these ladies and I went to school when we were younger. Now we're all grown up with kids of our own. One day you'll be grown up, probably marry a pretty girl and have kids of your own. That will make me a grandma."

If Samuel can explain aerodynamics to Adam, she can explain how she will become a grandmother. They reached The Grinder and went in, gathering around a large table. She ordered a regular coffee for her and a chocolate milk for Adam. Their server brought a booster chair for Adam and some crayons for his paper placemat.

"So what is new since you've been back?" Sonya asked her.

She explained about fixing up her dad's house and the arrangement she made with Samuel about fostering the kittens.

"I can't believe you got that hottie to foster cats. He is so cold inside. I would have bet he didn't like animals."

"Umm. It's hard to resist a trio of cuddly kittens. Even for Samuel." She remembered how he was weakening from his emphatic no before she made her rash offer. She believed he would have eventually caved into Barb's request. Given enough time.

"So many women have tried to hook up with him, and he shoots them all down. He's a real loner."

Sonya giggled. "A lone wolf. He keeps to himself and doesn't say much when people enter his lair."

"He's like one of the books in the store. He's got a fantastic cover, but between the pages is just a mystery." Talia let out a long sigh.

Dawson shifted, aware all three had tried to charm their way into Samuel's arms. Was she the only woman in Cedar Falls to feel his touch, taste his kiss? She dare not tell these girls what all she and he had done. She felt blushing beat creep up her neck, and she took a drink of the coffee, thinking to blame that if they mentioned it.

The whole conversation was starting to feel a little too much like high school and she hastened to switch the focus. "I have enough Scrooge at home with my dad, so let's change the subject, okay. Tell me what's going on with you two." She wagged a finger between Talia and Sonya.

An hour later she and Adam returned home It had been difficult to steer the conversation away from Samuel and it was clear all her old friends fantasized about him, married or not. She had to wonder if his arrival in town was one of the biggest events of the decade, at least from the ladies' point of view. She ran her tongue over her lips, still able to taste his kiss and smell his scent on her shirt. What would happen if her friends found out?

"They just won't, right buddy?" She parked the truck. "Let's see if Grandpa can watch you a little bit so I can get the groceries in, dinner started and then start a plumbing project."

The employee at the hardware store gave her a trick to try for the toilet that never seemed to stop running. Hopefully, all she had to do was put a straw around the flapper chain inside the tank. He seemed to think that would solve the issue and it would take one project off her list. She hoped it would be that easy. Because she knew the next one would be more difficult.

CHAPTER 4

Samuel parked the truck and looked up the steps to Mrs. Broome's house. Her walk was swept, and smoke curled from her chimney. Both were good signs. After realizing Lloyd had been sitting in a house without heat and no useable firewood, he made it his job to drive by in the evenings after work to check on the elderly and singles in the area. He brought some non-perishable food along, just in case. He also hoped the drive out through the cool air might clear his head.

He'd been uptight since he agreed to go to the festival and tree lighting tomorrow. What was he thinking? He didn't do Christmas stuff. He usually locked the shop door at noon and went upstairs to his apartment and hid out from all sights and sounds of Christmas for the day. He pulled his window blinds down and turned on the radio, playing every CD he had so to avoid the endless holiday tunes. So why was he agreeing to put himself through the emotional anguish tomorrow…just to spend time with Dawson?

He cut the engine and heaved a sigh. Instead of clearing his head, it seemed it was getting more muddled. He walked up to Mrs. Broome's door and knocked.

"Hello, Mrs. Broome. How are you?" He spoke up because he knew she was a little hard of hearing. Her husband, who had died two years ago, had been deaf.

She smiled, big and wide and pushed the storm door open. "Come in, Samuel. Good to see you."

The house was warm, lights were on, and fresh apple pie cooled on the table. His mouth watered.

She beckoned him to a chair, and he explained he had decided to just check on the people who were alone and lived out of town.

"Samuel Johnson! That is just the sweetest thing for you to do! I'm doing fine, as you can see, but surely there are others who would welcome your visit. Let me get you some apple pie before you go. And you can tell me what's new in the store. I've been wanting to stop in for a bit now."

As she plied him with fresh pie, thick with apples, and drizzled liberally with caramel, he explained what new things he had in the store, including some romance books he knew she liked. As he was leaving, she packed up another big slice of pie and promised to stop in after Christmas for a little post-holiday shopping.

He left, feeling good for his efforts. The pie was most welcome too. It smelled good sitting on the truck seat next to him. These local people supported his store, and in a sense, he felt he owed it to them to be looking out for them. He felt bad he hadn't caught Lloyd's condition. What would have happened if Dawson hadn't come into town? What if she had stayed married to Adam's father?

It was hard to say what would have happened to Lloyd. And his world would be a lot darker.

His body recoiled painfully when he straddled Adam to kiss Dawson. She'd looked nervous but soon warmed to his touch. She tasted sweet like butterscotch and he loved her berry lip gloss. What he especially liked was the low moan from deep in her throat. Her eyes closed, she moaned and then tightened momentarily in surprise. He almost lost the kiss to laughter!

But when she relaxed again, giving herself to him, he was the one who tightened with desire. The things he pictured. When they parted, he swore he caught a glimpse of those wishes in her eyes too.

Was it possible she could fall for the kid no one wanted? She was impressed with what he'd done with the store. That was basic business 101. He was impressed with how she kept plugging away with her dad's house and evidently, they were not getting along any better. He'd bet once that house was suitable and stocked, she was going to be out of there like her tail was on fire.

Except, where was she going to go?

Samuel returned home an hour later, satisfied he'd thoroughly covered the southeastern part of town, checking on a total of eleven residents. They'd all welcomed him warmly, and their houses were well stocked. He did shovel the walk for one guy. He could see the old feller had tried but Samuel made light work of clearing away the slippery spots. And every single house was decorated for the holiday and two more people sent him home with extra food.

He entered the store and locked the door behind him. As he navigated his way through the dimly lit interior, three furry beasts raced out to attack his ankles.

"Thank goodness I have boots on. It feels like there's three baby cougars, not kittens. That's enough." He set down his food gifts and found the bag of treats Barb had brought. He poured a handful out and scattered it on the floor. The kittens rushed in and the crunching echoed around the room.

As he reached the stairs to his apartment, he glanced back. Blinking sat, watching him walk away. Samuel's glance swept over the piles of toys scattered around the floor to the clean litter box and the food and water dishes both full. The heathens could ask for nothing. Still, Blinking sat and stared, a single treat sitting by his white paw.

"What do you want?" he asked the feline. Thinking he sounded unnecessarily gruff, he added, "What you need is a decent name." With that, he took his food and climbed the stairs.

Saturday Samuel worked all day, his store busy with merry shoppers and his thoughts full of Dawson. He watched the clock, wondering how close to noon she would arrive. Despite her promise to arrive just before he closed, he kept a hope that she might show up sooner. The antique key wound wall clock chimed eleven-thirty when Dawson and Adam arrived. Like a breath of spring air, she breezed in and immediately filled the store with sweet fragrances. One look at her and Samuel decided it had been worth the morning-long wait.

She smiled at him and he felt like he'd been punched in the gut, air almost escaping his lungs. How could a smile have such an effect on him? He watched as she helped Adam shed his outer layers. He'd been helping Miss Faith Appleby select gifts for her family that were all arriving over the weekend...all nine of them. She joked and said the baseball team was coming. And she wanted a saucy romance novel for herself...for once they all left.

As Miss Appleby weighed the decision between a grammar guru or a journal and pen set for her oldest niece, he stepped aside and let out a breath. Had he been going around all morning, holding his breath in anticipation of Dawson's arrival? One would think he was a giddy teenager going on his first date!

Dawson sent Adam to the box of toys he had added to this morning and began removing her own outer layers. In his mind, she was caught in slow motion, every movement screen ready. And he could not stop staring. Her blonde hair was curled in big waves. First, she pulled off her gloves and put them in the pocket of her red jacket. Then she removed her plaid scarf. She slipped off the red jacket like it was a coverup at a beach. Her pink sweater sparkled in the fluorescent lights, echoed by the pink teardrop earrings that swung from her ear lobes. His heartbeat rocked in rhythm to the glittering jewels. His body responded to her seductive dance and he swallowed convulsively.

"Samuel?"

Miss Appleby calling his name jolted him back to reality. He swung back to her. "Ma'am?"

He helped carry some of her additional choices for the baseball team to the counter where they were slowly piling up.

Dawson set to work, scooping up the energetic kittens as they swarmed around her and cuddling them against her pink sweater. One swatted at her earring. She laughed, musical notes teasing his ears, as she fended off their playful advances. He caught the faint whiff of peach and lavender.

"Candles."

"Umm? I'm sorry. What?"

"Candles." Miss Appleby gave him a knowing smile. "You should have some candles here."

He nodded. "That's a good suggestion. I have my supplier looking for literary themed candles already. Since we shouldn't burn scented books, right?" He grinned at her.

"No, of course not. But a candle would be perfect for my older sister."

He felt bad at her crestfallen look. "Maybe I can have some in stock in time for her birthday." He made a mental note to check back in with his supplier after the holidays. He would need to restock the store by then.

He glanced over at Dawson. She was filling the kittens'

dishes. Down on her knees, he could see the shape of her firm behind in the molded denim. His stomach curled in response to the tempting sight. Would noon ever get here! And then what? He'd be alone without the distraction of customers.

He glanced over at Adam, who sat on a mat by the window. He pushed two racecars around in a circle, making engine noises. Samuel smiled, imagining the great match race going on in the boy's mind. There was nothing so wrong with Adam that time and patience would not help. He felt his lips thin at the thought of the boy's father who so casually erased him out of his life. What a dick.

Miss Appleby laid her hand on his arm. He snapped his attention back to her, heat fanning his face.

"I'm sorry. I seem to be distracted today."

She wagged her head at him. "Perhaps it's because there are so many things vying for your attention." She inclined her head to Adam and over to Dawson who scooped out the kitten's box and was oblivious to them. She lowered her voice to a whisper, and he dipped his ear to hear.

"Samuel, I think it's wonderful that you are keeping the little fur-babies here for the rescue group. And now that Dawson is back in town, with her own baby boy, it's just so good of you to have them be around." She patted his arm. "You are such a good man."

His heart lurched. "Thank you, Miss Appleby. That means a lot to me." He cleared his throat and took her elbow, escorting her to the counter. Once her purchases for the baseball team were bagged and he slipped in her saucy romance novel, he made change and helped carry her bags out to her car. He returned, checked the time, and turned the sign on the door to 'closed' and dimmed half the lights. Dawson looked up from where she sat brushing the kittens.

"Ready?" he asked, sounding far more confident than he felt. "The festival awaits."

She climbed to her feet, gently moving the furry kittens aside. Her anxious smile sent a mule kick to his chest and he wondered what he was getting into. He braced a hand on the bookshelf in front of him and the truth hit him with a mighty blow. He was scared.

"Let's walk," Dawson suggested as all three of them stepped out onto the sidewalk. She held Adam's hand and Samuel wished it were him holding her hand. He thought about reaching for her free hand in the black gloves but decided against it. As they walked, he felt the crispness in the air, accented by her peach and lavender perfume. He could hardly tear his eyes away from her shiny lip gloss and he wondered what flavor it was. He could know with a kiss...

Further up the street he heard laughter and a chorus of Christmas songs in an off-key melody. A part of him suddenly wished to be safely home, up in his apartment, ensconced away from all things Christmas. His heart rate spiked. He went rigid. Then he swallowed against his fear. He could do this!

Because another part of him planned to squeeze every part of pleasure he could out of time spent with Dawson and Adam. If this was what it took, then he would do this. He gulped down the anxiety clawing up his gut and curled his fingers into fists and stuffed his fists into his jacket pockets. He was a grown man and he was going to act like one.

"Samuel. Hey, are you in there?"

Dawson's concerned voice reached him. He blinked and her wide-eyed stare swam into view.

He felt the heat rushing up to his face and he scrubbed his jaw. "Sorry. I've gotten into a bad habit of drifting off lately. You were saying?"

She looked a little dubious at his casual excuse but let his fading away go. "We have some time before Santa arrives so how about a sleigh ride?"

A sleigh ride sounded easy enough. Now his ears caught the jingling sounds of sleigh bells. Old Bob Pickett and his sons brought their big draft horses to town for every Christmas festival. The sons gave sleigh rides with their antique sleighs and Bob would bring "Santa" in later with a smaller, specially decorated sleigh.

"Sure. That sounds like fun."

They went to the corner when Bob's sons had the two sleighs, one larger and one smaller. The larger sleigh was just coming back from a ride, with the passengers laughing and singing as they climbed down. The other driver and the more intimate sleigh waited. Samuel waved to the driver, thinking it was fortuitous they caught the smaller ride.

"Come on up. Sparky and I will give you a tour like you've never seen."

"Sparky must be the horse," Dawson said as she gestured to the large brown horse waiting patiently.

Samuel took Dawson's hand and helped her step onto the metal footstep and up into the sleigh. Then he gripped Adam by the underarms and swung him in. Once they settled, he sat down next to Dawson, and opposite Adam. "Okay, we're good."

The driver tapped Sparky and the horse jogged forward, his bells shaking merrily. The driver introduced himself as Jeffrey and he drove them along the northern part of Main Street, with its many rows of shoppes, past the school, the church, the hotel, and numerous homes. They jogged along the outskirts of town. They passed Cedar Falls, where the water splashed along ice-covered rocks and followed the creek as it wound along its way.

Dawson pointed out the school and the church to Adam as they drove by. She shared stories of people she knew and events that happened. Samuel was not sure how much Adam understood but her stories painted vivid pictures in his mind. He saw the little girl grow up to a teen to a young woman and finally to the fiercely independent mother she had become. What he saw now intrigued him. Her breath came out in frosty puffs as she laughed with Adam. Her lips shined and he sorely wanted to kiss those lips.

To take his mind off Dawson's plump lips, he watched Adam's youthful delight in the town's Christmas decorations, the rush of the falls, and the gently falling flakes. He remembered a time when he was the young boy and thrilled with the holiday and all things Christmas and Santa. That was before he learned some hard truths and lost his zeal for Christmas. Watching Adam still with his zest so strong and his pure innocence caused an ache inside him, that squeezed his very heart.

Sparky and Jeffrey took them further out of town. The sleighs runners cut smoothly through the snow. They entered a patch of evergreen trees and the horse skillfully wove through the pines and firs.

"Twee!" Adam exclaimed happily, pointing as they went along.

Dawson nodded. Samuel was glad she never corrected his imperfect pronunciation of words. So far, he'd been able to understand the boy's short conversations. So many people wanted to teach a kid with a speech issue to talk the right way and he knew it usually did more harm than good. He'd bet anything that Adam would eventually work out most words on his own.

Dawson pointed to a pair of deer, startled by Sparky's bells. Adam's eyes lit up. The deer swiveled their ears, flicked their white tails, and bounded away. They soon vanished, melting into the forest. Through Adam's eyes, Samuel was being reminded of the enchantment of the season.

They left the forest behind and entered a small meadow that

skirted a pond. Samuel stretched his arm out and draped it around Dawson's shoulder. She smiled up at him, and his pulse rocketed. He leaned forward and smelled her perfume, inhaling cool peach and lavender. His gaze flickered to her bright lips and he would give a lot to know what flavor gloss she wore. This close, he swore he smelled pumpkin pie. The slow burning desire that smoldered deep within him licked to life, unleashing an intense heat all through him.

A group of turkeys flew up in alarm from under a bush as Jeffrey turned the sleigh back toward town.

"Bird!"

"Yes. Those are wild turkeys. Big birds."

"Bird. Tur-kee." Adam worked the words around. Then he flapped his tiny arms and looked at Samuel. "Tur-kee. Eat."

Samuel tilted his head to one side. "What do you mean, buddy? Yes, we can eat a turkey."

Beside him, Dawson shifted and lowered her gaze to peek at him. "We're having turkey for Christmas dinner. Would you consider joining us?"

The hot desire that consumed him a moment before snuffed instantly out. His heart stalled and his pulse skyrocketed. His mind went blank. *Christmas dinner.* He had avoided holiday meals for many years now. It was better, safer. He knew what the memories did to him.

He froze, remembering past meals. The turkey, the ham, the special dinners that never happened. The crackers crumbling in his palm as he rushed to devour them, the cake he tore the plastic wrapper away, the orange he peeled the outer skin from...

So many Christmas meals, almost thirty years' worth. So many colossal heartbreaks. His rock-solid vow to never celebrate another.

But he wanted to be near Dawson. He inhaled a long, cold

breath through his nose, and then another, letting each one out in measured amounts. He could do this.

"Sure." He heard the strangled answer escape his mouth like the frost of their breath. He must not have sounded as bad to them as to his own ears since they didn't look surprised. Except they were not aware of how fast his heart hammered and his chest tightened. "Do...do you want me to bring anything?"

"No, I've got it. Just bring your sparkling holiday personality."

While she sounded sincere, he knew she was being snarky with him. He let out an uneven breath, glad she was unaware of the anguish her simple request caused him. Or maybe she was and deliberately made light of it.

Dawson chatted, discussing the menu as Jeffrey and Sparky took them back into town. The snow that had been drifting down in lazy flakes now rained down in a steady pattern.

"Thanks, Jeffrey. Great ride," Samuel said once everyone exited the sleigh. He slipped some bills to the driver as Dawson and Adam patted the horse.

"Okay, now what?" he asked once they joined hands and walked away from the corner.

Dawson looked around. "It's a little early still for the tree lighting. And I think Santa might have arrived while we were out of town. Let's work our way to Santa's spot." She nodded her head to Adam, who failed to respond to the big elf's name.

Samuel caught the concern in Dawson's face and voice. She pulled those luscious looking lips into a worried pout. He took her hand and squeezed it tight. When she looked at him, he smiled and winked. "It will be okay," he whispered. "Let's go." He headed out to the makeshift workshop where 'Santa' held court with the local kids.

There were only two kids in line when they arrived. Dawson knelt at Adam's side and adjusted his outer gear. "Sweetie, you remember us talking about Santa Claus, right? There he is." She indicted the man in the red suit. "When it's your turn, go up to him, and tell him your name, and what you want him to bring you for Christmas. Okay, buddy?"

Adam nodded, his attention more on the lights and decorations than Santa. Samuel placed a hand on Dawson's shoulder, giving her another reassuring squeeze. She stood up and a frosty sigh escaped her. Soon it was Adam's turn and she gently pushed him in the right direction. Santa smiled wide and waved to Adam and greeted him with a hearty "Ho! Ho! Ho!"

"It's okay, Dawson. He will get better each year." Samuel wrapped his arm around her shoulder as they watched. "This is doubtlessly the first year he is aware of Santa. He's not quite three yet. Next year will be better."

"Maybe."

"And Santa is good with kids. It's kind of a prerequisite for his job."

She paused, then slowly turned around and looked at him. Realization dawning she lightly punched him in the arm. "Very funny, Samuel."

Within a few minutes, Adam came running back, waving a candy cane in his fist. "I saw Santa!" he exclaimed. Dawson knelt and he rushed into her arms. Samuel smiled at the tender scene, but his arms now ached due to the emptiness.

They walked along the streets, winding their way through town. Dawson and Adam frequently stopped to look at something. Dawson would kneel by his side, and they laughed if it were funny, exclaimed if it was amazing, and Dawson always explained a little about whatever it was. Samuel had walked these streets for years now, and for as many holidays, and he'd never experienced the awareness he did of his adopted town as he did today.

The afternoon wore on and the temperatures cooled. It

would soon be time for the tree lighting. And then their wonderful day would end. He felt a crushing pain in his chest.

"How about some food? I think they have the food tent ready to go."

Hands linked with Dawson and Adam, he led them to the large red and green striped tend set up along the southern end of Main Street. The white and multi-colored strands of lights that wove along the top of the tent acted like a beacon to guide them in, where the rich smells of frying foods enveloped them as they entered. Brightly lighted Christmas trees, each about four feet tall, flanked the entrance. Beyond that came the scent of frying meats and yeasty breads.

"Kind of sensory overload."

Dawson frowned at his comment. Adam inhaled and reached for the tree branch. Dawson caught his hand. "No, sweetie. Just like at home, look but don't touch. See the star on top?"

The food was set up buffet style, with tables and chairs set up for dining in. Dawson took a plastic tray and handed one to Samuel. He would bet they were on loan from the school. They selected hand-held pot pies, beef for him, turkey for Dawson and chicken for Adam. They had baked potatoes and rice bakes, assorted cheeses and breads and a dessert table. Tapioca pudding for Adam, butterscotch for Samuel and a cinnamon roll for Dawson.

At the beverage table, it was mulled cider for everyone. They took their seats and Samuel couldn't help the pride that filled him at the smiling glances the locals sent their way. Dawson seemed oblivious to the looks as she helped Adam and ate her own meal. He knew they looked like a normal family enjoying a meal at the festival, and he couldn't be prouder. Let the locals talk and tease him later, right now he was soaking in the moment.

"Cider isn't bad. I usually have a few drops of brandy in mine."

Dawson smirked. "By the time I finish that house, I'll skip the cider and just take a bottle of brandy."

He laughed. "Is the house that hard to work on?" He thought of the furnace issue with fondness.

"No, not really. My dad…" A heavy sigh escaped her. "I don't know exactly when we stopped being family. It feels like I'm staying with a stranger now." She wrinkled her nose. "Can you imagine not even recognizing your own dad?"

Yes, he could, but that wasn't a conversation for now. He forced back the memories and reached for her hand. "I'm sure it's rough. How is he with Adam?"

"Better than with me. I can usually trust him to watch him so I can get some work done. They watch television a lot. I suspect that's all Dad does anyway. I try to get him to come into town with us, or go do anything, but he's not interested." She dabbed at her eye. "I just don't know what to do other than plug away until I get the house done."

His heart picked up an extra beat. "And then what?"

"We pack up and go?"

She made it sound like a question. So he posed the one foremost on his mind. "Go where?"

"No clue. Somewhere. I can try to get a new job back in Virginia." She smiled. "Or I could hire on as a home repair specialist."

He laughed, deep and long. He loved her wit! Stopping, he touched a thumb to her cheek, cupping her face. He leaned closer. "I think you are very skilled in many things. Wherever you go or do, you will be a success."

She licked her lips and he smelled pumpkin. "Thank you, but I don't have your confidence just yet."

He ached to kiss those enticing lips. He yearned to make her smile again. "Or you could consider staying here in Cedar Falls?" He posed it like a question. His pulse picked up pace as she licked those luscious lips again. She was killing him.

She gave a shake of her head. "No, probably not. When the house is as done as I can make it, Adam and I are out of here."

He deflated like a popped balloon. She wasn't happy about that, but she seemed sure of it. He'd bet her strained relationship with her father was behind that sad expression. He glanced outside the tent at the gathering dusk. He started putting their leftover items on one tray and stacked the other two beneath it. "It's getting late. I'll clean up and we should get back out there if you want to catch the tree lighting."

"Twee!"

Samuel had to wonder how much Adam understood of the conversations going on around him. "Yes, buddy. And how about some cocoa for all of us to go?"

Dawson tidied Adam up from his meal while Samuel dumped their trash and grabbed three hot cocoas from the beverage table. He also placed three tree-shaped sugar cookies on a paper plate.

He returned to their table and Dawson smiled her gratitude, warming him inside out, better than the cocoa would do. She handed a cookie to Adam and held both their Styrofoam cups. Exiting the tent, they ran into four people dressed in nutcracker costumes. They danced, twirled, and kicked around the street. Adam laughed and Dawson giggled. Adam stomped his tiny boots in the piles of snow, delighting in making little footprints.

Samuel wondered what all he'd taken for granted until these two came into his life to make him see it all. Even the sweet sugar cookie and warm cocoa tasted more vibrant. Almond and buttercream and chocolate with marshmallows all exploded on his tongue in ways he never recalled these holiday staples tasting before. Had he been immune to them before?

Watching Adam and Dawson, he saw how they added colors to his life that he never knew he was missing. Had he been living in a dark hole?

As they walked, lights came to life everywhere. Streetlights flickered on, more strung strands of Christmas lights lit the paths to the town center where the tall evergreen waited to be lit. It was as if an old Christmas card came to life.

"Adam swears there's magic in the snow."

Samuel was beginning to wonder if that were true. There was magic going on around them now, there had been magic enveloping them during the sleigh ride, he was feeling magic sneak into the strangest places. So why not in the snow. "I can believe that," he simply said.

Vendors with their booths turned on table lights to show the last of their wares. Soon they would be packing up and probably going to see the tree lighting.

They passed booth after booth. One held homemade wreaths decorated with ribbons, bows, lights, flowers, and all manner of Christmas designs. Samuel stopped, unexplainably drawn to them. One caught his eye more than the others. A white grapevine wreath, ten inches in diameter and simply decorated called to him. He reached a finger out to trace the items. White poinsettias and red carnations nestled in a bed of pine boughs and holly, asymmetrically on the wreath. A silver star and a flowing blue gingham bow centered in the flowers. It was simplistic and still so...familiar.

"That's lovely."

He jumped at Dawson's voice at his side. "Yes, it is." He looked to the gray-haired lady sitting behind the table. "Um... How much?"

"Forty dollars."

He had no idea if that was a good price or not. He'd never bought a wreath. He just knew for whatever reason, this one needed to be on his shop door. Before he could analyze the feelings churning within him, he nodded to the lady and reached into his jeans pocket. He withdrew two bills and handed them over.

"What are you thinking?" Dawson asked. "I'd have thought you would go for the green monster there."

He followed her finger to a wreath decorated with colorful green, yellow, and white ribbons bunched in a circle and in the middle rested a green monster snarling like a wicked witch. Nope, the design held no appeal for him. He picked up his wreath, surprised to find his hand shaking. He flashed Dawson an unsure smile. "I'm really don't know what I was thinking, but this will look nice on the shop's door."

She grinned. "You know you'll be expected to keep it out every year now, right?"

He nodded, exhaling heavily. The sound of carolers beckoned them down the street. They linked arms so they could each hold their cocoa cups too. They paraded down the brick lined street to the center where the tree waited for lighting. The Christmas lights surrounding them created an ethereal glow. His fingers gripped the wreath as if he were afraid a gust of wind might rip it away. They stopped to listen to the carolers sing *The Little Drummer Boy.*

Dawson knelt at Adam's side and helped him sing a few words and the drum sound. Samuel's heart squeezed with conflicting emotions and tears gathered in his eyes. He blinked them away. His knees felt weak and he leaned on a lamp post for support. Cold sweat broke out on his forehead.

Festival. Dinner. Wreath. He shook his head in confusion. When had he emerged from his protective cocoon to experience Christmas?

"Paa-Rump-a-Pum-Pum." Dawson clapped her hands and Adam sang along, repeating the words. She looked up at Samuel and he melted. He had to grip the lamp post tighter. His breath stalled in his chest.

Whatever was happening to him, he knew one thing: he had to tell Dawson the whole story of why he shunned Christmas and why everyone thought he was a scrooge. He ached just watching her interact with her son, encouraging him to sing a simple song. He owed her the truth.

"Samuel, you okay? You look a little pale?" Dawson stood up and eyed him critically.

Cold sweat dripped down his back. He shook his head and pasted on a smile. "I'm fine. Are we ready?" He inclined his head further down the street.

They made their way to the center of town. Bricks swirled in a circular pattern, and the tall fir tree stood balanced in the center. Benches spread out from it and the town mayor, Mrs. Armstrong, sat on one bench, surrounded by young children. The light above her cast a golden glow on the opened book she held on her lap. The children had been fussing impatiently and as she cleared her throat, they stilled, sitting in rapt attention. They knew soon they would help light the big tree.

"'Twas the night before Christmas and all through the..."

Samuel listened to the mayor read the well-known tale. He recognized the book she held as one she'd purchased from his store his first winter in Cedar Falls. He watched, his attention between the mayor and her flock of enraptured children and Dawson as she watched Adam. Her expression hinged on bittersweet. She took a sip of her cocoa and her lip puckered into a thoughtful pout as he swayed to the mayor's words.

The melted marshmallows left a frothy mustache on her upper lip and heat suddenly uncoiled in Samuel's gut. He couldn't tear his gaze away from her lips. Having intrigued him all afternoon, they positively tormented him now. Whatever she was thinking about paled in comparison to the hot need overwhelming him. His pulse raced to a fast drumbeat.

She looked up at him and smiled. He was lost, sinking, and powerless. He took her hand, drew her up and inhaled her caramel, sugar cookie, and gingerbread scents in a greedy breath. Still with desire, he cupped her chin. His eyes stayed riveted on her foamy mustache. Did she have any idea how desirable she was?

His heart thudded. His hand dipped and he placed his lips over hers. It was the sweetest connection. She closed her eyes and leaned in. He grew bolder at her throaty moan.

The street noises surrounding them faded away. The lights blurred. It was just him and her. And the chocolatey caterpillar on her luscious lip. Before a rational thought could stop him, he leaned in more, pressed his lips against hers as he tasted cocoa and marshmallow sweetness. He drew the kiss out, gathering as much sweet flavor as he could from her moist lips. She relaxed in his gentle hold. He wished the moment they shared could last forever.

Finally, he withdrew, keeping a hand on her arm. He licked his lips and smiled. He wiped her lips with his thumb, liking how wobbly she appeared. She blinked up at him.

"Dawson, do you know how very desirable you are?"

CHAPTER 5

Dawson drove home, still licking her lips over and over. Whatever sparked Samuel's kiss and comment had not dissipated. She could feel his warm touch, a sharp contrast to the cool air. She tasted his own warm chocolatey kiss. She still felt the shivers caused by the dark light in his eyes as he drew her close, when the rest of the festival faded away and it was just the two of them, kissing.

Shivers slid over her as they pulled into the driveway. She was as giddy as a kid.

Do you know how very desirable you are?

No. Because no one, not even Adam's father, made her feel desirable. Needed, yes. Pretty, yes. Many things, but never desired.

She locked herself in the bathroom. She stood, looking at her image in the mirror. She gingerly ran her fingertip over her lips. They were still bruised from his rough-scruff kiss.

Oh, that kiss!

She smiled and the smile grew bigger in the mirrored reflection. He'd called her beautiful. The last time someone called her beautiful was her mom when she went to the prom.

She felt the tremble in his voice as he touched her face, the gentleness in his touch and the desire in his eyes. He smelled so good, a delicious blend of amber, cinnamon, and musk. She felt like a desirable woman! Like a movie star or runway model or acclaimed singer.

She lifted her hand to the mirror and placed her fingertips to the glass. She studied her reflection. What an afternoon it had been. The only thing that bothered her was his reaction to her invitation to Christmas dinner.

Most people are happy to be invited. He looked like she had wounded him. She wondered what had caused him such ache. She watched the uneven rise and fall of his chest as he worked through some internal dilemma. His face paled and his eyes darkened with sorrow. She wished she could have reached up and erased the furrow between his eyebrows. He drifted away, going someplace she didn't want to go. When he finally spoke, the angst almost tore her in two. It took everything inside her to pretend she'd not noticed and keep the moment light.

She would be surprised if he did show.

Aside from that moment, she had a wonderful time. And Adam never stopped talking all the way back. His two- and three-word sentences bubbled with excitement. Her heart swelled to know she and Samuel gave her boy a wonderful Christmas memory.

From a self-proclaimed anti-Christmas scrooge. Well, something made him react like he had about the invitation. And then something else made him buy that lovely wreath. What a contrast. He'd acted like a man in a dream when he stopped at the booth and bought the wreath. It meant something to him, though he wouldn't say what.

And then he kissed her. And called her desirable. She giggled at the woman in the mirror.

"You gonna be in there all night?"

She jumped at the sound of her dad pounding on the door.

"No. I'm coming." She flipped her hair and reminded herself she was twenty-six, not sixteen as she twisted the knob.

"Was there something you wanted, Dad?" she asked as sweet as she could. "You missed a fantastic tree lighting festival."

He waved a hand in the air. "I've seen plenty of them. Same old thing every year."

She begged to differ. Samuel hadn't been to the other festivals to light her up inside brighter than the town's tree. "Adam had a great time. He'd never been to one before."

"Are you going to make dinner?"

She blinked, rebuffed by his lack of interest in his grandson. "I hadn't planned to. Adam and I ate in town." She inhaled a weary breath. "Do you want me to whip you up something? An omelet and toast? Cheeseburger and fries?"

His face dropped. "You already ate?" Then he waved a hand through the air again, as if dismissing her. "Never mind. I still have a pot pie or two left."

Relief warred with concern. She would have been happy to cook him something but was glad he dismissed her. "Suit yourself." She decided to indulge the relieved emotion as she walked to the living room to turn on the tree lights and call Adam.

The scent of pine filled the room and the lights cast a soft glow. She listened to her dad bang around the kitchen and snuggled her son to her chest. She missed her mom. She missed Samuel. She wondered if she was making the right choice to stay here and work on the house. Maybe it was beyond her after all.

She blinked at the multi-colored lights and a tear ran down her cheek.

❄

Dawson's breath escaped in a startled exhale and she muttered a curse. She snatched her hand back and glared at the heavy toilet lid that just crashed across her knuckles.

"That hurt! This is nuts." She tossed down the wrench and examined the wound, swelling more by the second.

Desirable. The word could still spin her off into emotional circles. She cradled her hand to her chest and looked down at herself. "He might not see me as desirable now."

Dressed in patched coveralls and a green chambray shirt she found in a thrift store, and her hair in a twisted braid, she could hardly be considered desirable by anyone.

But last night still belonged to them...

"This is crazy. It's time for a break." She brushed herself off. How she managed to get cobwebs in her braid was beyond her, but there they were, sticking and defying her attempt to dislodge them. She wrinkled her nose at the thought of what else could be up there. And she sported a funky odor. Who knew plumbing was so dirty?

Forty minutes later, cleaned and smelling of cranberries and vanilla, she and Adam headed out to the bookstore. They parked a block away and took their time to enjoy the storefronts. Adam pounded every little snow hill he could find, smashing it into the brick sidewalk.

"Oh, look at this, Adam." Dawson pointed to Samuel's new wreath on the door. "Doesn't that look nice." In fact, it looked great. Festive. He picked a good wreath. Since it was Sunday, the store was closed. She bent over and fished the key out from under the white rock. Samuel used four rocks to set up sandwich boards or other signage. Two were gray, one was brown, and one was white, which also hid the spare key.

She knocked once, to alert Samuel if he were upstairs, and ushered Adam inside. She relocked the door and left the key on the low bookcase. "Adam, go play by the chair. This won't take long." She helped him out of his outer clothes and gave him a gentle push to the chair she wanted him to use.

It did not appear that Samuel was around. She removed her coat and scarf and the kittens scampered over to her, meowing loudly. She giggled at the sight of three fluffballs, rushing toward her with their broomstick tails all straight up in the air.

"You guys are growing like weeds. And you're so cute!" She scooped them up and nuzzled their soft baby fur. She carried them to their feed station and filled their chow bowl. She'd never seen it empty yet, despite their complaining mews to the contrary. But she heaped it full each time.

Next, she cleaned their water bowl and their litter box. By the time she returned from taking the dirty litter to the trash outside it was clear Samuel wasn't in. She sat down by Adam with a brush and started grooming them as they came at her. Their contented purrs and playful batting at one another made her happy. Adam stopped playing with the toy car and cuddled one kitten when it crawled into his lap.

"Gentle."

"Yes, honey, that's right. Pet the baby gentle." Dawson sighed. "I could weaken so easy. But I just don't know where we are going to end up. Forgive me?" She made a silent vow that once she and Adam were settled into a place, she would adopt a puppy or a kitten. Maybe both. "I never even checked the paperwork to check. Are you guys all guys?" She picked up her favorite solid gray bundle of fluff. "And which one are you? Winking, Blinking or Nod?"

She cradled the baby against her chest and went to the counter in search of the paperwork Barb left. The information and Barb's cards lay in the corner of the wooden counter, under a small paperback book. *Your First Cat: What to Expect.*

How thoughtful of Samuel to leave that out for any

prospective adopter. She shifted through the pages. Two boys and a girl. "And you, my little gray friend, are a boy. Blinking."

She held the kitten up to her face and planted a kiss on his nose. "What a silly name. I hope whoever adopts you goes with something more appropriate." The kitten patted her nose with his paws, and she breathed in the clean kitten smell. Like clean laundry dried in the sunny breeze.

Ten minutes later she locked up the store and replaced the key. He'd left his truck outside so he must have walked somewhere or ridden with someone else.

"Twee!" Adam pointed down to the town center where the tree stood like a dark green sentinel.

"Lights?" He frowned, looking so incredibly sad she squeezed his hand reassuringly.

"Yes, the lights are still there. It's simply hard to see them in the daytime. But I promise you tonight, when it's dark, they will shine just like they did last night."

He tugged her along the brick walk and she gave in. "Okay, we can go look at the tree."

Adam walked with such purpose, not even bothering to squash the tiny mounds of snow. She was proud of him. Whatever his purpose to have to see the tree now, it was clear in his mind. They reached the tree and he sat on the bench where the mayor had sat, surrounded by the children. Adam looked around and then stared expectantly at Dawson.

She glanced around. What did he want? People strolled past, many carrying packages. A few cars went by. Being Sunday not many stores were open, and most people were either in church, gathered with family or preparing for their holiday. She waved at a woman with a familiar face, not exactly sure who she was either, then back at Adam.

"Stor..ee."

He sat primly, little hands folded in his lap, attention riveted on her. She bit her lip in thought. Stor...ee. Then the light bulb went on. "Oh you, want a story. Duh, Dawson." She sat down next to him and took him into her lap, inhaling the little boy smell she loved about him. It had been a while since she recited the Christmas tale. Would she remember it? She had other things on her mind last night, Samuel things. Then she looked into her son's trusting eyes and she cleared her throat.

"Okay, it was the night before Christmas..."

Adam leaned his cheek against her shoulder as she finished the story. Clapping drew her gaze to the left. *Samuel?*

"That is by far the best I've ever heard that story told."

She studied the man as he slowly approached them. He wore his dark blond hair close cropped, his clean-shaven face showed off a square jaw with a mole and he had blue eyes. He towered over them, so she guessed he was near the six-foot-tall mark. His smile was bright and even. A note of familiarly struck her.

"Hardly, I missed a couple of key parts." She pushed her hair behind her. "Sorry but do I know you?"

"Dawson Patrick, right?"

She gave a slow nod, her other arm automatically curling tighter around Adam. Her son cuddled closer to her, but he was naturally shy and wasn't displaying any unusual distress.

The man didn't seem bothered. He grinned. "It's been a while. We've both changed some. I've found a good barber and you just got better with age. I'm Kurt Duskey."

"Kurt. Duskey." The pieces fit and she gasped, her hand going to her mouth. "Kurt! You look..."

"Different. Yeah, I know. You remember me when I was channeling my inner mountain man."

She laughed. "Yes, you cleaned up and lost a lot of hair. You look good."

"Thanks. I heard you were back in town, at your daddy's, with a little one." He inclined his head at Adam.

"Kurt, this is my son, Adam." She angled her head to face Adam, who stared suspiciously at the new man. "Adam, this is Kurt. He's an old friend of mine. We went to school together." She turned back to Kurt and motioned to the adjacent bench. "We went to school, dated, went to the prom, and then you broke my heart."

He staggered back. "After prom, you broke my heart." He sat down and held up a hand to stop her comeback. "Hey, it's cold out here. Why don't we go somewhere warm, have some coffee, catch up and decide who broke whose heart?"

It was Kurt asking. He leaned forward on the bench, elbows on his knees, and an expectant smile on his face. She'd given her heart to Kurt in high school. He was her first real crush, first love, first everything, until it ended. Then he was her first heartbreak. There was a time she could never deny him when he asked like he was asking now. Just coffee this time. She looked into his blue eyes and remembered...so much. Her heart did a little flip flop and butterflies lifted off in her stomach.

"All right."

They walked up the street to Laughter and Lattes Coffee Shop. Dawson couldn't believe she was walking with Kurt. It was as if the years peeled back and they were seventeen again. Except she had Adam now.

They took seats and she ordered a chocolate milk and blueberry muffin and a regular coffee for herself. Her stomach was too tied in knots to try to eat. She grinned at the funny latte Kurt ordered.

He shrugged. "I developed a taste for them while I was in L. A."

"What did you do there?"

Again, he lifted a shoulder in a shrug. "I left here with the intent to begin acting. Then surfing. I did get small parts in a few movies, which led to behind the camera jobs for bigger movies." He sighed. "It wasn't as magical as I thought it would be. But the surfing was great." He grinned, looking every bit the boy she remembered. "But the coffee was something else. Now, what about you?"

She caught the subtle look at Adam and briefly explained about her marriage, and divorce to Peter and how she was contacted by her brother and ended up here.

"Sounds like you are better off." He set the coffee mug aside. "Do you remember what you and I liked to do in the winter?"

A few things came to mind. She crossed her arms on the table. "Can you be more specific?"

"Sure." He drew the word out, a husky drawl in his tone that caused a shiver up Dawson's arms. His eyes shone as he continued. "Do you remember us ice skating?"

Samuel returned home sore, and hungry. Hank Thomas, a Cedar Falls senior resident had stopped by and asked him to help with some trees that had fallen in his yard. Normally his sons would have helped with that sort of task, but they were out of town for a few weeks on their job commitments. Mr. Thomas looked so nervous, wringing his hat in his hands as he asked for help, Samuel didn't have the heart to say no. As much as he had wanted to see Dawson when she came to town, more so he had to go assist a resident in need.

Mr. Thomas suggested he drive, saving Samuel the trouble of using his truck. And he promised to give him lunch and bring him back afterward. While he could think of better ways to spend a Sunday, he gladly accepted the offer. Mrs. Thomas fed him a large lunch of thick sandwiches, fried potatoes, apple pie for dessert, and strong coffee.

By both using chain saws, Mr. Thomas and Samuel powered through the fallen timbers and cut them up for future firewood. The sons could split and stack the wood for drying once they got back home. And Samuel had to admit, it felt good to be outside in the brisk air, hear the buzz of a chainsaw, and put in a hard day's labor with a neighbor.

It was nearly four when Mr. Thomas brought him home. "Here," he said as Samuel opened the truck door.

It was a fifty-dollar bill. Samuel looked at it for a moment and handed it back. "Thanks, but I didn't help for the money. It did me good to be out with you today."

"Nonsense. Your time is worth something. Certainly, I took you away from something valuable today, even if it was just watching television."

More like watching Dawson and Adam, but he smiled, nonetheless. "Let's just say I was extending the Christmas spirit, okay?" He closed the door, shutting off any further arguments, but not before he caught the look of surprise on Mr. Thomas's face. Even he knew that Samuel Johnson had no Christmas spirit. But that was before Dawson rolled into his life with her tacky sweater, insulted his tree, and flashed a smile that oozed Christmas spirit.

He let himself in the front door and relocked it. The kittens came running to greet him. The place smelled clean. As they twirled around his ankles and tried to kill him, he shuffled to their dishes. Yep, they still had food left to carry them till tomorrow. He bent over and picked up Blinking.

"Come on, you're coming upstairs with me. At least for a little while." The kitten settled into his arm and closed his eyes with a contented purr. "And we're doing something about that name too."

Upstairs he sat the kitten down on the chair. It blinked and protested with a loud meow. Samuel chuckled. "Bossy thing, aren't you?"

He pulled out the large skillet and a package of chicken thighs. Within minutes he had the meat browning. He poked and tossed a baking potato in the microwave and washed and tossed a salad. Rosemary and lemon permeated the room soon after he added them to the frying chicken. He kept glancing at the kitten. It just sat watching him, his fluffy tail curled around his front legs. Samuel took a sheet from his grocery list pad and wadded it up.

"Hey, Blinking, wanna chase this?" He tossed it to land a couple of feet away. Blinking pounced, lightning fast, and grabbed the paper in both paws.

"Wow, you're fast for a little guy." He watched as Blinking tossed the into the air and deftly caught it. He swatted it to the end of the chair, and then on the floor. He jumped down after it, hunted it a minute before climbing back up to the chair with his prize in his mouth. He whacked it twice more before resuming his original position watching Samuel.

"That was very entertaining, Blinking. Good job. It won't be long, and you'll be able to jump up to that chair." He knew from memories and his reading on the subject, kittens grew and soon learned to jump vertically to near impossible heights as well as horizontal lengths. Furniture, cabinetry, and all manner of high places soon become fair game to a cat.

The chicken was soon done, and he added fixings to the salad and baked potato. Preparing a plate and a cup of warm tea, he moved to the small dinette table overlooking the street. Blinking followed, climbed up on his lap and curled into a ball, purring happily.

Samuel tore off a small piece of chicken, blew on it to cool it and offered it to Blinking. "How about some real meat?"

The kitten reached for it, sniffed it cautiously, took a tentative lick and then accepted it. Samuel offered three more bites of chicken and even a piece of potato. As he ate, he gazed out the window at the scene below.

Houses and apartments glowed from interior lights and candles flickering in the windows, some doors sparkled with illuminated wreaths and streetlights shone. In the distance he could see the lights from the church's nativity scene and the tree at the town center. He had the urge for cocoa for dessert. He could almost smell the apple streusel, and candy canes. The glow of the moon glistened off the snow. A magical feeling reflected off the lights, creating a look of sheer fantasy.

He pushed the plate away and rubbed the kitten's belly, earning a gentle kangaroo lick. The tiny paws latched onto his fingers and the rough tongue felt like sandpaper. Samuel swore he felt part of his heart crack.

He cleared his throat, swallowing a lump. "How do you feel about Sampson?"

A short time later he carried Blinking/ Sampson back downstairs. He went to bed, lying with his arms curled behind his head. He stared at the ceiling. A knot formed in his stomach. Tomorrow he was going to Dawson's for Christmas. It was just a dinner, but it was Christmas dinner. He wasn't sure what he was feeling more: fear or elation.

Adam pounded on Dawson's bedroom door, rudely pulling her away from a cocoa sweet dream of Samuel's kiss. Roused, she fumbled for her watch on the nightstand. 6:19. She blinked, and the pounding continued.

"Mom! Twee. Come see."

Despite the early hour, she smiled. Ever since the afternoon at the tree lighting festival, Adam was trying to put more words in his sentences. She had to believe it was Samuel's patient and accepting influence. She absolutely could not fault him when it came to his dealings with Adam. Samuel was better than Adam's own father had been once it became clear Adam wasn't considered 'normal'.

"Mama!"

She rolled over and swung her feet to the floor and quickly thrust her toes into the moccasin slippers. Adam was recently also developing new senses, like urgency, thoughtfulness, and animation. While she was glad to see him developing anything new, the sense of urgency sometimes grew old quickly.

"Yes, Adam. Give me a minute." She called through the door as she stood up and let the room settle a second. Mama was his newest word, copied from Samuel. So far, he was alternating between calling her Mama and Mom. Eventually he'd settle on one. For now, she swore she heard a tiny huff of frustration on the other side of the door. She grinned. It would probably get worse over the years.

She brushed her hair away from her face and wondered what he would be like next Christmas. He'd be almost four and hopefully would experience a lot of growth over the coming year. And where would they be in a year? Probably not in Cedar Falls. Another knock goaded her to the door.

"I am coming. Hold on."

She had carefully outlined the day's events last night as she and Adam had sat in the living room, bathed in the glow from the tree lights. First, Adam could open one present. Her dad promised he'd get the boy something so she was banking there would be at least two presents under the tree by morning. After that came a hearty breakfast of French toast, sausage and scrambled eggs with fruit and juice. After that came showers, or a bath in Adam's case. Then he could open another gift. Lastly, he and Grandpa could go do something fun outside while she prepared dinner and worked on the house.

The turkey was previously thawed and stuffed and just needed to go in the oven. She had already done as much prep work ahead as possible and she was utilizing her mom's old slow cookers to make the sides. Basically, dinner was pretty much done. And Samuel had already said she didn't need to come into town Christmas Day for the cats, so she had lots of spare free time to work on her current house project. And he would be joining them in time for a three o' clock meal.

Her heart fluttered. Would he like what she cooked? Would he like the decorations? Why was he so against Christmas and still live in a town that celebrated it for weeks?

She opened her door and her heart melted. "Oh, sweetie, you look like an angel." His blue eyes sparkled, and his cheeks glowed with cherub dimples. "All you need is wings."

She ruffled his blond sleep-tousled hair. "Doubtlessly Grandpa will be around by now. Let's see what he got you." She hoped he did get Adam something like he said, and that it was appropriate for her son. Yes, they had their differences, but Adam was his grandson and he deserved to be treated as such. They reached the living room hand in hand. Her dad sat in his chair, reading a newspaper. She brushed her hair aside.

"Morning, Dad. Merry Christmas."

"Merry Christmas." He set aside the paper and pointed to a box, roughly the size of a breadbox, beside the tree.

"Me!" Adam placed a finger to his chest, his smile big and bright. He broke free of Dawson's hand and rushed to the box. He eagerly tore the paper away and Dawson exhaled.

"That's very nice, dad." She studied the remote-control toy car. "Adam, what do you say to Grandpa?"

Adam climbed up in the chair and threw his arms around his grandpa and offered him a kiss on his cheek. Dawson swiped at the tears building in her eyes. Grandfather and Grandson, together at last. She noticed similarities between them: their chin, nose, and eyebrows.

A short while later, she called Adam away from the remote car. He was particularly enjoying the flashing headlights and real horn. She had to wonder if her dad knew about the horn when he bought the car.

"Breakfast, buddy. Put the car away for now." She had to fight from smiling at his disgruntled expression. Right now, he was all boy, wanting his car. Whether three years old, thirteen, or twenty-three, some things never change. She pointed a finger in the area she had told him to store the car when he wasn't playing with it. "Now, Adam. Breakfast will get cold."

She returned to the kitchen and soon heard running water as he washed up in the bathroom. She removed the French toast from the skillet to a plate and poured the warmed syrup into a gravy boat. She set the butter dish on the table and added glasses of orange juice It was all ready.

"Dad, do you want to join us? French toast and sausage."

She didn't hear a reply, so she sat down and waited for her son.

"What do you think of your car?" she asked after they began eating.

He smiled. "Fast."

"Your car goes fast? That's great. What else can it do?"

He mimicked the sound of a honking horn. She said the words and tried to get him to repeat them. After a few unsuccessful tries, she gave up with a hopeful smile. 'That's okay. Next time maybe."

He did so well with his vocabulary, colors, and numbers, and then he just stopped, like he ran into a wall or something. She wasn't sure how to respond or what to say, and maybe what not to say at those times. It made her crumble inside, just like his successes made her want to cry out to the heavens in delight.

"So here is the plan," she continued, ticking each item off on her fingers. "After I clean up, I'm taking a shower. And you get a bath. Then you can play with your car again. Then I'm going to work on the house for a bit until Samuel gets here. Did you know Samuel was coming for dinner today?"

He shook his head side to side. "Kibins?"

"Not today, buddy. We go back tomorrow and see the kittens. But you can open another gift once I get out of the shower and you get your bath. Okay?"

He nodded happily and took a big bite of sausage.

After her shower, she spritzed on cinnamon buns and mulberry scented body spray, another special she found unopened at the thrift store. She rubbed on matching body lotion and smiled at the scent lifting into the air. Then she dressed in a long-sleeved thermal top and overalls but took care on her hair. She added volumizer and curled the ends and fluffed her bangs. Later, when her repair duties were done for the day, she would change into that special red dress.

Samuel was really going to find her desirable when he sees her in that red velvet dress. That was her best find so far at her thrift store shopping sprees. For only eight dollars, and it still had the tags attached, she felt she scored a great deal. She only wished she had pretty shoes to wear, but those were left back in Virginia, so she would have to make do with her high-topped boots.

Since she was spared having to run into town today, and dinner was fully prepped, she had enough spare time to knock a couple projects off her list. Cleaning the sticky kitchen drawers with WD40 and replacing one drawer slider were first on the list and she didn't think it would take long. No electricity this time.

If she still had time, she could tackle the loose cabinet knobs with some thread lock.

She was enjoying each item she could tick off her list, even if each finished project took her one step closer to leaving Cedar Falls and Samuel. And taking Adam away from his grandfather.

Two hours later, as she was tightening the screws for the new drawer slider, her dad's heavy footsteps clomped up to her. She froze.

"Dawson? You have a second?"

"Sure, Dad. Everything okay with Adam?" She stood and dusted herself off, her heart thumping uneasily. Her dad stood still, hands in his pockets. He shifted uncertainly, his gaze dropping to the ground.

Cold fear jabbed her. "Dad?"

"I know you and I don't always see eye to eye."

She waited, her breath held, her chest constricted. He seemed to be waiting for something, so she gave a slow nod. Was he kicking her out? Now?

"You have a good son. You should be proud of him, even if he doesn't talk much. It's okay to be quiet."

"Thank you." She didn't know what else to say. Her mind raced as she wondered what was behind his somber expression. Cold sweat dripped down her neck and ran down her back.

"Josh was always quiet."

He was comparing her son to Joshua? She didn't recall Josh or her ever being particularly quiet. Not like Adam was. However, her mounting anxiety prevented her from saying anything. Her dad shifted again. Her stomach tied in knots and she braced herself.

"What I mean to say... is...Merry Christmas, Dawson." He withdrew a box from his pocket. It was not gift wrapped but it bore the name of a jeweler. Her hands shook as she accepted it and lifted the lid.

Her breath left in a whoosh. "Dad! This is mom's jewelry set!"

"Yes," he agreed, kicking at a spot on the floor. "She loved it and now it's yours."

Dawson's hands trembled as she lifted the silver necklace from the blue velvet nest. The heavy medallion glistened in the overhead light. "I remember Mom wearing this. She said it made her feel beautiful and loved." She replaced the necklace and fingered the delicate oval earrings.

"I bought that set for our silver anniversary. She wore them every chance she could. I considered having them buried with her, but I figured one day you might get them."

She held the earrings up to the light. The tiny diamond that hung suspended from the oval sparkled like a star atop a Christmas tree. She remembered her mom wearing these and her youthful attention oftentimes riveting on the sparkling diamond as the earrings swayed at her mom's ears. Tears pricked her eyes. She replaced the earrings and took out the final piece, a silver link bracelet with tiny diamonds set in the center. "These will look very nice with the dress I'm wearing at dinner tonight." She returned the bracelet. Closing the lid was like closing the door on her mother's life.

"You said Samuel Johnson is coming to dinner?"

She nodded. "Yes. He had no family or plans, so it felt like the right thing to do."

"I've never heard of him talk about any family. Have you?"

"No. He never talks about anything personal like that. I have no idea what brought him to Cedar Falls. I just know he bought the bookstore on his twenty-fifth birthday."

Her dad grunted and turned to walk away. "I hope you enjoy that as much as your mother did."

❄

"That's beautiful, sweetie. Let's just plop the head on and get this guy dressed." Dawson helped Adam attach the volleyball sized snowball atop the soccer sized one beneath it, which sat upon a basketball sized base. She rocked back on her knees and handed Adam sticks, helping him stick them in the snow for arms. Then she handed over a carrot raided from the fridge and two large black mismatched buttons from her mom's sewing kit. One of Josh's baseball caps was the stand-in for a derby hat.

Adam methodically placed each item in the appropriate location and named each part. "Arm. Eye. Nose. Hat."

Dawson praised his skills, and his first snowman, and just wished she had a spare scarf and something for a mouth, but Adam didn't seem to notice they were missing.

"Give me a big hug, buddy," she said when they finished. She high fived him. "What a super snowman. Good job."

"Magic."

She tilted her head to examine the three-and-a-half-foot tall creation. "Maybe. One never knows." She wished she had Adam's innocent belief in magic. She needed some. He patted her shoulder and tears pricked her eyes. "I love you, sweetie. So much so." She hugged him tight, wishing the moment didn't have to end.

"Okay," She wiped at her tears, "let's go get changed for dinner. It's Christmas dinner and a special meal. Samuel will be here soon."

She couldn't wait to see Adam cleaned up, smelling his little boy smell she loved, and dressed in that adorable outfit she bought at the thrift store for four dollars. The fit was a perfect size for him: the tan trousers, white shirt, red suspenders, and a tan bowtie with white snowflakes.

She also could not wait to slip into that red velvet dress, splash on a few more drops of cinnamon buns and mulberry scent and see Samuel's face when he arrived.

CHAPTER 6

"Oh my word, how does Dawson do this! Gahhh!" Samuel plugged his nose and swallowed against the bile churning in his gut.

He'd come downstairs ready to tend to the kittens, glad that he could offer Dawson a day off. Feeding the furry beasts wasn't hard, as they made the location of their food known loud and clear. He easily figured out how to scrub their water dish. Then he tackled the litter box. Hot bile rushed through his senses as he knelt at their box and inserted the plastic scooper. His eyes watered and he pulled his shirt up to cover his mouth and nose.

"That is terrible. Which one of you three stooges had something crawl up your fluffy butt and die? Surely not you, Sampson?" If so, that might be a dealbreaker.

He finally got the box scooped, tied the bag with two knots and sprinted out to the trash can. He yanked his shirt down and sucked in a fresh breath. They may be cute, and possibly cuddly, but combined they were a formidable tribe of vile-smelling, stinky fluff.

Once inside again, he grabbed the carton of baking soda and dumped a liberal amount in the box. Barb said it helped neutralize odors. He'd stop at the store tomorrow and grab a couple more boxes. He also had a whole new respect for Dawson. She cleaned their septic tank litter box every day and never raised...a stink...over it.

Finished with the creatures, he headed back upstairs to shower and get ready for dinner. He'd driven over to Higgins last week and bought a suit from their menswear outlet to update his formal look. After his shower, he trimmed up his beard and dabbed on Five o' Clock aftershave. It was his favorite scent for many years; leather, lime, amber and fir blended with earthy, woodsy tones. He loved it. And he'd had a few lady customers comment how good he smelled. Today was all about making a good impression on Dawson.

And surviving Christmas. That had him worried the most. Hopefully, he would have a chance to talk privately with Dawson today. He grabbed Lloyd and Adam's gifts and headed out the door. "Behave you heathens and I'll give you a special dinner tonight. Tuna. Yeah, sounds good, doesn't it?"

He was losing his mind. Kittens. Tuna. Gifts for Adam and Lloyd. Suit for dinner. Dawson had just flipped his happy little world upside down and dropped it on its ear.

He drove out of town, passing only two other cars. He waved at the locals, figuring they were like him, traveling to someone's home for a meal. "Over the bridge and through the woods, to Uncle Lloyd's place we go." He chuckled at his dry humor.

He reached the Patrick house and immediately spotted Adam's snowman in the front yard. He liked the Portland Sea Dogs baseball cap perched on its head. He'd bet that was Josh's.

He knocked at the door, his heart pounding. He wasn't a kid anymore. He could handle Christmas as a grown man. He was no longer dependent on others to provide him happiness or disappointment. He would create his own joy and make new memories to push out the old ones still clinging to his psyche. So maybe Dawson shoving him into all things Christmas might be good for him. He shifted uneasily as he waited, and he wondered if he should knock again.

Lloyd opened the door. "Welcome, Samuel. Glad you could come."

"Glad to be invited. This is for you." He handed over a bottle of wine, wrapped with a basic bow and in a brown paper bag.

Lloyd took the wine, shook his hand, ushered him in and took his topcoat. "Dawson's in the kitchen. We can go to the parlor. The boy is in there now. She'll be along."

"Sounds good." Samuel set Adam's gift on the entry table and followed Lloyd's lead and they wound through the house. The rich smell of burning firewood and evergreen greeted him. As they passed near the kitchen, he hoped for a glimpse of Dawson but only smelled warm apple, cinnamon, turkey, and gingerbread. They reached the living room and he inhaled butter rum and nutmeg.

"Eggnog, Samuel?"

"Sure. Thanks." The rich flavor coated him in silky warmness. He sipped the creamy drink like it was warmed whiskey. They sat down and he studied the tree. "She did a good job decorating it."

Lloyd nodded, ignoring the tree. Adam called his name and rushed over to give him a hug. "How you doing today, buddy? Was Santa good to you?"

Adam nodded and climbed off Samuel, fetched his car and brought it over. He proudly showed him the horn and lights and all the directions it could go.

Samuel laughed. "Adam is going to be a master driver one day."

Again, Lloyd grunted. "Dawson feels sure he'll be good at a lot of things someday."

Samuel bristled at the words. He drew in a breath, reminding himself to be calm. "And doubtlessly she will be proven right. Adam just needs people to believe in him."

"Do you?"

Lloyd's direct question took him by surprise. He watched Adam play with the car, making sounds and decisions how to maneuver the remote clutched in his small hands. He turned back to Lloyd, conviction making his chest tight.

"Yes, I sure do."

Lloyd grunted again. "I'm trying to. He's no Joshua but he seems okay."

Samuel figured that was as high of praise anyone who wasn't Josh would get. He knew from previous visits old Lloyd didn't even rate Dawson as high as "okay" very often. It must have been tough on her after her mom died. And yet she still came back to help. She was a good woman. A good daughter. And a good mother.

"There you are. I thought I heard voices."

He looked up as Dawson came into the room. His heart stalled and his pulse skipped, and he was sure his face flushed. His hand was shaky, so he set the eggnog glass down. Quickly. He rose to his feet in welcome and almost fell back down. "Wow. Um, hi. You look fantastic."

Her red velvet dress nearly took him to his knees. It hugged all her curves that her overalls usually hid. It fluttered off her shoulders to reveal creamy arms and the hem ended just below her knees. Satin rosettes dotted the neckline and silver jewelry sparkled in the glow of the tree lights. He wanted to kiss her. His lips ached to touch hers.

He inhaled a ragged breath and took in the scent of mulberry and sweet cinnamon.

"You look nice too. Merry Christmas." She reached for his hand. Spider webs of tingling spread up his hand and arm.

"We're so glad you could join us."

Her smile was more brilliant than the tree. He flushed and self-consciously rubbed his vest, aware of her lingering look at the pink, double-breasted baroque fabric, which matched his tie. "It's the best I could do. I think the pink makes it look like Cinderella's fairy godfather."

She stepped close and brushed off his shoulders. "Nonsense. Mauve is a manly color and perfect for the holidays. I genuinely like your look. It pairs well with the tan trousers."

She made him feel like a bottle of wine, pairing well with a meal, but he smiled. She sometimes had an odd way of saying things. He liked her funny little habit. He cleared his throat. "Merry Christmas, Dawson."

"Dinner is done. Are you hungry?"

He was, but not for food. "I...ah...brought a gift for Adam. Would it be okay to give it to him now?"

He watched the surprise pass over her face and then a slow smile. "Absolutely. That is great." She turned to Adam. "Sweetie, Samuel has brought you a present."

Adam lit up, abandoned his car and rushed over to Dawson, staring at him in hopeful expectation. He remembered feeling that way. And he remembered the pain that came when the expectation failed. "Hang on, buddy, and I'll be right back." He rushed from the room, blinked back a few tears, and returned with the brightly wrapped package. He sat down on the loveseat and Adam scrambled up next to him.

Everyone watched as he slowly peeled the pretty blue, green, and yellow paper away and revealed a brown box beneath. He slowly turned the box over and over and Samuel helped him open the box. He pulled the screen out and studied it.

"That looks impressive. What is it?"

Samuel grinned. "It's a touch screen learning toy that adapts from an iPad to a laptop. It teaches words, colors, numbers, shapes, sounds, and more. And it grows with him, teaching more as he learns." He took his gaze off Adam's excitement as he pushed buttons and looked up at Dawson. Her appreciative smile stole his breath away.

"Thank you."

Her eyes shown dewy soft and her lips parted, and he was going to die if he didn't kiss her soon. But first... confession time. She held his gaze just long enough to squeeze his heart, then she called Adam and her dad to dinner. He climbed up and picked up Adam and carried him to the table. Dawson looked surprised at first but again, her dewy-eyed smile told him she was pleased.

They gathered at a long, oak table decorated with a beige lace runner, vanilla and peppermint scented flickering white and red striped candles, greenery and a few coils of ribbon and bright, glittery Christmas balls. In the center of the table sat a large turkey, golden brown and smelling like heaven. Samuel's stomach growled. Crockery dishes held heaping servings of mashed potatoes, broccoli, green beans, stuffing, cranberries, and a full gravy boat. Napkins with Christmas motifs and sparkling silverware sat at each of the four china place settings. Samuel sat Adam down in his booster seat and pulled out the chair for Dawson before taking his own seat next to her.

She reached for his hand, shyly meeting his eye. "Shall we pray first?"

Lloyd led the prayer, short and to the point. Samuel grinned as he echoed Dawson's amen. Then Lloyd stood to carve the turkey, beginning with the legs and thighs.

Samuel opted for a breast portion. Dawson passed around the mashed potatoes. They smelled of garlic and thyme. The stuffing and broccoli echoed the garlic and herb scent while the green beans lemon scent wafted up when he scooped some onto his plate. Dawson offered him a basket of muffins, packed with cranberry, topped with lemon glaze and toasted almonds. Lastly was the rich, brown gravy.

"Wow, this looks great and it all smells so good. The table is festive. How'd you find time to do all this?"

Dawson blushed as she cut up food for Adam. "Here and there between him and other things. I used Mom's crock pots for a lot of this. I prepped as much as I could all this week, so there wasn't much to do today but cook the turkey and do a few odds and ends. Dessert was baked yesterday, as were the muffins, and they both just needed to be frosted today."

"Dessert too?" Like he'd have room for dessert after this.

"Um humm." She passed the plate to Adam and swirled her fork into her potatoes. "Boston cream sponge cake."

In all his years of Christmas meals, many were bad, and some were acceptable, a couple were good, but none were mind-blowing beyond expectation as this was. Every bite was delicious. The turkey was moist, the stuffing was flavorful, the vegetables crisp and everything was cooked to perfection. One thing was clear, Dawson was one heck of a cook.

And the conversation around the table was good. Lloyd said little, opting for succinct comments when necessary. Adam kept the conversations alive with his two- and three-word sentences. Dawson blushed when he complimented her, made efforts to get her dad to talk and engaged frequently with him and Adam.

As the meal wound down, he helped clear the plates and prepare for dessert. The sponge cake looked sinfully delicious. He rolled up his sleeves and rinsed the dishes.

"Oh, hey, the garbage disposal works now, so you can just scrape all the leftovers from the plates into it."

He closed his eyes for a moment. The garbage disposal hadn't worked either. He'd love to see what still remained on her to-do list. But then again, maybe he shouldn't. "What was wrong with it?"

"Just a jam and a couple leaky seals. Compared to some things around here, it was relatively easy to fix once I figured out the problem. Besides, I think I'm running a path from here to the hardware store in Higgins."

She sounded proud of herself. Doubtlessly she was learning a lot about home maintenance. Her velvet dress clashed with the overall-clad handy woman he knew her to be. He smiled. "If all else fails, you could get a job as a home repair expert."

Her smile faded and she placed her hands flat on the counter. "If all else fails, I will probably go back to Virginia and see if I can get a job working in make believe again."

He caught the jab at her dad's callous mention of her career choice. He'd investigated and knew her software engineering job required a lot of education and commitment. He dried his hands and came over to her. He cupped her chin and tilted her face up to his. "I know your dad gets to you, but I think you're doing one heck of a super job here. I've never had a finer meal."

She blinked, tears misting her eyes. "Thank you. It's nice to be appreciated."

He could not take it any longer. Her sweet and tart scent surrounded him, and her dress set off fireworks in his mind. "You are so much more than just appreciated, Dawson."

He touched his lips to hers, bringing his hands to touch her soft shoulders. Her skin was satiny soft. Her lips yielded under his and he felt her mold herself to him. She was soft where he was hard. Her hands moved up and under his vest, her fingers crawling over his shirt and teasing his stomach muscles. He inhaled as her fingertips floated over his heated skin in feathery strokes. Her chest crushed to his and he swallowed a moan of pleasure.

Dawson Patrick could make a man think just about anything when she was in his arms.

"What is going on in there?" her father called out. "The boy is getting restless."

Better than cold water blasted through a fire hose, Lloyd's words pushed them apart. Dawson sighed and returned to standing at the counter with her hands flat on the surface. He backed up to the sink and began scrapping a dish into the newly repaired garbage disposal. He peeked over at her and she met his eyes. She licked her lips and they shared a co-conspirator's smile.

Five minutes later Samuel had the dishes rinsed and ready for washing. No dishwasher here, these would be hand scrubbed. Just as well, if Lloyd had one, more than likely it would be one more thing Dawson would need to fix. He just was in awe of both the sheer number of things that needed repair and the fact that Dawson was teaching herself how to become a regular Miss Fix-It.

Dawson carried the sponge cake out to the dining room table and Samuel carried the coffee and cups. He brought a chocolate milk for Adam. She cut the cake and doled out pieces, cutting him a large wedge. Hazelnut rose into the air from the coffee, laced with more vanilla. She had a beaker of snickerdoodle creamer and he added a liberal splash.

The cake was delicious, as the meal had been. Already a fan of both Boston Cream desserts and sponge cakes, the two combined into one was sheer delight.

"This is really good," he praised as they finished. "Don't you think so, Lloyd?"

The old man pushed his unfinished plate away. "It was okay I suppose. I've had just as good down at the diner."

Before he could think to respond, Dawson exploded. She leapt to her feet, threw down her napkin, and stared at her dad for a sum of thirty seconds. Her mouth opened to an O of surprise and hurt filled her face.

"I have never met a more unappreciative old grouch. Mark

my words, this will be the last Christmas I cook for you. And don't even think I'll make you anything special for New Years!"

Deliberately, she turned around and walked away, her back straight and her head high. Samuel could feel her pain as she exited the room. When she reached the front door, she let it slam with a loud bang.

"Excuse me, Lloyd. Can you watch Adam a minute?" Without waiting for a reply, he followed in Dawson's wake.

He found her on the swing, knees pulled up to her chest, the dress showing lots of curvy leg. She glanced up and he cringed at the tears rolling down her face.

"Are you okay?" he asked as he sat down next to her and wrapped one arm around her shoulders.

She sniffed. "I just don't get him. I don't understand." She paused, sniffing again. "He gave me this jewelry set today for Christmas. It was my mother's. He had bought it for her on their twenty-fifth wedding anniversary. He was so nice when he gave it to me earlier." She sniffed and swallowed and pounded her leg with her fist in clear frustration. She blinked back the tears. "And then he turns into a mean old grump again! I mean, what makes him that way?"

"Oh honey, you know he didn't mean it. It's just his way."

"I don't care. Doesn't he know how much that stings? How it hurts me? Can't I have one day he doesn't belittle me? Just one day where he says he's happy with something I've done. For him!"

She buried her face against his chest and sobs racked her. "I know I'm not the great and mighty Joshua, but I can't be all that bad. Can I?"

His heart broke. He liked Lloyd fine, but right now he was mad enough to take him out back and have a man to man chat. No one had the right to hurt Dawson like that man just hurt his own daughter. He'd experienced his share of child comparison and he knew the sharp, twisting pain it caused.

"Dawson, you are not bad at all. You are the most wonderful person I've ever known."

She snorted. "Some don't agree." She blinked more tears away and pounded her leg again. "I'm just trying to be a good daughter to him. But he makes it so damn hard."

He gave a harsh laugh. "Dawson, you are being a fantastic daughter." He reached over to snag the blanket from the rocking chair and draped it over her shoulders. "What can I say, Dawson? I hate to see you like this."

The silence stretched as she sobbed onto his vest. Finally she pulled her head back and studied him. Her eyes were red and puffy and trails of tears streaked down her cheeks. She probably never looked so beautiful and sad at the same time. He tried for a smile and failed miserably. He slid his thumbs over her cheeks to collect the tears and took her hands into his and kissed her knuckles. She winced and he noticed the black and blue bruises covering one hand.

"Dropped toilet lid," she said by way of explanation.

He felt the heavy sigh building up inside and he let it out with a weary sound.

"Dawson, I am so in awe of you. The whole time I was enjoying that fantastic meal you prepared, I kept telling myself you are one hell of a woman. Seriously, you can cook a dynamite holiday meal, you can fix a broken-down old house, you're a great mother, you're dependable and devoted to those cats, and you are one fine looking lady." He grinned at her frown. "I just can't figure out why I'm not trying like crazy to get you to notice me."

Now she smiled, a little lopsided, but he would take it.

He ran a fingertip along her jaw, delighting in the spark in her eyes. He drew her lips closer, then he inclined his head and kissed her. Gentle. Easy. Long. Eager. He inhaled the sweetness, and let it linger on his tongue.

"You are one hell of a woman, Dawson," he said as they ended the kiss. "And don't ever let anyone belittle you."

She blinked and swiped at her eyes. She sniffed. "I know. Dad's just dad. But just once I wish…"

"Yeah, I know. I understand," he said as her voice trailed off.

She tilted her head to one side and studied him. "I believe you, Samuel. How can you understand?"

He inhaled a breath and tried for a smile. "Because I'm training to be a grouchy old man. Just ask the folks in town."

She shook her head. "No, I don't believe that. You might want people to think that about you, but I see another side. One who is caring and sympathetic. One who knows more than he's letting on. And this is not the first time I've thought this about you."

Samuel shifted, wondering if this was the opening he should take. "Well, actually, yes, there is some… parts in my past that…could…"

"Samuel."

Her gaze stilled his babble. He released her hand and looked out across the yard, then back to her. "I have never talked about my life to anyone in Cedar Falls."

"I'm not planning on staying in Cedar Falls."

Dawson's matter of fact statement cut him sharply. He couldn't blame her, but he sure wished he could change her mind. And after he said what he needed to; she would be doubly sure to want to leave.

"Okay." He breathed in a ragged breath and wondered where to start. The beginning. He exhaled. "I do understand a lot about Adam's condition and your dad's seemingly callous behavior and a few other things in your life."

She crossed her arms over her chest. "And can you explain to me how?"

"Because I was born in a prison."

Dawson could not imagine a more shocking statement. Her arms unfurled and she looked at Samuel, sure her jaw dropped. She stared at him, momentarily lost for words. Finally she asked the only question she could think of. "How does that make you so able to understand Adam, my dad and other parts of my life?"

He rolled the sleeves of his shirt down. "Because I lived a lot of it. My mother was pregnant with me when she was arrested and sentenced to twenty-five years. She was a heroin junkie who made some bad choices, and I came four weeks early. When the medical team asked what her plan was with me, she reportedly said she didn't have any and didn't care. They offered her the adoption option for me, if I was to even live, and she supposedly said fine, whatever. Those were the words on the prison records: fine, whatever. When asked about my name or my father's name for the paperwork, she allegedly didn't know his and simply said "Same old same" for me. "Same old same." They transferred me to the local hospital preemie unit, and she went back to her cell."

He stopped and she was sure her heart was stopping too. She could not begin to imagine the pain that knowledge caused him. He took a shuddering breath and she placed a hand on his arm. He shook his head.

"No, Dawson. You wanted to know, so let me get this out. Everyone has a story, and this is mine. The hospital staff came up with Samuel as a first name and Owen as a middle name, reworking the first initials from her casual comment. And this all happened in a county called Johnson."

"That's why your last name is Johnson? Because you were

born in Johnson County?" She balled her hand into a fist and held it to her mouth in shock and horror.

His smile was grim. "How is that for an original way to name a kid?"

She thought it was terrible. She recalled how she lovingly searched through baby name books and online forums, looking for the perfect name and making lists, investigating origins and meanings. Adam's name was the product of months of careful exploration. Samuel's mother's cold casualness was nothing short of deplorable.

"Once I was fit enough to leave the hospital, I entered the foster care system. The first few years weren't too bad, mostly since I don't remember them. Because she'd used heroin and other substances while pregnant, I was slow to develop. It also made me less desirable to be adopted."

He looked away and she took an involuntary breath in.

"I was on the autistic spectrum too, just like Adam. I was labeled middle to high functioning and given an average chance for independence."

"But you're fully independent. You run your own business." Could she dare to hope her son could one day be as independent as Samuel?

"Yes, but I wasn't always this way. And I still struggle with mild dyslexia. But I had some good foster homes that worked with me and got me the services I needed. Services that would benefit Adam now. I also had a bunch of bad foster homes, with people who should not have had kids. I could assure you there is hope for Adam if he had some professional services to help boost him along. But if he were surrounded by people like your ex-husband, he would probably never pull beyond the lowest expectation they had of him."

Again, Dawson was so thankful she got Adam away from Peter's disparaging behaviors. And she did not want Adam to ever understand his grandfather's remarks. There was another reason to leave before he got much older.

She dropped her hands to her lap and laced them together. "I am so sorry you went through all of that as a child. That is terrible and no one should have experienced any of that. But I still don't understand why you dislike Christmas though. Were you born on Christmas Day?"

He smiled sadly. "No. My birthday is in the spring. April. Like all kids, I loved Christmas at first. I made gifts for my foster parents and believed in Santa and all that stuff."

She nodded, to encourage him. Slowly, as he gathered his thoughts, his shaky voice continued.

"One family I lived with was good. They even put up a tree and baked sweet stuff. I was about five. I had made some stuff at school that kids are supposed to give their mom and dad. I gave it to them. The teacher read us stories all week about how Santa comes to visit all the boys and girls and leave them presents. Except Santa never made it to my foster house. My people didn't believe in giving gifts and once Christmas was over, they threw my little school project away, the treats were frozen, and we had them with dinner over the next few months. And two days after it went up, all the decorations and tree came down."

While sad, and disappointing to a five-year-old boy, Dawson didn't see how that could make a man shun Christmas.

"That was just one example. When I was around seven, I was moved to a new foster home. I really liked the woman who lived there. Again, I made a gift at school and the man had decorated a couple of weeks prior. Two days before Christmas they requested I be moved. I learned later she had cancer and was dying. But to a seven-year-old, I wondered what I had done wrong. The truth came much later. I stayed in some homes where Christmas was not celebrated at all, somewhere food was scarce, sometimes having to be stolen, and there were never fancy dinners. I had a couple of foster families who abhorred Christmas to the point I was forbidden to even speak of it, upon penalty of a beating."

Beating? She opened her mouth to say something, what she wasn't sure, but he stopped her with his hand on her leg. His eyes searched hers and she swore he saw into her soul.

"The thing to remember, Dawson, is school, television, media, and other kids all make a big deal of celebrating Christmas. We're bombarded with decorations, food, songs, exchanging gifts, seeing Santa, and all that typical holiday stuff. It's a gala event every year. However, it's really the parents and family that bring all that promise to reality. If the family in the kid's home isn't into the celebration, there won't be a celebration despite what everyone and everything taught the kid. Reality sometimes sucks."

She grinned at his wry comment. "Yes, it sometimes sure does." She heard the heaviness in her voice and winced. She looked down to where his palm rested on her leg. It was warm and comforting but she ought to be comforting him. "I am determined to make Christmas as positive for Adam as I possibly can."

"I know you are. And I applaud you for that. One day Adam will too." He raised his hand, removing it from her leg, and burrowed it under the blanket to trail it up her arm. Warm shivers followed in his wake.

Then he sighed, exhaling a deep breath and returned his hand to her leg again. "For me it wasn't just Christmas, though that has particular bad memories. It was Thanksgiving, birthdays, Valentine's Day. Basically any celebration that involved gifts or parties. On my tenth birthday I'd been in a new home for about five or six months. I'd hinted strongly about how much I wanted a particular gift since my birthday was coming up soon. It was a popular toy though I can't remember what it was anymore. I just remember going to school that day, spending all day hoping it would be waiting for me. When I got home, no one remembered it was my birthday. Both foster parents were busy with the other kids or some other obligation. I went to my bedroom and cried because I'd been forgotten again. I ended up leaving that home before the school year ended."

Her heart cracked and she licked her lips. "Were all your home placements bad?"

"No, as I got older, and more help for the dyslexia and autism, they seemed to get better. I also had lower expectations than when I was younger. When I was seventeen, I landed in a great home with a semi- retired business couple. Their kids had grown, and they liked having teens around the house. The dad was super with finance and business management. I was studying business and finance in school and we really connected. It was probably my first true bond to a foster parent. I don't know what it feels like to have a real dad, but that is probably close to it."

She smiled, glad he finally achieved some peace and happiness in his youthful years.

"When I graduated and aged out of foster care, they let me rent my room and stay with them while I attended college. I took a part time job to pay the rent and help with bills and save up. I wanted to buy my own business. When the time came, and I had my bachelor's, my foster dad made me an offer. When I found a suitable place, he would put up the capital to get me started and I would pay him back with a reasonable interest rate. So once I heard about some promising businesses for sale in Portland, I made the trip. On my way back, I drove through Cedar Falls and stopped at the bookstore. I had time to spare and liked books. It just happened the bookstore was for sale too.

They say in business not to let your emotions rule and not to make decisions based on feelings, but I fell in love with the bookstore and felt like it would be a better fit than the Portland properties I'd looked at. I went back and talked to my foster dad and he came up here with me and ended up buying it. We closed on my birthday."

"Your twenty-fifth. That is fantastic, Samuel. I am so glad you finally got to have some happiness in your life."

"More than happiness. This next chapter has included you and Adam."

His eyes darkened and he cleared his throat. He trailed his hand down her leg, exciting tiny shivers of delight with his touch. Her pulse pounded, galloping through her throat and chest. He didn't seem finished just yet.

"I know you've been wondering about me," he continued, his voice silky soft. "Why I don't do Christmas, why I know about Adam's condition, why I do or say a lot of things. I hope what I just shared helps you get me and gives you optimism about Adam's future. And I hope it helps you better understand your dad when he shows you that old grumpy side." He paused then tilted his head. "Or at least tolerate him if not understand him."

She grinned. "It helps. All of it helps."

He looked away a moment, his gaze sweeping the yard blanketed in snow, lighting on Adam's snowman, and then back to her. "Has your brother said anything to you about your dad's mental faculties?"

Her galloping anticipation slammed to a heart-shuddering halt. Mental? "Like what?" Did her voice just squeak?

He drew small circles on her wrist, slow and rhythmic. "Like forgetfulness. Irritability. Unprovoked hostility. Denial despite obvious evidence. Things like that."

"He mentioned dad was getting older. He noticed he was less robust. But I've seen a lot of that irritability and hostility aimed at me."

"Are you sure it's aimed at you personally?"

She laughed. "Yes, One hundred percent sure. Why? Where are you going with this?"

Again, the sweeping gaze and then he looked back at her, his brows followed into a V. "I suspect your dad might be starting with something like dementia."

She went cold. "You mean Alzheimer's?"

"Not all dementia equals Alzheimer's. There are lots of other causes. But yes, something in that general family. I'm no doctor of course, but I've seen enough people with various forms of dementia to recognize some of the symptoms with your dad. I thought with your brother's medical knowledge he would have picked up on it right away."

"Let me tell you about Joshua the Great. Even if he had noticed something with Dad, his M.O. would be not to tell anyone, but to slide some unsuspecting person in to take care of the situation while he returns to his borderless location."

"Like he did with you?"

That Joshua. Realization slapped Dawson across the head. "Yes, just like he did with me," she agreed slowly. "Does that mean I can't leave him?" What if she and Adam were stuck here indefinitely taking care of her dad?

Samuel let out a long breath and looked down at his feet. Dawson felt herself tighten with anxiety with every moment he stared downward. Joshua left, why did she automatically have to stay? She couldn't have Adam exposed to her dad's mood swings and when he degraded her. What if he started belittling Adam?

"No, you don't have to stay. I'm not even sure if that's your dad's problem. I just see his apathy, how he turns his mood around on a dime and how he never noticed the house issues. It might be something else. The prudent thing would be to have him see a doctor to be sure."

Okay, she could do that. She'd contact Doctor Armstrong's office and get an appointment. Then she would know. Then she could plan. She nodded at Samuel and eased out a shaky breath. "Thank you for pointing out your observations. I just assumed he was a spiteful old man."

He gave her a grin. "Well, there might be some of that too. Word in town is I'm well on my way there."

"You are not." She grabbed the pillow behind her and smacked him with it. "You are absolutely the sweetest guy in town, the most helpful and caring, and everyone knows that." Except for the girls she went to school with who considered him cold as ice. But they were jealous they couldn't land him for themselves.

"Everyone?"

"The ones that matter."

He grinned and leaned in, brushing shoulders as he ducked his hands under the blanket and tickled her ribs. She let out a surprised squeal and then uncontrollable laughter.

"Oh! Stop! No! I'm ticklish!"

"I was hoping you would be."

His smile was broad, and he didn't stop. Dawson bent over, finally dropping to the porch floor, laughing all the way. She crawled over to the steps and into the snowbank. The cool snow felt good. Samuel followed.

"Smarty pants," she accused him, as she inhaled a huge breath. She grabbed a handful of snow, turned, and smeared it into his face like a cream pie.

"Hey!"

She smiled in retaliation. "Ha!"

He scooped up a handful and tossed it at her. She ducked but still got sprayed. "Oh, that's cold!" She whipped a handful back at him. He returned the favor. Their laughter spilled out and Dawson felt tears rolling out of her eyes, a contrast to the cold snow.

She dunked his head in a snowbank. Fortunately, the snow was fresh powder, airy and light. But it was still cold on her legs.

"Okay, uncle. I call uncle. It's too cold for this."

Immediately he helped her up, bringing her close to him. His warm breath fanned her face. His bright smile, alive with joy, light a fire in her heart.

"Mercy, that was fun. Look, I'm still breathless."

He nodded as he rubbed his hands along her arms. "It was fun, I'm glad we did that. But you're in that lovely dress and not exactly suited for a snowball fight."

She punched his arm. "Next time I will be dressed proper and you will get the snowball fight of your life."

He reached over to snag the blanket and drape it over her shoulders. He ran the tip of his finger down her cheek, erasing the tears. "I do not doubt it. Next time." He bent his lips to hers, claiming her bravado assertion.

She leaned in for the kiss, taking his warmth and his excitement, and returning her pleasure. A moan escaped her. And then a shiver.

"You're shivering." Immediately Samuel broke the kiss and moved her up to the porch. "Inside, before you catch cold."

Dawson wasn't sure if her shivering was due to cold snow or anticipation. Either way, he had a point. She cut him a coy smile. "You know what's good after a romp in the snow? Hot cocoa by the fire."

He moaned and patted his stomach. "I'm not sure I can get any more in my stomach since your fantastic meal, but it does sound tempting."

"Come on, I have to check on Adam anyway." She took his hand and guided him inside, to the kitchen. There she prepared four mugs, heating the milk on the stove, measuring cocoa powder and sugar into the mugs, and stirring the boiling milk. In a couple minutes she poured the milk into each mug and stirred.

"Here." She passed one to Samuel. "I'll join you in the living room. The fire probably needs tending by now."

He evidently took her hint, gave her a wicked grin and a salute. She headed off to find her dad and son.

She found them in the family room, watching an old western movie. "Dad, Adam, I made hot cocoa." The mugs warmed her hands and the rich aroma tickled her nose, reminding her of Samuel's spontaneous tickling. Who knew? "Come in the living room if you want. Samuel and I want to enjoy the tree and fireplace."

"I do!" Adam jumped to his feet.

"Take your robot, honey, and I'll bring your cocoa." She was pleased he was playing with the robot she bought him. Like Samuel's toy, it was also educational and would teach him colors, shapes, words, and more. It seems they were ganging up to ensure her son had a good education before he started school. She smiled at both the thought and her son's bright smile.

"Dad?"

He reached out for the mug, his face drawn into a frown. "I thought I saw your mother around earlier. Do you know where she went?"

Her heart plummeted. Her mother? "Dad, Mom died a long time ago. Remember?"

"No, she was just here this afternoon. Did you see her? She was wearing her favorite jewelry. Did she give it to you and go away?" He pointed to her bracelet.

She coughed down the lump in her throat and thought of Samuel's comments. "Dad, Mom isn't here now. Do you want to join Adam, Samuel, and me in the living room? The fire is going, and the tree is lit."

He shook his head and took a sip of cocoa. "I'll wait here in case she comes back."

Dawson hurried from the room and back to the kitchen. She

set Adam's mug down and braced her hands on the counter. Was her dad losing touch with reality? She hung her head and let the tears fall. Had Joshua known and deliberately not told her? What was she supposed to do? How was she supposed to feel?

She had no clue, but she had a child waiting for her. She blew her nose, wiped her face, and carried both her and Adam's mugs to the living room. Adam rose from where he had been explaining his robot toy to Samuel and eagerly took his cocoa.

"Be careful with that, baby." She watched as he sat down on the floor with his legs crossed and stared at the tree. With the overhead lights off, and just the glow from the tree lights and the flames licking the oak wood, the room was cast in a dreamy radiance.

"Are you okay?" Samuel asked as she sat down next to him. He stretched out his arm to invite her close and she gladly accepted. She curled her legs under her and leaned into his shoulder. The cool satin of his vest felt comfortable against her cheek. His other hand reached to take her cup and set it on the end table.

Her chest constricted and her eyes burned. "I think you might be right. Samuel. Just hold me."

She closed her eyes, listened to her son slurp his hot cocoa, and let Samuel's gentle touch just envelope her in a safe cocoon.

CHAPTER 7

It was dark when Samuel finally parked his truck. Emotionally depleted he sat and stared at the brick fronted bookstore, the white grapevine wreath on the door, and his apartment above. A light covering of freshly fallen snow gathered in the corners of the windowpanes, giving the building a Currier and Ives look. Four years and he'd been happy with his choices, content in his life and with this little town, even when they overdid the whole Christmas thing. He was willing to overlook and tolerate them if they overlooked and tolerated his anti-holiday scrooge. So far it has worked out fine. He never felt as if anything were missing.

Tonight, for the first time in memory, he felt complete.

Dawson Patrick blew into his life like a pink sparkly blizzard and cut a space in his heart with her happiness, laughter, and compassion. Tonight she poured herself out and filled that hole with her vulnerability, her independence, her sense of humor, and so much more.

This evening, he finally felt like he was part of a family, a piece of the puzzle. And call him crazy, but he thought Dawson and he fit together well.

He'd been flabbergasted when they tumbled into a snowball fight. He was surprised, considering she was still wearing that beautiful dress and sparkly jewels, but like a true tomboy, she acted as though she were wearing her overalls instead. He grinned at her laughing screams while he tickled her. Oh, he would absolutely keep in mind she was very ticklish. Would she giggle and carry on like that if he were to tickle her feet, or behind her ear, or blow in her ear?

He really wanted to find out.

He let out a breath and gripped the wheel. He was concerned about Lloyd. He was no doctor, but he was sure some of the old guy's behaviors were not normal. He knew Dawson just thought her dad disliked her, or favored Josh over her, which there probably was some truth to that. And when she came into the room with the cocoa, she'd been crying. Her eyes were red and puffy though she tried to hide it.

She whispered the brief conversation between herself and her dad and he felt a knot of dread in his stomach. He wanted to be the one to solve those problems, but he didn't know how. So he offered Dawson what he could; sitting with her in his lap, his arm around her shoulder, and be surrounded by wood burning, tree lights blinking and Adam happily slurping his cocoa and playing with his toy.

The moment was frozen, and Samuel began to believe in magic. When Dawson nestled against his chest and relaxed in his arms and uttered a tired sigh, he believed in home.

Especially after another short conversation with Dawson. Nestled against his chest like one of the kittens, she whispered another thank you for Adam's Christmas gift. He smiled and assured her he was happy to get it, and he thought Adam was a neat kid. Then she softly asked him if he ever thought about having kids of his own.

He didn't know where that came from. Left field he

supposed. A feather could have knocked him over. He didn't know what to say. "Well, I like kids, but I've never considered having my own. I suppose with the right mother for them, and the right timing in my life, yes, I'd be open to that."

What he wondered now was whether Dawson would be the right mother. She was the perfect mother for Adam. He had no doubt she'd be the perfect mom with any kid she had, but what about *them* as parents?

He thought of his own mother and he went cold. Would he be a better parent than her? Whatever happened to her? He had no idea. Her twenty-five years was up four years ago.

But Dawson hadn't been done. She wanted to talk more about Adam's disorder and their combined educational gifts. "It seems vocabulary is his biggest hurdle. At least right now."

The angst in her voice almost killed him. He tried for a smile. "I have noticed he mainly has trouble with r's and t's. Those can be tricky letters." He placed his hand on her knee. "Just give him some more time."

She nodded, and he could feel her chin rubbing against his breast. "He's talked more in the last three weeks here than he ever did back in Virginia."

"Maybe he just needed a fresh start."

Now he blinked at the snowy scene outside the truck window and heaved a sigh. Quite a day. Maybe they all needed a fresh start. He exited the truck and unlocked the shop door. He moved quietly through the dimly lit interior and nearly tripped over the furry trio of hairballs.

"Hey!" he yelped as he reached out to catch himself on a bookcase. "If you kill me now, you'll starve before tomorrow. Back off."

He reached their food bowls and let out a disgusted huff. "You still have plenty in there." He pointed to their dishes. Still he refilled both food and water, then grabbed a bag and scooped their box, gagging on the stench. "Aggghhh. Gross."

Finished, he took the bag out to the trash and returned, sitting in Dawson's chosen chair. He swore a whiff of her scent lifted into the air and curled around him like her gently curled tresses today. Sampson climbed up and commenced to purr and massage his front feet on Samuel's leg. Soon the other two joined in.

"All right, I like you guys too, but you're getting hair all over my suit." He brushed them off and swept the hair away. "I'm going to bed. Sampson, you wanna join me? I'll leave the door open."

Ten minutes later the suit was off, and he wore his sweats. He slipped into bed and Sampson climbed up, sitting on Samuel's chest. He tucked his tiny paws, closed his eyes to slits, and purred as loud as a motorboat.

Samuel chuckled and scratched the kitten's ear. "My chest has been a popular place tonight, but to be honest, I'd rather have Dawson next to me again."

He stared up at the ceiling, and listened to the purring rumble, and wondered what he was going to do about all these crazy new feelings zipping around inside him.

"Mama. Play."

Dawson peered down on her son as he held the robot toy. Vertigo hit and she clamped her hands around the ladder. "Sweetheart, I'm thrilled you want to play with the robot, but I am just a little busy up here."

"Me up?"

No!" she all but shouted as Adam approached the ladder. "No, sweetie, ladders can be dangerous." Didn't she know that! She almost fell twice already. Well, toppled, but either way, she would be glad when she was done balancing on it. "When you're an adult, you can climb all the ladders you want, but for now, stay away from them."

He smiled and she wondered how much he understood. Did he know one day he would grow to be an adult? Sometimes just not knowing what he grasped and didn't about killed her. "Where's Grandpa? Maybe he wants to play with you and robot." It was worth a shot.

"Out."

Out? Where he had gone that he didn't say anything? And she didn't notice. Of course, keeping her balance on this six-foot ladder, while trying to splice and rewire the broken light fixture was a challenge. Splicing, another new skill she could add to her DIY resume.

She set her tools and the fixture in the cavities and holes on top of the ladder. Now, after all these years, she knew what those features on top were really for. She climbed down and took Adam's hand. "Show me where Grandpa went out."

Adam led her to the front door. Sure enough, his truck was gone from its semi-permanent parking spot under the oak tree. Thank God Adam hadn't gone with him. She'd have had a meltdown of epic proportions. In the meantime, where was he?

She retraced her steps and took Adam inside. She gave him some crackers and sat down to think. It was clear he slipped out and didn't say anything to her. What if he went to find her mother?

She dropped her elbows on the table and watched Adam finish his crackers and juice. "Well, kiddo, I guess this is a good place to stop and go into town. We can see if maybe Dad's at the diner or some logical place and then we can stop in and see Samuel."

"Kibins?"

"Yes, of course. Them too."

They reached town and first on Dawson's list was the diner. Her heart sank when she failed to spot her dad's truck in the lot. Next, she checked the grocery store, thinking he might have gone shopping for more frozen dinners and pot pies. Again, his truck wasn't in the lot. She cruised up and down Main Street and doubled back to the grocery store again. She stopped, heaved a sigh, and looked back at Adam.

"Well, kiddo. I don't know. Those were the two most likely places. And if he were already heading back, we would have passed him. So, do you have any ideas?"

"Kibins."

She grinned. "I did ask, didn't I. Okay." She turned the SUV back to Samuel's store.

"Hi, guys." He welcomed them with a smile when they walked in.

He was busy helping a customer, a man with assumedly his teenage daughter, so Dawson offered a half wave and helped Adam with his coat and things. "Sweetie, go play for now." She pointed him to the box of toys Samuel now kept out for all the little kids to play with. She set to work on the cats, noticing the teen girl was more interested in holding the black and white kitten instead of listening to her dad and Samuel. Once she filled the food bowl, all three kittens came running, their tails up like flagpoles.

She stayed busy, her mind racing with worry for her dad, as Samuel helped the customers. Another man came in just as Samuel was ringing up the first customer's items. She was utterly amazed at how busy his store remained, and she looked around, deciding it had to be the wide selection of things he offered and the great personal service he provided. Higgins had no bookstore, and she was sure many of the surrounding small towns didn't, so surely many of his customers came from outside of Cedar Falls too.

"Hi, you're doing okay?" He knelt beside her where she sat brushing Blinking and the black and white kitten. The grey tabby scurried over to climb into Samuel's arms. "You look a little stressed."

"Dad's gone." Without preamble she blurted out the story of how he left without saying anything and all the places she just checked. "I know he's a mean old grump, but he is my dad. What if he drove off somewhere looking for Mom or gets lost or—"?

"Hold on." He deposited the kittens on the floor, picked her up and resettled her on his lap. "One thing at a time. First, settle down and give me some timelines. When did you first learn he was gone? When had you last seen or heard him?"

She thought back and answered to the best of her memory. "I lost track of how long I was up on the ladder, that splicing is tough on my train of thought." She sniffed, about to cry.

"Now, I'm going to call the police and have them keep an eye out. They might find him during their patrols. They can also post someone by your house in case he comes home on his own."

She held out her phone but kept her fingers curled around it. His hand wrapped around hers, and she took one moment to relish his warmth. "But what if he just went somewhere simple and gets mad at me for alerting the police and freaking out?"

He released his hold on her hand and cupped her chin, and his eyes softened. "Dawson. Your father is missing, he has recently proven delusional, and you have every right to be concerned and contact the police. When he is found, he should be grateful you cared to search, however, if he decides to be unappreciative, that is on him, and not you. You are doing the right thing, okay?"

She soaked in his brown eyes. They were soft as silk, and his breath was cool with mint. She could just drift away on his gentle, rumbling voice. She nodded. "Okay." She held her phone out, palm up, still watching his warm eyes.

The emergency dispatch picked up and he relayed the information and included a description of her dad and his truck. Finished, he returned her phone, taking a minute to curl his fingers around hers.

"You cannot own someone's mistreatment toward you, Dawson. Any more than you can take responsibility if they choose to say bad things. It's on them."

She nodded, knowing it was true. "But it still hurts."

"I know it does."

He drew her into a hug, and she welcomed the comfort he provided. She knew a customer could walk in any moment and Adam was playing nearby but right now she needed to have this close contact with Samuel.

A shrill scream rent the air and she jumped, inhaling sharply. She and Samuel both swiveled around.

"Adam! What happened?" She leapt to her feet and rushed to where her son stood by a table, tears pouring down his face as he wailed.

He held his tiny hand out to her, and she saw the crooked trail of blood, perhaps three inches long. She cradled his injured hand in hers. Out of the corner of her eye she spotted the black and white kitten darting away, heading for the carrier they kept behind the desk.

"Oh baby, the kitten scratched you, didn't it?"

"Kibin bad!" he cried, nodding his head vigorously.

"How's it look?" Samuel joined her and they examined the wound.

"I don't think it's deep and he won't need stitches. But I'm sure it hurts." She hugged Adam to her chest and patted his downy soft hair.

Samuel agreed. "No doubt. That's a scary thing to happen." He nodded toward a set of stairs. "Take him up to my apartment and clean the wound. There is antibiotic medicine and wound adhesives in the bathroom."

"That's very kind of you." She stood, scooping Adam up and went upstairs.

The red brick walls greeted her first. She glanced around, looking for the bathroom. Finding it, she stood Adam up by the sink and ran his hand under the warm water. The soap was green and smelled like cucumber and melon. Once the bleeding stopped, so did Adam's crying. She sat him on the toilet and dried the hand and washed his tear-streaked face. Finished, she searched the medicine cabinet and found antibiotic ointment and bandages.

"There, sweetie. It's all better now," she said with a smile and then kissed the top of the bandage. She kissed the bridge of his nose, and tickled his side, eliciting a giggle.

"That's my brave boy." She picked him up and swung him around, and they went out to the living area. "This is where Samuel lives."

She took a moment to look around now that Adam was giggling instead of crying. The apartment was small but spacious. No pictures of him or family. Not much in the way of personal possessions. The kitchen was furnished with a stove, sink, refrigerator, and a few small appliances. Coffee pot, toaster oven, and electric grill. The walls were original brick and three abstract paintings hung on two opposing sides.

A small ladder bookshelf held a modest collection of books, two plants, and an old-fashioned radio. The chair was draped with a chunky blue two-toned blanket. She could imagine him nestled there at night, reading something, with the overhead lamp shining off his glasses. He could sit at the small dinette and watch the street below. She was surprised to see a yoga mat rolled up by the loveseat. The door off to the left had to be his bedroom. She was tempted to peek but decided against it.

While simple, the apartment was tidy and smelled with a unique blend of woodsy moss and leather, with clean lime and cloves.

"Come on, honey, we've seen enough. Samuel has embraced a spartan design style." Honestly, she wasn't surprised. A modest, simple design fit him.

She took Adam's hand and they made their way down the wooden steps. Samuel was with a customer and looked up as they came down. She smiled and returned to the chair.

"Let's pet the kittens, Adam, until Samuel is free."

He balked at first, grunting as he tried to pull away. He shook his head anxiously back and forth. "Kibins bad."

She had anticipated this and held firm. "No, Adam. Kittens will sometimes scratch when they are scared. I want you to hold a kitten properly, so they feel safe and you are safe. Like this." She scooped up the grey striped kitten and held it close to her chest, supporting its body. "See." She gently stroked the baby between its ears.

"Now you try. Sit down here." She had him sit and held the kitten out. "Take it gently."

He whimpered but reached out to take the kitten and followed her cues to support it and carefully pet it. Soon it purred loudly, and Adam laughed.

"See, he likes you."

The customer left with her purchases and Samuel came over. "All good?"

"Yes. The scratches should heal soon, and he's learning to face a fear and redevelop trust."

Samuel reached for her hand and squeezed it. "You're a great mom." He caught her gaze and winked at her. "He is one lucky kid."

"Maybe. But where is my dad?"

He shrugged. "No word yet."

As much as she wanted to stay with Samuel, she knew she should return home in case he was there or came back.

"I tried calling the house, while you were upstairs but there was no answer."

"I've noticed he doesn't always answer the house phone. I'm not sure if he doesn't hear it or just prefers to ignore it." Dawson sighed. The enormity of the situation with her dad was slowly dawning on her. "Maybe I should also start a search for Joshua. He's somewhere on the other side of the world. How long do you think that will take?" She laughed humorlessly.

He smiled, and it felt good just to look at his smile.

"Just remember, when you do find your dad, whatever mood he's in, just smile and overlook any negativity. Forgive him if he's upset. It might not really be him."

She nodded, tears clogging her throat. "Forgive. Got it. Thank you for everything but we need to go back home."

He walked them to the door. "Did you like my little place?" He cut her a rakish grin and inclined his head toward the stairs.

"It suits you."

Dawson reached the driveway and a police cruiser sat parked under the oak tree. Her pulse had been racing along during the drive and now, seeing the car, it skyrocked. "Stay here, baby, I'll be right back." She got out of the SUV and the officer did likewise.

"Dawson Patrick?"

"Yes. Did you find my dad?"

The officer, a beefy guy in his sixties smiled. "He found his way home about fifteen minutes ago. He stopped and wanted to know what I was doing here, so I said I was wondering how many apples he usually gets off that tree there."

She glanced at the tree, and back at the officer. Her brows knit in confusion. "That's an oak tree."

He chuckled. "Yes, it is. And your dad pointed that out after about three full minutes. If he's seeing a doctor, it might be worth mentioning that."

She saw where he was heading and smiled her thanks. "Yes, I will be sure to mention it. Thank you. Umm, beyond the tree thing, what sort of mood was he in?"

Again, the knowledgeable smile. It warmed her almost as much as Samuel's could.

"I'd tread carefully if I were you, but you don't need a hazmat suit."

Good to know. "Thanks." She brushed her hair aside and glanced at the house. She blew out a breath. The officer patted her shoulder.

"Have a nice day, ma'am." He saluted her.

He returned to his cruiser and she returned to the SUV. "We'll have a late lunch and I'll work on the house a bit and then we will have a movie before dinner. How is that for a plan, buddy?"

She and Adam entered the house. "Hi, dad."

He was in the kitchen, stirring coffee. "There's some police officer outside asking about apples."

She feigned innocence. "That's odd. We don't have any apples around here."

He grunted, took his coffee cup, and ambled off. She sighed and made a cheese sandwich for Adam. She cut up orange slices and added them to his plate. Since she wasn't hungry, she just poured a cup of coffee and sat with Adam for a few minutes.

Then she sighed heavily, pulled her hair back and stood up. "I'll be back in a few minutes, pumpkin." She refilled his milk, snagged the phone book and her cell phone, and walked outside.

The cool air felt good on her skin as she thumbed through the Cedar Falls and Higgins area directory. She found the number she needed, stared at it a moment, and dialed. "Joshua, you owe me so big time." Her heart thudded with trepidation.

When the receptionist answered, she explained the situation and asked for an appointment. Her heart sank when the lady said they had no openings until late February. She opened her mouth to protest, beg, cry, or ask for another referral when the lady came back.

"Actually, I see a cancellation for tomorrow at ten-thirty. Do you want that one? Or would you prefer to set up a February date?"

She didn't know. Tomorrow meant less time to think of a good reason to get him to ride with her to Higgins. February meant she was stuck in limbo here two more months. Her stomach knitted into knots. She knew she was hoping to delay the inevitable. "You're open the week between Christmas and New Year's? I thought most doctor offices were closed that week?"

"We're only open two days this week, Wednesday and Thursday So which appointment did you want?"

Dawson let out a heavy breath. "Tomorrow."

She hung up the phone, leaned against the porch railing, and sobbed into the wind. If only Samuel were out here with her.

"Why do you feel the need to haul me all the way to a doctor? If Joshua were here, he wouldn't be doing this."

Dawson bit her lip and her fingers tightened around the

wheel. Yes, if only Joshua were here. If only. She pictured the things she would be telling him if he were here. When she could finally ease the tension in her jaw, she smiled. *Forgive him. Forgive him.*

"Yes, if Joshua were here, things would be different. But he isn't here, and he asked me to come in his place. So, I am taking you to the doctor because I am worried about you." She could tell he wasn't sure what to think about that, but as she spoke the words, she was impressed with herself.

They reached town and the doctor's office. Her dad opened the SUV's door first. "I ain't so old I can't make it into the doctor's office by myself. I ain't a first-grade kid." He slammed the door.

"No. you just sometimes act like one." She turned the engine off and looked back at Adam as he happily played with Bear-Bear. "They have lots of information now, so let's hope they can work with him." She reclined the seat and closed her eyes.

An hour later he returned, rapping the glass with his knuckles. His frown set her nerves on edge. She unlocked the doors and waited until he climbed in.

"How was your appointment?" she asked as she started the SUV again.

"Hope you're happy. They want me to go to the hospital for tests."

Tests? Did they think they saw something wrong with him? Did she dare ask?

"If Joshua were here, he'd set them straight that there was nothing wrong with me. He'd tell them I'm fine. Instead, you tell them I'm feeble-minded."

Dawson pulled out into traffic and picked which battle to fight. "Joshua isn't here. So when do you need to go to the hospital, Dad?"

He snapped a paper at her. "Now."

She bit back a moan. She really needed this information timelier, and with maybe a bit less complaining. Where was the hospital in Higgins? "Ok, we'll find it and you'll go." There was bound to be a cafeteria inside or someplace she could get Adam out for a walk and a snack. "Did they say how long the tests would take?"

"Two hours."

She did the math. It was already eleven-thirty. It would be almost noon before they found the hospital and dad got to where he needed to be. Two hours would be two o' clock, and another two hours home would be four. Then running back to town for Samuel's kittens would be almost closing time. She had to call him.

Half an hour later she deposited her dad into the care of two people in scrubs. They seemed quite competent to deal with him and were unfazed by his surly comments. They directed her to the hospital cafeteria and once Adam was engrossed in his tuna sandwich and chocolate pudding, she called Samuel's store.

"Don't worry about the cats. I can get a gasmask and take care of them. How are things with your dad?"

She lowered her voice and explained the situation.

"I wish I could be there with you."

"Me too. This is rough." Emotions rose and she wiped a tear away. "I don't know what to think."

"Do you want me to come out to the house after I close? Sort of be a peacemaker if need be?"

She thought it over. It was so tempting to say yes. She could make a meal and tell dad Samuel had been invited to dinner. And just to have him nearby was priceless. Yes sat on her tongue, ready to launch out.

"It would be great, but he's my dad and he has to accept it's me here, not Josh, and we need to find a way to face whatever is going on. Right now I need to find out how to get looped into his medical team."

"So is that a yes or a no?"

She smiled at the chuckle in his tone. "It's a thank you for the offer, I appreciate it but don't worry. Take care of the cats and we'll be there tomorrow."

She heard the disappointed sigh as much as she felt the hollow taste in her mouth.

"Okay. In that case, have a good evening. Call me if you need me."

She ended the call and smiled wearily at Adam. "Hey, buddy, how's the chocolate pudding? Can I have a bite?"

He giggled and shook his head. She reached out, forced a laugh, and stole a bite anyway.

Dawson stared at the dusty skates and gingerly touched a finger to the white leather. Once upon a time these meant the world to her. Mom had bought them for her fifteenth birthday, and she wore them every winter. Once the fire department froze part of the park each winter, she took her skates to town.

She met friends, boyfriends or just skated with whoever happened to be there. She flowed freely over the ice, going forward and backward and even spinning a time or two. Skating was her escape from her dad and brother. Escape from bad school days. Escape from teenage girl troubles.

She picked them up and blew the dust off. She'd left them here when she moved away, and it looks like they've never been touched. She had come down to the basement looking for some more tools and stumbled across this lucky find. Would Kurt want to skate like they used to?

They used to hold hands, and glide over the ice with the hair blowing through her hair. It was a magical time of her life. Ice skating made her feel alive and free.

The blades were still in good shape and the leather boots were good. They just needed a good cleaning and they'd be as good as new. This project suddenly moved to the top of her list over hunting for tools. While her dad was busy giving her the cold shoulder, she could clean these pieces of her past up, restore them, and leave them in the back of her SUV. Just in case. If she was going to be stuck in Cedar Falls for the winter, she'd find Adam a pair of skates and teach him how to glide over the ice too.

An hour later she had the skates restored. The white leather felt supple beneath her fingertips. It smelled like new leather. The blades sparkled in the fluorescent lighting and the new laces she found in the odds and ends drawer fit perfectly. She smiled in satisfaction as she carefully placed the case in the SUV. Now she could return to her tool hunt before she went into town. Bent curtain rods awaited her now.

"Samuel, hi, how are you doing?"

Samuel smiled. Mike, his last foster dad, always sounded like he was having the best time. He stopped unpacking a shipment of inventory and sat down at the desk to take the call. "I'm doing good. Mike. Good to hear from you. How's Evelyn? How's Aruba?"

"Evelyn's fine. I don't know about Aruba, though I suspect it's still there."

That surprised Samuel. As far back as he knew, Mike and Evelyn had always taken the weeks before Christmas until the middle of January off and gone down to Aruba. "You're not in Aruba now?"

"No. Evelyn wanted to stay home this year. We were hoping you could come back and visit. It would give you a chance to get away from Cedar Fall's Christmas-palooza."

Samuel grinned. It certainly was that. He could hear the carols and songs from the street seeping through the windows and pouring in the doors each time someone opened the front door. "I don't know, Mike. It's been super busy here."

Mike chuckled. "That's the perfect time to close up temporarily. Didn't you learn that in school?"

"Yes." Ideally, it was a good time, and a great excuse to escape the never-ending holiday. But did he really want to be away from Dawson now? Especially with her dad just starting medical tests and being exceptionally difficult to her. He hesitated, aware of Mike breathing at the other end of the phone. "It's complicated. I...uh... I'm fostering some cats for the rescue group."

"Cats. That's a bit unusual for you."

Didn't he know it. "Yes, but I was kind of coerced into it." He explained Barb's persistence and glossed over Dawson's offer of assistance. "Let me think about it, Mike. I appreciate the invite and I'd like to see you and Evelyn again. How many kids do you have now?"

"Two. They're both rather good and aren't as rough as some have been."

Samuel understood rough. Some foster kids arrived with enough PTSD baggage to require a moving truck to carry it all. He raked a hand through his hair as he listened to Mike highlight the kids. The more he thought about it, he'd love to see the only foster parents that had ever felt like real parents, but he hated to leave Dawson. They ended their call and he promised to call back in a couple of days with an answer. He blew out a heavy breath and raked his hair again. Maybe he could talk to Dawson when she came in today and see how things are with her dad.

But then again, Dawson was the type she'd just smile, cheerfully tell him to please go see his family, and pretend everything was okay. She was so selfless; she'd never let on how something might affect her. It kind of drove him crazy.

Samuel was with a customer when Dawson came in with Adam. He waved and resumed his help with Mr. Judd. Dawson appeared happy. Was it because her dad and she were doing okay together or because she was able to come to town and get away from him? He sincerely hoped it was the former, and not the latter.

Stealing glances at her, he thought of his conversation with Mike. He'd like to see his foster parents again, but he would really miss her and Adam. He knew it was true when he said so to Mike but watching them now smacked him hard with the truth. Dawson and her son have firmly entrenched themselves into his life.

The question was, what could he do about it? They didn't need him in their life. The truth was, he needed them in his. He needed their joy, their innocence, their great hearts, their laughter and so much more that they naturally carried within them. He could, by contrast, offer them so much less in return.

"I think that should do it," Mr. Judd said in his deep baritone voice.

Samuel clutched the stack of books he'd been holding and followed Mr. Judd to the counter where his customer set down his own armload of post-Christmas goodies. Mr. Judd looked over at Dawson, tipped his hat and smiled.

"Ma'am. Watching you gives a new meaning to the term wrangling cats."

Dawson laughed as she pushed the cats away from the bowls

she was trying to fill. "Yes, they don't understand it's better to fill the dish when they don't have their furry heads all buried in it. Babies, what can you do? At least there is only three of them."

"Good point." Mr. Judd studied her a moment. "You look familiar. Do I know you?"

Dawson had furrowed her brow in thought as well. "Maybe. Dawson Patrick, Lloyd's daughter."

Judd snapped his fingers. "Yes, of course. I know Lloyd. How's he been? I haven't seen him since probably before Halloween."

Dawson's face fell and Samuel's heart dropped. He leaned closer to hear her reply.

"He's having some problems, which is why I came back home for a while. Hopefully, it won't be anything serious."

Mr. Judd appeared bothered. "Tell your dad I say hello. I'm Earnest Judd. I don't live in Cedar Falls any more, but I will make it a point to stop in and see him. In fact, do you think he'd mind if I dropped in before I leave town?"

She smiled. "He would probably enjoy your visit. Thank you."

"Good." Judd tipped his hat again and turned back to Samuel. "Right. And what are the damages today, my good man?"

A few moments later Samuel came around the counter and enveloped Dawson in a hug. She laughed, then sighed, and leaned against him. He inhaled her perfume, that peppermint and vanilla scent he liked. She was warm and soft, and he wanted the moment to last forever. Since anyone could come in any second, he closed his eyes, determined to savor this feeling of holding her and the emotions it erupted within him, for as long as he could. The only sounds were the kittens crunching through their food and Adam making motor sounds by the window.

"Umm, this feels good." She reached up and rested her hand over his.

Fresh spikes of desire snapped through him. He swallowed.

Breathed in. Breathed out. Breathed in again. "How'd it go last night?"

"Dad isn't talking to me right now. I consider it a win."

He smiled at the humor in her voice. He also heard the sorrow. He silently applauded her bravery. As much as he hated to admit it, she was a better person than he was. If he were in her shoes, he doubted he'd stick things out like she was. Again, he was struck with how she deserved more than the man he was.

CHAPTER 8

Dawson blew out an irritated breath and walked outside. She stood on the porch, crossed her arms over her chest, and glared at the sunshine glinting off the snow. She was mad. She was mad enough to do something drastic. But she couldn't. And that's what really bothered her.

Dad was talking to her again, just enough to remind her she overreacted on her medical concerns and to rub it in nothing would be happening if Josh were here. She snorted. He got that much right. *Nothing* did get done when Joshua was here. She had hoped he would be in a better mood when his friend, Earnest Judd, came for a visit. Instead, the reverse seemed to be true. He even went so far as to insinuate Adam's daddy wasn't here because of her tendency to exaggerate situations. That was when she had to leave the house.

And Adam, her sweet-tempered loving baby, was his grandfather's grandson today. He woke up grumpy and continued to fuss about everything she tried or suggested, and he cried over nothing and refused to tell her what was going on with him. Tummy ache? Headache? She had no clue.

Between the two of them, she'd had enough by the time

breakfast was finished. She left the dishes on the table and her son in the care of her dad and stomped out to the porch. She wished it were a lot further away. She paced along the length of the planked boards, careful to avoid the rotten ones. One more danged thing she'd eventually get fixed. If she were still here when the weather warmed up.

Lord, she sure hoped not.

Right now, she didn't want to still be here tonight.

She punched the post, wincing when her bruised knuckles connected with the wood.

"Great, Dawson. That was smart. Break your hand, end up in a cast, and you'll be stuck here that much longer."

She cradled her hand, sure it was only sore now, and not actually hurt. She could put ice on it, but that would require going back inside. Instead, she sat down on the bottom step and plunged her hand into the pile of snow she had shoveled off the porch two days ago. She sucked in a sharp breath at the cold bite but then it felt good and she relaxed.

What the devil was she going to do? It might be a good day to replace the bad socket on the stove burner. And finish the rest of the electrical projects on her list. In her mind, it might not be so bad if she electrocuted herself.

Three and a half hours later she and Adam drove into town. Adam was marginally better and seemed content to play with Bear-Bear. Dad was still on the warpath and she was glad to just get away. She considered asking Samuel to dinner tonight so she wouldn't have to deal with him alone.

She parked the SUV a block from the town's tree and together she and Adam walked to Samuel's. Adam stopped at every other shop and stared at the window displays. Instead of admiring the decorations, he pointed and asked for candy, food, and toys. When she said no for the seventh time, he dropped to the sidewalk and proceeded to wail like she'd just slapped him.

"Adam, what is going on with you?"

Others stopped and stared. She felt heat rushing to her cheeks as people gave a variety of glances at them. Some looked sympathetic and others were almost hostile. Fear soon replaced the concern.

"Adam, come on." She picked him up, and he hugged her neck, still wailing. "If you keep this up, we're going to the emergency clinic. I wish you could tell me what was wrong."

She carried him to Samuel's. hating she was bringing a crying child to his store. She entered, hoping he didn't have customers.

He did. She gave him a wide-eyed look to match his double take and raised eyebrows.

"I can take him upstairs if you want. Or we can leave."

He shook his head, held a finger up to his customers, excused himself, and came up to them.

"Hey, buddy, what's going on?" He asked the question of Adam, but he looked at her.

She shrugged her shoulder. "I don't know. He's been fussy all day. Dad's been on the war path. I don't know." Tears of her own threatened to fall. "Shall we—"

She was about to suggest they leave when Samuel scooped Adam out of her arms. She sagged against the bookshelf and heaved a breath. She watched as Samuel walked back to his customers, softly talking to Adam, and rubbing big circles on his back. Like he'd held kids all the time, he rocked Adam off one hip as he engaged with the customers. They smiled and chatted to Adam. Dawson was stunned to see him revert to sucking his thumb but still smile and chortle with the customers and cling to Samuel's neck like a lifeline.

She'd never felt so out of control or spellbound in her life. The temptation to have Samuel come to dinner and sooth dad too was growing exponentially.

She made her way over to her favorite chair and watched as

her son melted into Samuel's embrace, as Samuel deftly handled a cranky toddler and two bemused customers and finally, the customers carried their books and novelties to the counter.

Samuel still held Adam and he stepped behind the counter to ring up the sale. He worked well with one hand. Finally he sat Adam on the counter and the little rascal helped bag the purchases by handing Samuel each item as he asked for it by name. Dawson watched in awe as Adam transformed from a grumpy baby to a happy, smiling child. The customers smiled and waved bye-bye to Adam as they left carrying their bags. Dawson heard them laughing as they opened the door and entered the street. Christmas refrains drifted in.

Alone, Samuel held his hands out to Adam again and the child eagerly scooted into his arms, going for the neck hold again. Samuel patted him and whispered at his ear. Then he came around the counter and approached Dawson. Her heart jumped like a kick drum. She stood up and held her arms out. Adam reached for her, cooing softly.

She wrapped her arms around Adam and fingered his soft blond hair. She smelled the strawberry scent of his shampoo. She and Samuel locked eyes and for a moment, she forgot to breathe.

"Do you like spaghetti and meatballs?" The question tumbled from her mouth before she could think. Her thoughts were too focused on Samuel's dark eyes and easy smile.

"Yes."

"Six o' clock. Suit not required, but it's optional."

He chuckled. "I can bring dessert. Or wine." He lifted a dark brow in question.

"I need something a lot stronger than wine."

Half an hour later Dawson and Adam left Samuel's shop. She still had no idea what caused Adam's bad temper, but thanks to Samuel, it seemed to be gone.

"Thank goodness," she said to Adam. "Because you're too cute to be a sour puss."

"Sour."

"Yes, sour." She stopped and made a face. "Like you've been sucking on a lemon. You and grandpa been making lemon smoothies?"

"Yuck! A lemon smoothie doesn't even sound good. Who likes those?"

She whirled. "Kurt! You surprised me."

"I used to do a lot of that. Remember?"

She looked at his Cheshire cat smile and did remember. He had a habit of just appearing out of seemingly nowhere, scare her, and then stand there innocent with his hands in his pockets and a whistling tune on his lips. "Never was there a more blameless person than you, Kurt."

He skipped a step forward. "I had a great thought. Let's go skating." He nodded at the skates looped over his shoulder.

"Well, I did find my old skates. And they are in the back of my SUV." She glanced down at Adam, who was back to being attached to her leg. "However, I haven't had a chance to look for skates for Adam."

Kurt shrugged. "We can go now, he can watch, and maybe later he can join us."

"I can't just leave him sitting on the sidelines. He's not old enough."

"We'll think of something." Kurt reached for her hand. "Where did you park?"

Suddenly Dawson was seventeen again. Once they touched hands, all the frustrations of the day melted away.

Once they stopped on a bench to lace up their skates,

Dawson insisted Adam accompany them onto the ice. She said she could push him along and he could slide on his boots.

"It will help boost his confidence and teach him balance," was her argument.

"Okay. Whatever." Kurt sailed off and made three wide, arching loops around the ice rink, did a few jumps, and danced across the ice like a ballet performer before he finally came back to slow down with Dawson. She ignored the butterflies fluttering in her stomach as she watched him glide so freely over the ice. She tried to ignore the sense of desertion when he left them to fly like a bird.

"What did you do over Christmas, Kurt?" she asked when he returned to them.

He stuck his hands in his pockets, turned backward to face Dawson, and easily propelled himself in reverse. "Made the rounds with the family, I have a lot of siblings, grandparents, uncles, aunts and cousins. It takes a few days to visit each of them and eat all that good food and get all those great presents."

She felt a pang of envy. One of the things she'd liked about Kurt was his large family. Coming from a small family, she found his large circle as refreshing as he was. The ones she had met were welcoming and fun to be around.

She tried to talk about her troubles with her dad, and the doctor visit. Granted, some of the things she said were spoken in code or spelled out, but he didn't have the interest Samuel had. Within a couple of minutes he shook his head. "My older sister is one of those, the doctors who deal with old people and their mental problems."

She braked to a stop, catching Adam. "You have a sister who is a geriatric psychologist? Seriously?"

"Yeah, I guess so. Why'd you stop?"

"Because I need to put a geriatric physician and a geriatric psychologist on retainer. And speed dial. And my Christmas card list. Or wear out a path to Higgins. That's why. Where's your sister work?"

"The Higgins Hospital."

Dawson could not believe it. "Could I have you and her come to dinner one night?"

"I don't know about her, but I'd love to come to dinner any night?" Kurt leaned in. "How about tonight?"

Meatballs. She remembered her invitation to Samuel. "No, tonight's not good. Talk to your sister and see if she's willing to help me out and if so, when would she be free."

"Okay, okay, fine. I'll ask her. How about you and me—"

He bent in again, and she smelled the sweet scent of soda on his breath and she pushed him away again. "Let's skate. Come on, Adam." She gave him a gentle push and kicked off. With Adam only being able to push himself along on his boots and with her guidance, Dawson was limited how far or fast she could fly. Kurt kicked off, raced by, waved, and spun into a double axel. He certainly wasn't rusty. He looked like he just stepped off an Olympic competition. She remembered a time she did too. Together, they spent hours skating on this frozen pond, until spring came, and it melted once more. But for a few months, their laughter and friendly rivalry kept the locals entertained.

"Sweet baby, you need skates of your own." She longed to see her son zipping along like Kurt was now. She yearned to be free again.

Samuel turned back around and returned to his store. He was sorely tempted to turn the sign to closed. He tore off the "back in five" note and wadded it up. Spotting the kittens, he tossed it to them, and they pounced on the crinkled paper like it was the golden mouse. He watched them but this time their antics gave him no pleasure. Inside, he was devastated. How could he unsee what he just saw at the ice rink?

He'd helped a customer carry her purchases to her car, unfortunately her car was halfway down the street. He deposited the bags in the back seat, thanked her, and turned to leave. It was a lovely day out, not too cold, and abundant sunshine. He breathed in the fresh air and turned in a slow circle to see what was going on around town.

Sometimes he got stuck inside the shop for endless hours and by the time he looked outside, it was dark and cold. So he decided to take advantage of the pleasant, sunny day and the fact he had a few minutes to spend. The ever-present holiday music filtered on the wind and laughter turned his attention from the center's tree to the ice rink to his left. And his heart stopped. Cold.

Dawson and Adam skated along the ice, with Dawson wearing a pair of white skates and guiding Adam as he gamely tried to keep up. Normally that kind of scene would have warmed his heart, made him laugh and go over for a closer look. It was reminiscent of Norman Rockwell. What chilled him and froze his steps today was the guy who skated in circles around them, literally in backward circles around them. He looked like he could be a professional ice skater to judge by his finesse.

Suddenly sick, Samuel rushed back to his shop and sat down at his desk. With no customers currently, he could work on inventory, cleaning up, or a slew of other tasks. Sampson climbed up his leg and begged a scratch.

"Not now. I'm not in the mood." He deposited the kitten back on the floor, wadded up a small piece of notebook paper and tossed it across the room. The three siblings raced after it.

Dawson looked beautiful out there. She was having fun. Oh how she deserved a respite from everything she'd encountered lately and just experience some pleasure. She was radiant. She was playful.

Samuel was glad she had this time. She needed it. What bothered him was the guy who gave it to her. Why couldn't he be the one to provide a reprieve, a chance to laugh and play, and let her worries go if only for a few hours? Why wasn't he the man out there dancing on ice with her instead of that other guy?

Maybe he sounded jealous, and maybe he was, but as much as he believed Dawson needed this time, he needed to be the one providing it even more. Except he couldn't. What did he know about just relaxing, letting things go, and simply wrap one's self in the moment? What did he know about sheer bliss? If he was out of his element in understanding such happiness, how could he provide it to another or share in it with her?

He slammed his palms down on the desk, feeling the shockwaves radiate up his arms. He was hopeless. And too tightly wound, as Mike and Evelyn had frequently told him, to understand the lighter side of life. At the skate rink, he heard and saw the lighter side of life through Dawson.

Three hours later he parked his truck outside her porch and exhaled. This dinner might be harder than Christmas dinner had been. Tonight he wasn't fighting the demons of bad holiday memories. Tonight he was tormented by images of Dawson smiling and sailing carefree and happy across the ice. And he wasn't a part of it. And he knew he couldn't be.

He walked along the path, noticed Adam's snowman was missing his hat and one stick arm. Had birds made off with them or had Adam removed them for whatever reason? He was no slouch on the ice, nor was he an Olympic pro like that other guy, but he could hold his own enough to teach a toddler to skate. He knew for a fact Pete's General Store carried ice skates for kids. He didn't have a huge selection, only one section of a short wall, but there ought to be something suitable to get Adam started for this season.

He knocked and Dawson was almost immediately at the door. She gave him a big smile and his heart kick started.

"Hi, glad you could make it."

"Adam ok? How's your dad?" Why did he have to launch into an interrogation? Couldn't he just smile and say hello and you look lovely? She did look nice, in her white cable sweater and skintight blue jeans. Her hair was curled again. She stepped back and her eyes widened a little at his direct go-for-the-throat greeting.

"Adam's fine. Dad's the same."

The carefree glow she wore before was gone and even her happy smile could not hide the lines of stress and worry he'd seen so often. Maybe he'd never noticed until today when she had that opportunity to really lose them. But why couldn't he be the one to give her that chance?

"Are you okay?" she asked as she stepped aside and reached for his coat.

"Oh yeah, just still wrapped up with work."

"Umm, end of year stuff?"

"Yes," he agreed as he handed his jacket over.

"Dinner is nearly done. I just have to take the bread out of the oven. Why don't you go say hi to Dad and Adam? They're in the living room."

He hated to step away from her mulberry scent, but he agreed. Passing the kitchen, he breathed in tomatoes, yeast, and spices of basil, garlic, and onion. He wiped the drool away as he headed on down the hallway.

What repair project had Dawson worked on today? No wonder she looked stressed. This house was a veritable quagmire of projects. She must feel like she'll never see the light at the end of this long tunnel. And her dad… He sighed. She was one hell of a woman.

Two hours later Samuel returned home. Once again, his experience far exceeded his expectations with the Patrick's. Dawson took something as common as spaghetti and meatballs and turned them into a culinary delight. She could be a chef on one of those cooking shows. Maybe he was just biased, but he'd never enjoyed finer 'ghetti and balls.

Lloyd started out in a bit of a grumpy slump when he'd first arrived, but before long they were engaged in some stimulating talks about the Panthers and the Warriors. Lloyd thought the Warriors were all washed up this season, but Samuel politely disagreed. It was the Panthers who needed to pack it up and go home, which Lloyd opposed with him. It was fun to debate sports with the old guy. However, he still sensed the undercurrents layered beneath the forced civility each time Lloyd and Dawson came within six feet of each other. It was the only thing that made the dinner difficult. He wished he knew some way to repair the rift between them. He saw how Lloyd's seemingly insensitive comments upset and hurt Dawson. Maybe she just needed to know if her dad really meant what he said or if it was a by-product of some medical condition.

At least she didn't run out on the porch in tears this time. But he was a little disappointed their porch time tonight didn't turn into another snowball fight.

And Adam. The more he was around that kid, the more he fell in love and gave away more of his heart to the little tyke. The boy's father had no idea what a good family he walked away from. And Samuel knew with every beat of his heart what a great family he could never have. Ah, but wasn't that the story of his life? It was pretty much all he knew.

He prepared for bed, exchanging khakis and button-down shirt for his roomy sweats again. Sampson had followed him upstairs and sat on the bed in a bread loaf shaped Zen-state of feline bliss.

He climbed into bed and pushed Sampson aside. "My side. Go back downstairs."

Once he was settled, the kitten bounded up on his chest, kneaded his front paws three times, circled once, and lay down back into his bread loaf position, his eyes fixed on Samuel.

"The problem, Sampson, is my heart and mind are on two different agendas. My mind knows I can't have Dawson or get serious with her. She's only here for a little while, and I'm here indefinitely. She deserves someone fun like that guy at the rink, not some over wound, serious all the time, afraid of Christmas and commitment guy like me."

He exhaled deeply, rubbed Sampson under the chin and smiled as the cat blinked slowly back at him. "And my heart says she's a beautiful woman with a super kid who needs a man figure in his life. And the problem is my heart doesn't want to listen to what my mind tries to tell me."

Dawson slid into the foamy bubble bath, eased out a tired sigh, and closed her eyes. Mercy but she was tired. It seemed every muscle from her neck and shoulders down to her ankles were sore and complaining. Eucalyptus and lavender permeated the room. She slowly swished the Epsom salts with her feet. Candles flickered, lifting scents of gardenia and citrusy notes while flutes and piano music played on her phone app. For a little while, this was heaven.

She lifted her hand up, cupping the water and bubbles. The scent reminded her of strawberry fields. Maybe Epsom salt and bubble bath together were overkill, but tonight she needed both of them.

Both Adam and her dad were off to bed, Samuel was long gone, and she was done working on the house for the day. She'd gone out for a walk, watching the stars come out, and twinkle in the darkening sky. The moon flirted with the wispy clouds and the air was crisp and felt good on her skin. She walked to the end of the driveway, stared up one direction of the road that led to town and then turned and looked up the other direction.

What was she going to do with her life? With Adam's life? The impact of her situation was really striking home and she felt the strands of panic rising.

She and her dad were not going to see eye to eye. Whether it was due to him having any kind of mental disorder or not remained to be seen but even if it was, she didn't see him taking medicine daily and working to remain civil. And on that note, what if he was mentally unable to provide for himself? He'd already proven he was not able to cook, clean, and do the basics in care? Was she just going to pack up the car and drive away while waving and wishing him luck?

Could she be that heartless?

She'd leap blindly at the chance to come here, but now that the initial adrenaline from the divorce settled and she took an objective look around, she questioned the wisdom of her choice.

She was proud of her work on the house, but today, her body was reminding her she wasn't a carpenter or handyman. Home repair was hard, physical work. Another knee-jerk reaction she now questioned.

Adam was doing well, using more words, and thoroughly engaged in his interactive learning toys he received from her and Samuel. His growing vocabulary was also no doubt due to Samuel. Her baby boy was blossoming before her eyes and she loved to watch him grow. His birthday was next month. She could stay here, throw a little party with her dad, Samuel and maybe Wendy's kids. She could make a nice dinner, roast chicken and vegetables kind of thing, and bake a sheet cake and let him blow out the candles.

But what about after that?

She swirled her hands through the water, stirring up the scents. She really liked Samuel. Probably too much. If she left, she'd miss his bright smile, husky laugh, and gravelly voice. She'd miss his dry humor and honest acceptance of her and Adam. He was thoughtful and she'd not seen that in her dad, her brother, or her husband. It was a treasure to see in Samuel and she would mourn its absence.

But if she stayed, she'd be forever working on the house, and forever at the mercy of her dad's moods and biting words. What if Adam picked up on it? How would she react to that?

She wished she could get ahold of Joshua. They really needed to talk.

She held up a palmful of bubbles, breathed in the strawberry scent and blew them away. As she watched the shiny orbs drift up and pop, a tear slid down her cheek. She wasn't strong enough to do all this on her own after all.

Dawson studied her list and drew a line through the word showerheads. They were both cleaned and working well now. She could see real progress on her list. She nibbled the end of the pencil as she read what was left. Repair holes in drywall, fix wallpaper seams, cover up ceiling stains and repair popped drywall screws. Clean gutters. Caulk bathtub. Reglaze and paint the cracked windows. Overhaul the loose deck boards and wobbly railings.

It wasn't too bad of a list. The items were becoming more time consuming and more technical compared to stuck doors, leaky toilets, and sticky drawers. Reglazing. That was going to be tough.

She spent the morning scouring the garage and basement for caulk, drywall saw, and drywall materials. She had a short list of things she needed. Thank goodness her hardware shopping lists were getting shorter.

After a quick trip to Higgins for supplies and lunch, she and Adam would drop in and see Samuel and the kittens again. He would never know how valuable his support was to her in the face of her dad's opposition, but she knew and treasured him for it.

Two hours later she had the SUV loaded down with supplies once more, and Adam cheerfully playing with the toy from his drive through meal box, and she was almost to the outskirts of Cedar Falls. She looked for a parking spot near the bookstore. Even being mid-week, and early afternoon, the town was full.

"Well, baby, it looks like we'll have to walk a little bit."

Hand in hand they walked the brick sidewalk of town, stopping to watch anything with lights or music. Being 1800's circa buildings, many buildings kept their covered porch entries. Adam jumped up the front step, gripped the post and leaned out into the sidewalk. Dawson laughed as he tried to catch snowflakes. Then they would step down and continue to the next building to capture Adam's interest.

They crossed over to the block where the bookstore was, and Adam unexpectedly broke out of Dawson's hand. She gasped, horrified as he rushed down the street.

"Adam! No! Stop!"

Deaf to her cries, he continued, and she raced after him. He shot forward like a bullet. A thin young man stepped out of a store and directly into her path. They collided and ricocheted off each other. The man's phone flew out of his hand, clattering to the bricks.

He began to apologize and reached to help Dawson, but she scrambled up, mumbled an apology, and rushed after Adam.

"My son..." she said as she rushed off. The bookstore was only two doors away and she marveled at how Adam artfully dodged pedestrians and obstacles. She shouted his name again, but he did not slow down.

A customer exited Samuel's bookstore, holding the door open a moment to turn back into the shop. Adam darted through the open door. Dawson rushed up as the customer began to close the door. She breathlessly snatched the handle.

"My son," she panted to the astonished patron. Dawson could only guess the portly woman had not witnessed a two-foot-tall child duck in while she held the door open. The woman excused herself and moved aside as Dawson hurried through the doorway and collided solidly with Samuel.

"Oh!" Air left her lungs as if she'd slammed into a concrete wall. His hands caught her by the shoulders and steadied her.

"Easy," he said gently by her ears. "Take a breath."

"Adam," she gasped, her lungs burning. She'd only sprinted a block, but it felt like miles. "He broke away."

"Yes, he's right over there." He propelled her to where Adam sat on the floor with the kittens climbing over him. He chortled and gently pet them. She fisted a hand to her mouth at the sweet scene and then looked back at Samuel.

"I saw him whiz in like a bullet when Mrs. Rosenberg left the door open. I knew you couldn't be far behind."

His smile was tender. "We had to walk a little bit," she explained. "About four stores down he broke from my hand and wouldn't stop. I was so afraid."

"Umm humm." Samuel drew her close. "No doubt. He seemed to know exactly which door to come in."

She listened to his own heartbeat, so calm compared to her

own. She was glad Adam had known which doorway to enter, but he shouldn't be breaking away and running off.

"I'll watch him, and you go upstairs and make yourself a cup of tea, mug of cocoa, coffee, whatever it takes to settle your nerves," Samuel suggested as he rubbed circles over her jacket. He pulled her out to arm's length. "You're trembling. You had a scary event just now, and you need to slow down that adrenaline. Adam will be fine." Then he gently pulled her scarf and gloves off and set them aside. "I got this. You go upstairs." He nodded toward the staircase.

Surprised to find herself shaking, she nodded. She climbed the old wooden staircase to his apartment and stood in the efficiency kitchen with her arms wrapped around herself. What did she want? Tea, cocoa, coffee? She was drawn to the copper tea kettle and she filled it with cold water. The heat from the burner felt good. She popped the top from a decorative tin canister on the counter and sorted through an assortment of herbal teas. Then she pulled down two large mugs from the open shelving above.

Within a minute the kettle whistled, and she poured the hot water into the cups. Lemongrass, honey, and ginseng swirled around her as she steeped the bags. She hoped he was in the mood for tea. She spotted a container of raspberry dessert cookies and added three to a small plate. Once the tea was steeped, she drained the bags, balanced the plate and the mugs, and returned downstairs.

Adam sat on Samuel's knee and Samuel read a story to him. He looked up at her approach, concern on his face, then he smiled as he accepted the second tea mug

"Thank you, that was thoughtful."

She shook her head and extended a cookie. 'Thank you," she said and nodded at Adam. She gave Adam the second cookie and kneeled next to Samuel.

"Baby, you can never run off on me again. Bad things could happen, and I would be very sad." She stroked his soft hair as he nodded at her and nibbled the cookie. When he finished the treat, he climbed down and went back to the kittens. Adam got up and offered Dawson the chair. He leaned against the wall and cradled the tea mug.

"He can't just take off."

"No, and hopefully he will remember today."

She took a sip of tea. Honey and lemon. "If he understands."

"How was Adam diagnosed?"

His direct question surprised her. She thought a moment. "It happened quickly. It was mentioned by someone at his day care that he wasn't as developed as some of the other two-year-old's. I took him to our pediatrician, who thought he might have autism. I took some pamphlets and website addresses home." She stopped and raked a hand through her hair and took another sip of tea. "Next thing I knew his dad was filing for divorce. I guess he spoke to our lawyer over the weekend."

"Weekend? Dawson, lawyers don't usually work on the weekends."

"They were friends. They played squash or singles or something on Saturdays."

Samuel's jaw dropped. "I don't know a whole lot about family law, mostly because I've always been the pawn that just got moved around. But I do know that is clearly a conflict of interest. No wonder you got robbed."

"I didn't get robbed. I got Adam."

Samuel smiled. "Yes, but what he did was wrong both ethically and morally, and maybe criminally." He kneeled by her side. "And not every kid is born reciting Webster's. Just because some are slower than others to develop skills does not automatically put them on the spectrum. When did he receive an official medical diagnosis?"

She thought about that. "He didn't. Our pediatrician thought he might, but we never pursued it because …"

"Because he filed for divorce and the rug was yanked out from under you. You went into survival mode."

She nodded, now realizing her error for not following up further into a diagnosis for Adam. "What if he isn't?" Her heart skipped at the thought. "On the spectrum?" Her voice cracked.

"Then he will catch up to other kids his age at some point and be just fine." He gently cupped her chin and stared deep into her eyes. "Either way, Dawson, Adam will be fine. He is a smart kid and you are doing a fantastic job raising him."

Her heart stalled as she got lost in the depths of his eyes. Her pulse skipped and raced, until she was sure he could hear the blood roaring in her ears. The place his fingertips touched her skin warmed through to her bones. Oh, Samuel!

Then a shadow passed over his face, clouding his eyes. He abruptly withdrew, taking his warm touch and lemony breath. He stepped back a step and looked around, his gaze landing on where Adam was playing with the kittens by the tower at the window. His gaze softened once more. Adam carefully stroked the gray kitten from its head down to its tail and back again, much to the cat's delight.

"Adam sure does like Blinking," she said, resuming her teacup.

"That's Blinking? I thought the striped one was Blinking."

"I'd checked once, but I could be wrong." She stood and went to the counter and located the kitten info. "Yes, the solid gray one is Blinking. The striped gray tabby is Nod. And the little black and white—tuxedo—is Winking." She looked back at Samuel. "Why?"

"Nod? Really? That's as stupid a name as Blinking." He looked solidly at the gray tabby kitten and shook his head. "No, there's no reason."

She didn't believe that. "You weren't thinking of adopting one, were you?"

His face flushed and he looked away, scrubbing at his chin, his dimples puckering. Finally he met her gaze. "I think I already have. Sampson's been sleeping with me at night. I thought he was Blinking."

Sampson? She followed his finger to the tabby. "I, umm, think that's wonderful. To be honest, I'd be tempted to adopt Blinking if I could. He'd be a great pet for Adam."

A silence settled between them, growing uncomfortable. Still unnerved from Adam's uncharacteristic bolt, the awkward silence between her and Samuel intensified her anxieties. She set the empty cup aside. She had to say something. "Well, I plan to handle the gutters next on the house."

His head whipped around to her. "Up on a ladder?"

She blinked. "Yes, that's normally how one reaches the gutters."

He paled, and his lips thinned, but he did not answer. She watched him, growing more uneasy as the quiet stretched. She looked over at Adam for a minute, peeking at Samuel as a tic in his jaw throbbed away.

He inhaled deeply, sunk his hands in the pockets of his jeans, and exhaled. "Dawson, have you considered finding someone for you? I know the divorce is recent, but someone who can be a positive male figure in Adam's life. A man who can go out and do things that teach him male lessons and who can be a steady rock for you. A man who can connect all the missing pieces in your life."

She'd rather thought Samuel fit those descriptions, but she had a feeling he wasn't talking about himself. An uneasy feeling slid over her and she licked her lips. "He looks up to you so much."

Samuel nodded, and looked around uncomfortably. "Yes, and

I adore him. But you've said yourself you don't plan to stay. And I am tied here." He exhaled again, his eyes clouding over. "You might not want to get so caught up on me and look for other options."

She reeled backward, stunned at his words. Her mind struggled to process all the meanings that could be attached to them. He looked wounded but she was the one who felt she were bleeding.

"Samuel, I don't understand where you're going with this."

He opened his mouth, then closed it, seemingly unable to answer her. Just then the bell on the door chimed and they turned at the sound.

A woman, medium build, probably in her early fifties, with dark hair, and eyes, entered. She glanced around ever so briefly, and her gaze flickered to Dawson before landing squarely on Samuel. She sighed, as if relieved.

Samuel took a step forward. "Hello, can I help you?"

"I hope so. Are you Samuel Johnson?"

"Yes."

She sighed again, then smiled and extended her arms. "I'm your mother."

Dawson inhaled as she looked to Samuel. His eyes went round, his mouth worked like a fish out of water and he stepped back two paces. His hands went up, palms out and he shook his head.

"I don't think so."

The woman smiled ruefully. "I understand you might have strong emotions about me." She glanced at Dawson. "Is there somewhere or some time we could talk privately?"

Samuel vehemently shook his head. "Dawson is a special person to me. She knows the circumstances of my birth. And my tour through the foster care system." She wanted to hug him for the introduction but winced at the bitterness in his final words.

She almost stepped closer to him but decided a few feet was a safe distance.

The woman exhaled. "Yes, and I am sorry about that. It was actually the best thing for you."

Samuel laughed harshly, cutting her off.

"You wouldn't have wanted to grow up behind bars. That's never good. At least in foster care, you stood a chance. Samuel, I am sorry I couldn't be your best mom, but I am your mother. And I've been clean and sober since your birth."

Samuel stood, arms crossed over his chest, not looking overly impressed. His jaw tightened and his eyes narrowed. "Congratulations. So why are you here? How did you find me?"

She shrugged. Dawson felt bad she didn't even know the woman's name. She tried to imagine being in prison and having Adam. She couldn't imagine handing him off to anyone. Yet Samuel said this woman sent him off with a callous wave. Except that was many years ago.

"Hi, I'm Dawson Patrick." She stepped forward, offering her hand. "I see some similarities between you and Samuel."

Samuel frowned. "Dawson," he warned, his voice a low growl.

"Hi. Sandy Jarvis."

"Now that we're on a first name basis, what are you doing here?"

Dawson cringed at Samuel's sarcasm. Sandy seemed to take it in stride.

"I wanted to meet you. See you." Sandy paused. "Maybe get to know you."

"Well, here I am. Look away." Samuel spread his arms out. "How did you find me?" he asked again.

"Three years ago I hired a private investigator. I was out, clean, and working at a steady job. I'd never forgotten you and found out you'd never been adopted. At least there were no court adoption records. My dad loaned me some money to hire the PI.

I had your date of birth, your gender, your place of birth. You never left Maine, so it wasn't hard. The PI was actually in your store two weeks ago to confirm it was you."

Dawson watched Samuel's brows furrow and doubtlessly he was thinking back two weeks ago, doing a mental catalogue of the customers. She had just started coming in the store then, so everyone looked new to her.

"Glad you got your money's worth."

Sandy sighed at his barb. "Your dad had a biting tongue too."

Samuel laughed. "So you know who my dad is? According to prison records, you didn't."

"I'm sure. Now. Things are much clearer than back then. I had dated this one guy for almost a year. You have some of his features. And his sarcastic humor. He didn't know I was pregnant when we were arrested."

"So where is he now? What's he got to say about having a kid now?"

"I'm sorry but he died in a prison riot at Warren fifteen years ago."

Samuel grunted. "So he never knew about me."

Sandy shook her head. "No."

Samuel's grunt and eye roll spoke volumes. Dawson felt his hurt, his sense of betrayal—again. She wanted to go to him, to comfort him and ease the rigidity from his jaw and wrinkles from his brow. But his guarded look warned her he would not welcome her touch now.

Not to mention his suggestion mere moments before that she look elsewhere for male friendship. What brought that on? They had shared so much together, of themselves, and enjoyed much fun and laughter. What made him make such a recommendation? Her own heart ached and bled for her and Adam.

"If you two ladies will excuse me, I need to leave. The store is closed and so am I." He turned to Dawson. "Lock up on your way out please." He strode to the door, flipped the open/closed sign, and stiffly marched upstairs, never glancing their way again.

Dawson forced her jaw shut as she followed his exit with her gaze. She was in utter disbelief. Stunned, she turned to Sandy, who wore an equally disappointing expression.

"I'm sorry," Dawson said. "I've never seen him like this."

Sandy smiled ruefully. "That's alright. I assumed my showing up out of the blue would shock him. I don't know what I expected. It was a pleasure to meet you."

"Yes. Maybe with time, he might come around?"

"Maybe." Sandy looked over at the stairs and back to Dawson, tears wetting her eyes. "I'll see myself out. Thank you."

Dawson set about taking care of the kittens and checking on Adam, who thankfully had fallen asleep in the corner and had missed both exchanges. When she finished with the kittens, she gently woke Adam, dressed him for their walk back to the SUV. Exiting the door, she looked at the closed sign, turned off the lights, locked the door and slid it shut. The click of the lock echoed a snap within her soul.

CHAPTER 9

S amuel stood at the window overlooking Main Street. His foot propped against the brick wall, and his shoulder resting against the cool glass, he watched over the influx of people come and go. He saw his mother leave the store, stop momentarily outside the door, and then walk to the east. She got into a nice condition, older model car and sit behind the wheel for several minutes. Then she drove away toward the east.

He knew he should feel bad for acting the way he had and treating her and Dawson so poorly, but right now he was too stunned to feel much of anything. It had ripped his heart out to suggest to Dawson to look elsewhere for a man. He'd meant maybe her skating partner, but he couldn't force the words out. The look of pain and bewilderment on her face about ripped him in half.

And then *she* walked in. With her bold declaration that she was his mother, who went to great pains to find him, and evidently wanted to create this happy little relationship with him now. And by the way, his dad never knew about him and died in prison over a decade ago. Fantastic. That was simply great.

He had no clue how he should feel about any of *that* or what he should think of suddenly having a mother drop into his life. He'd bet there was no book downstairs that covered this situation.

And then Dawson and Adam stepped outside. He leaned his cheek against the smooth pane to better see them. She reached for his hand, and he would bet she had an iron-clad grip on him. They walked west, stopping to momentarily peer into every other shop window.

He owed her an apology. He had no right to dump his business on her when she was only responsible for the cats. And technically there was nothing stopping him from taking care of their food and litter. Except it was a guaranteed excuse to see Dawson every day.

He moved to the door and opened it in case Sampson decided to pay him a visit. Or Nod, as Dawson had correctly pointed out. Nod, Blinking, whatever, they were all stupid names for a cat.

He picked up his cell phone and returned to the window. He dialed Mike's cell phone. Mike picked up on the third ring. He cleared his throat, blinked twice, and swallowed a lump.

"Hi. It's Samuel. If that invitation is still open, I'd like to come visit. I can be there tomorrow morning."

He could be there tonight, but it would be too late to barge in, so he'd leave now, spend the night along the way, and show up at their place in the morning. He hung up, grabbed a duffle bag from the closet and dropped some clothes and toiletries and phone charging cord into it. He wrote a note to Dawson that he would leave with the key outside. By the time she found it, he'd be back with his family. The closest thing he'd ever known as a real family.

He carried the note and his bag downstairs, making sure the door to his apartment was shut. He took the garland Adam gave him off the tree and left it coiled on the counter. He made another note and taped it to the front window explaining he'd been called out of town and would return later. The few lines he'd scribbled to Dawson said he didn't know when he'd return. Let the rumors begin.

The last thing he did was to take the wreath off the door and carried the Christmas tree out back and leave it next to the trash can. It was time he returned to his Christmas scrooge.

"Bye, Sampson. Keep an eye on things for me." He patted the kitten and scratched it behind its ear. "I'll miss you." With his eyes burning, he locked the door, tossed his bag in the truck, and drove out of Cedar Falls, not sure when he would be able to return.

Dawson pulled into the driveway at home and turned the engine off. Her mind still spun with the events of the last hour. Samuel's words bit the hardest, leaving a painful sting.

She felt bad for Sandy. As a mom, she knew the unbreakable bond between mother and son, even if the son was almost thirty years old and they had never meet. Had Sandy held Samuel at birth? Nursed him just once? She'd never forget those first, precious moments with Adam. From what Samuel described, based on records and what he'd been told by the foster system, she'd never bothered with him from his first breaths.

Horrible! How horrible for them both.

"Mama?" Adam kicked the seat back impatiently. He pointed out the window. "Magic."

She followed his pointing finger at the snowman in the yard and she sniffed. "Yes, baby, we all need some magic right now. Lots of it." Only, the real magic and not just more snowfall.

She got out and removed Adam from his car seat. She'd come back for the repair materials later once he was occupied. "Come on, little man." She dropped a kiss on his nose before she deposited him on the sidewalk. He giggled and her heart soared at the sweet sound.

"Bout time you get yourself back here."

Her dad's growl caught her at the door. She froze, weights dropping on her like balloons full of lead.

She inhaled slowly and let it out gradually as she helped Adam undress. *Be nice. Polite.* "Yes, I am back. Is there something you need?"

Her dad grunted, sounding like a bear coming from hibernation. He hobbled back down the hall.

"Are you hungry? I was going to make sandwiches. Do you want one?"

He turned around and shook a finger at her. "What I want is for you to return at a reasonable hour when you leave and stop treating me like you're in charge."

She looked at him, knowing her face had to be twisted into a puzzled frown. "Reasonable, like a curfew?" she asked.

"Yes. That's a start. I'm still your father and head of this household."

She struggled to make sense of him. Was he thinking she was still seventeen and needed a curfew and she was late? Or an adult who treated him like a kid and she needed to be in charge? Which one? Darned if she could make sense of it.

"Dad, do you remember how old I am?"

Again, he grunted, and looked at Adam. "Old enough to think you know a thing or two about life."

Oh the things she knew about life!

She was growing tired of trying to guess the reason behind his obvious sour mood. She felt a headache pulsing behind her eyes. "Dad, yes or no on the sandwich?"

She guided Adam to the living room, brushing past her dad. Adam headed for the robot toy and she turned to the kitchen and pulled three plates from the shelf. She started a pot of canned tomato soup on the stove.

Her dad followed. "The doctor's office called. Seems you convinced them I'm senile."

She unwrapped the bread and unscrewed the mayonnaise. Right now she would have to agree with the doctor. "And what did they say?"

"That I'm senile."

Must be the test results. "I'll call them after lunch and set them straight." Or get the straight answers. She stirred the soup and slathered condiments on the three sandwiches. As soon as one was finished, and loaded with chips, she pushed the plate at her dad. He grudgingly took it, eyeing it as if she had added poison.

"If you're not hungry, give it to Adam. He will appreciate it." Yes, she was snarky, to her dad no less, but this time he deserved it. She stirred the soup again and assembled a second sandwich. Her dad took the offering and sat down at the table.

Lunch was stressful, with a quiet that stretched on forever. Like a yawning cavern. Once Adam and her dad were finished, she cleaned up and tossed her unfished food into the fridge. She went out with the excuse to get supplies and called the doctor's office. She got a recording and left a message. She sounded desperate to her own ears as she relayed the message and asked for a return phone call as soon as possible.

In the meantime, she could start on her next project.

Right after breakfast Dawson prepared Adam for their drive to town. She'd spent a restless night rehashing Samuel's words to her and the visit from his birth mother. A sense of urgency gripped her to go earlier.

"We're going to town now, Dad. I'm not sure when we'll be back." She had hunted him down to the living room to relay her message and found him reading his paper. She waited to see what comments he might have. This time he chose to ignore her after giving her a cursory wave good-bye.

She wasn't sure which was worse, being ignored or degraded. Both bothered her. No matter now, she had a road trip with her little man to look forward too. She found a radio station playing children's holiday songs and they both sang along and laughed on the road to town.

Dawson pointed out things they saw that matched the lyrics in the songs. Sometimes she saw the connection in Adam's eyes and sometimes she saw a blank wall.

Samuel's comments about a real diagnosis rang in her ears and when they reached town, she would call the pediatrician's office and see about getting an appointment for him. She might not stay here forever, but she could get her son started on any assistance he needed, which could be portable with him to a new location.

She parked one block away from Samuel's store and firmly took Adam's hand. "You stay at my side. No running ahead."

They reached the Chapter Twenty-Five door and Dawson's heart sank. She read the 'out of town, closed indefinitely' sign. So much for having another conversation. She bent for the key and found a tightly folded note. Her heart sank even further as she scanned the brief lines.

Dawson, I don't know what to think or do. I'm leaving town and I don't know when I will be back. I hope you will continue to care for the kittens. If you want to stop, call Barb and have her come pick them up. I'd understand.

She was glad he understood something because she was floundering hopelessly, understanding nothing. She didn't get her dad's inconsistent behavior, she didn't know what to think about Samuel's parting comments, and she didn't know what her son could understand and not. No one was making sense around here lately.

Adam fussed and she pocketed the note and let him in. "Go play with the car please. I have some phone calls to make."

She spotted the garland they'd made for Samuel's tree, neatly folded on the counter. As she fingered it, she looked over to where the tree had been. She realized it was missing and then she realized she hadn't seen the wreath over the door either. Had he given up on the thin thread of Christmas he had finally held? She would almost bet the tree and wreath were in the trash.

Determined not to let his faith in Christmas die, she rushed out to the garbage and retrieved the wreath and tree before they were picked up. She carefully set them in the small storage room. They'd be safe in here for now. Then she returned to the front.

She grabbed the phone book from behind the counter and dialed the town pediatrician, a two-person practice. One doctor was booked through the end of February, but one had a few openings in early January. She snagged January seventh at ten am.

Next, she called the doctor back in Higgins about her dad.

She hung up the phone and walked over to her favorite chair. She sank into its cushiony softness and sat with her hands folded in her lap. The kittens climbed into her lap and she stroked them, snuggling with Blinking. So Samuel had an affection for Nod? Sampson. It fit the striped, wide face and round green eyes. Cuddling the warm, purring bodies, she let the tears fall. It felt like her whole world was falling apart—again in just a few weeks—and she was at a loss on what to do.

Adam came over to her, drawn by her sobs and patted her arm. She drew him into her embrace too. Her world was fractured, but her solace was soft kittens and clean boy smell.

Half an hour later she finished tending to the kittens and called Adam away from his toy.

"Time to get dressed, honey. Let's you and I go to the ice rink?"

She needed some time to mentally prepare before she headed back home.

They reached the rink and she laced up her skates. She entered the ice and held Adam's hand as she pulled him along the ice. Scared at first, he soon relaxed and caught her rhythm.

"Sweetie, we need to get you some skates of your own before the ice melts." She longed to fly free but realized that was a long way off. Even when outfitted with skates, Adam would need time to master the basics and then time to become good enough to keep up with her. "Maybe next winter, baby."

"Fancy meeting you here."

"How long do you intend to mope around?"

Evelyn's voice penetrated Samuel's fog and he looked up sharply. "I wasn't aware I was moping."

She placed her hands on her ample hips and nodded. "You aren't aware of it, but everyone else most certainly is. What did you leave back in Cedar Falls that has your thoughts?"

He forced a smile. "Just the store. Business has been great, so I'll have lots of inventory to replace."

Her smile was warm and genuine. Samuel had missed her smile like a favorite blanket.

"That's good to hear. I'm glad it's working out so well. And you like living there?"

He nodded. "It's not bad at all."

"Even with the never-ending Christmas celebration?"

"They wrap it up around March or April, until they start

winding up again in mid-October." He grinned. "I get a few months' reprieve."

"Super." Evelyn dropped her hands and sat beside him. "So what's really bothering you, Samuel? I'm not your mom, but you could always talk to me before when you were bothered by something."

Yes, he frequently shared concerns with Evelyn and Mike. Such things as teen boy angst to business dreams and fears. They listened and offered the benefit of their wisdom and never judged him for his thoughts or feelings.

"Evelyn, the last few weeks have been complicated. And it has nothing to do with the business."

She waited, so he collected more of his wandering thoughts. "A woman moved back to town, with her little toddler. She's a town native who moved away about six years ago." He ran a hand through his hair. "She's remarkable and the kid is awesome. She thinks he might be on the spectrum."

"Does she know about your past?"

"Oh yeah, I've told her almost everything. And she's fine with all of it. The more I'm with her, the more I want to be. She even got me to foster three kittens for the local rescue group, to give presents this year for her, her son, and her dad." He paused for a big breath. "And I bought a wreath for the door at the tree lighting festival. It reminded me of the white willow one you'd put up."

"Wow, Samuel, that's all so amazing. I'm kind of floored actually."

"I know." He nodded and exhaled. "I know. She's amazing. She's fixing up her dad's run-down house, and she's doing it all by learning as you go through books. That's how we met."

"This sounds like it could be a good experience for you. How do you and the son get along?"

Samuel went on to explain his deep feelings for Adam and

how the boy was embracing him independently and learning more words. He even told how Adam broke away from his mom to run to his store.

"That all sounds wonderful, Samuel. I'm thrilled for you. All your dreams are finally coming true. It appears Dawson and her son are bringing fresh air to your life. So what is the reason you're so down and out?"

He could not bring himself to admit he suggested Dawson find another man, not when he wanted to be her man. Evelyn might have a hard time understanding his logic. Instead he shared the other heavy weight on his heart.

"My birth mother came to visit me."

Two days later Samuel was sitting on the back steps listening to the bird calls. Evelyn always fed the birds and there was a variety of feathered friends dropping in. He watched as they chirped and fluttered over the assortment of feeders and bathing stations Evelyn dutifully maintained. He counted four red cardinal pairs, three bluebirds, three sets of yellow and black goldfinches and countless brown sparrows. A blue jaw swooped in and cawed loudly. The others scattered. The jay grabbed a peanut and swept away in a blue blur.

Beyond, in the yard, the latest foster kid residents were engaged in a heated battle of basketball in the shoveled off court. He remembered the time he lived here, and had jumped, literally, at any chance he could play against another kid, or Mike. Of all the places he lived as a kid, this was the best one.

Mike came out, shut the door with a bang, and stood next to him. Samuel remembered when he thought Mike was the size of a giant; eight-foot-tall, two-hundred-seventy pounds and ripped as steel bars. He'd been in awe of the man who looked like he could haul bags of concrete all day long or be a bar bouncer.

Now, as an adult, he saw Mike as just a regular guy, five foot nine, two-ten, who educated himself, married well to a great woman, and tried to be a decent person. Mike once told him his goal was to have a good business life, be the best husband possible, and leave the world better than he'd found it. Sage words of wisdom.

He rose a hand in greeting to Mike.

"Noisy things, aren't they?" Mike said finally, motioning to the birds fluttering around them.

"I suppose so." Truthfully, he'd never minded them. When he lived here the small ones kept him entertained with their friendly antics and he enjoyed all their colors and songs. He watched as three black and white chickadees flittered to the feeders and tweeted loudly.

"I don't like all the noise or the mess, but they give Evie a lot of pleasure. Therefore I accept them."

"The kids are well-mannered." Samuel nodded to the kids on the court.

"Umm hmm. We got lucky this time. The older Evie and I get, the younger the kids seem to be. You'd think the foster system would one day run out of kids."

Samuel stiffened. He recognized Mike's subtle lead-in. "She told you?" Of course she had. He'd never known either one to keep things from the other. Beyond their business role models they showed him as a youth, it was their communication as a married couple that impressed him the most.

Mike nodded and sat down beside Samuel. "She mentioned you've had an interesting couple of weeks."

Samuel would bet anything she said more than that. He let out a long sigh, shook his head and looked over at Mike. "Where should we start?"

Mike grinned. "Anywhere you want to. How about with your birth mother? Sandy, right?"

Samuel told Mike about her surprise entrance and her claim to be clean, now drug and alcohol free for nearly thirty years.

"I don't even know how I'm supposed to feel about her. What is the etiquette on something like this?"

Mike chuckled. "There is no etiquette. Whatever it is you feel is what you should be feeling. This is one of those no right or wrong things."

Samuel nodded. He felt a lot of things. "Am I supposed to just welcome her with open arms, forgive and forget everything? Just let all those bad years in the system disappear because she's..."

Mike dropped a hand to Samuel's knee. "Samuel, nothing is ever going to erase the years you spent in foster care, or your childhood. The good, the bad, and the in between are all what made you the man you are today. Evie and I have played our parts in that too. Regardless what you and Sandy do or don't do, those years are a part of you. Now, what does Sandy want to do?"

"I've no idea." Mostly because he stormed away before she could say. "Get to know me I guess."

"Would that be so bad? You're a neat guy to know when you finally let your stoic guard down."

Samuel frowned.

Mike laughed again. "Okay, just think about it. She might be interesting to know too. Who knows? You two might have more in common than you realize."

Samuel doubted that.

"So tell me about the woman and the little boy. Dawson?"

His heart swelled. He missed her already! He inhaled and exhaled his gaze locked on the fluttering birds.

"She's perfect, everything I could want in a woman."

"So naturally you're chasing her away." Mike shook his head. "Samuel, sometimes I just don't understand you."

That made two of them. Samuel had a habit to sometimes do things that made him wonder if he was starting with early dementia. "As a child in the system, I didn't play with other kids. No one wanted to play with a foster kid."

"Yes, sometimes that's how it goes. Unfair but the reality for many."

"Especially for a slow kid. And then as an older teen, I no longer cared about hanging out or being with the fun kids. My goals were academic: getting good grades, taking the right classes, getting into the right college. Then as an adult, it became all about college and chasing the degrees. Then I got the bookstore and my whole life has been wrapped in building it up."

"What's your point, Samuel?"

"I don't know how to hang out, or where to go for a fun time. Dawson and Adam need someone who can show them a terrific time, take them on adventures like ice skating, be a male role model for Adam and a protective figure for Dawson. I can't do any of that."

Mike blew out a breath. "Samuel, there is never an age limit or requirement to being a friend and a role model. If there was, Evie and I would be in big trouble. Sometimes hanging out can be done from the sofa with a movie and sharing a bag of popcorn. When you're around people you love, things just naturally evolve. No special skills or classes required."

Samuel coughed. "Love?"

"Yes. Love." Mike got up and held a hand out to Samuel. "Come on, there is something I want you to see."

They drove the short distance into town, and then out of town. "There's this little piece of property I've been keeping an eye on," Mike explained on the drive. "It has great potential and just went on the market a few days ago. It's just below the appraised value."

They arrived in the town of Dustin, about twice the size of Cedar Falls. Already the holiday decorations were coming down. It felt foreign to stand on a sidewalk and not hear Christmas tunes drifting on the wind. It was almost refreshing.

"Here it is." Mike stopped walking in front of a set of glass doors. "This place covers most the city block. It's the bookstore and the adjacent coffeeshop and bakery. There are four apartments above. The one above here is a two-story apartment, quite roomy and super clean. Above the bakery are three smaller, one-and two-bedroom studio units."

Samuel studied the building fronts, the foot traffic and he gazed up to the apartment windows. "That's a lot of property to oversee. And Dustin isn't in a direction of your other businesses. It's kind of...out of the way for you."

Mike nodded. "That's right. I considered that problem. And the best solution I could come up with is for you to buy it. I can float you the down payment if you need it until Chapter Twenty-Five sells. You could run one business and hire a full-time manager for the other. You could live in one apartment and rent the other three out. Expenses are higher here than Cedar Falls, as are the taxes, but the potential for income is quadrupled. I've pulled some numbers if you're interested."

Samuel's gut twisted. From a business point of view, the properties were tempting. He could do a lot with them. But the idea of leaving Cedar Falls, and leaving Dawson, pricked painfully. Even though she made it plain she intended to one day leave.

A movement caught his eye and he watched a woman and a small boy step out of the business at the end of the street. She wore thigh high black boots and wore the same red jacket as Dawson. Her blonde curls bounced in the wind, tamed only by the scarf she wore. She held the hand of a little boy with red mittens and a coat like Adam. He barely resisted the urge to call out and go after them. But it was crazy to think they were way over here in Dustin. Still…his chest compressed.

"Samuel?"

Mike's concerned voice reached out and touched him. Exhaling a deep sigh, he tore his gaze off the retreating pair. "I don't know."

"Don't forget the added bonus that this town isn't Santa's little year-round village."

There was that. Still…

"Unless you're married to the Cedar Falls property. Chapter Twenty-Five?"

Married. What a funny term to use.

"I would assume it needs a lot of cash up front. I might have to liquify what I have in Cedar Falls, even with your float. There's still the startup expenses."

"Tell you what. I'll front the down payment and cover your startup costs. You pay me back, with interest once you sell Chapter Twenty-Five and show a profit with this." He lightly punched Samuel's arm and grinned. "This could be the start of your first million, Samuel."

And the end of any future with Dawson and Adam. Which was destined to happen anyway.

"Let me think about it, okay?"

CHAPTER 10

W hat followed for Dawson were the longest and hardest days of her life. She banged and pounded and wrestled through the house repairs from just after breakfast until long after the sun went down. She hauled the pre-split firewood that Samuel so thoughtfully provided inside each night. The crackling fire was one of her moments of peace.

She drove her dad to Higgins and back for more tests and doctor visits. He flat out denied there were any problems and assured her Joshua would set her straight when he returned. Apparently, his doctors felt differently, and she hoped each new day might bring a surprise return of the highly esteemed Joshua. She had a thing or two to say to her dear brother when he did show.

Her dad's moods ranged from professionally civil to cantankerously harsh, and they could change by the day or even by the hour. She felt like she was on thin ice with him. Sometimes she just looked at him, at an utter loss for words. What happened to those sentimental moments Christmas Day when he gave her those beautiful pieces of jewelry? She treasured the gift, and the moment, but she'd trade her mom's jewels for one day of that moment with her dad.

Her only breaks were when she and Adam escaped to town alone for a few hours. They stopped at the bookstore and she let Adam play while she sat in the dimmed room and cuddled the kittens. Sampson seemed especially lonely, so she gave him extra attention.

"He sure spoiled you, didn't he?" she asked one day, nuzzling the baby's fur. She sniffed, hoping for a scent of Samuel but she only sniffed fluffy kitten. Clean, warm, and cottony soft. Watching the babies tussle, tangle, chase, and bat give her heart a happy lift and let her laugh through her tears.

What was going to happen when he returned?

Twice Adam climbed into her lap, hugged her neck, and patted her cheek. "Samuel?" he asked, pointing to the counter or to the upstairs apartment.

"No, baby, he's not here right now. He had to leave for a little while." She sniffed back the tears and he puckered up into a pout. One time he brought her the garland Samuel had left coiled on the counter.

"Twee?"

"The tree is gone, sweetie. It was time to put it away." Never mind their tree was still up. She'd left Samuel's Charlie Brown tree in the back storage where Adam wouldn't see it. But he found the garland.

"Come on, sweetie, let's go skating." She was finished with the cats for the day, had brushed them within an inch of their lives, and couldn't stand sitting in the empty bookstore any longer. Sometimes it felt like it had been abandoned. Well, she supposed it had been.

Skating with Adam was her other reprieve. She splurged and bought him a pair of after-Christmas priced skates at Pete's General Store and began his first lessons. Kurt usually met them there too. She wasn't sure if he just happened to show up when they were there or if he stalked them when they came to town. Maybe he just happened to spend a lot of time there.

She still couldn't skate with Kurt, free as the wind like they used too, but she liked to watch him glide effortlessly. He made it look so easy.

"See that, Adam? One day you can do that."

He gave it a good try. He stuck his arms out, wind milling to find his balance. He learned how to push off, laughing merrily when he got it. He mastered how to turn, fall, and stop. He was just...slow at all of them. In her heart, Dawson knew it took time to learn and master a new skill. And Adam was enjoying the lessons Samuel would patiently teach.

"Isn't he ever going to get this?" Kurt asked one day. "It isn't that hard."

Not for someone who had done it every winter for years. His words seared her heart. "This is his first time. You were a rookie once too," she said, jumping to defend her son. Kurt sniffed and sped away, sailing across the ice like a sailboat over the lake. A piece of Dawson's heart quivered and split like dry wood, "Don't you worry, honey, you are doing fine." She tapped his nose with her finger.

"Mean," Adam said after Kurt pushed off and made another sailing sweep around the rink.

A truth hit her, almost knocking her to the ice. Once upon a time she had adored Kurt for his brazen behavior. She felt wild and free with him. Together they were unstoppable. That was years ago. She was a mother now, she had responsibilities. Kurt skated and acted as though they were still teenagers. He might be fun, but she needed stable and reliable.

She needed someone like Samuel, who has closed himself off so much that he left town.

"Come on, sweetie. Back to the car."

Kurt caught them as she was removing their skates and putting their boots back on.

"Hey, why you leaving so soon? We barely had a chance to skate."

"We need to go back home. My dad's waiting."

Kurt leaned against the tree where the bench sat. "Yeah? I was going to ask you out to dinner. I thought we could see if our old spark was still alive."

There was no doubt the spark was still alive, but it was now tempered with maturity—the one thing Kurt lacked. "Kurt, tell me in all honesty." She fixed him with a hard look. "How do you feel about my child?"

He blinked, taken aback. He looked at Adam, momentarily working up an answer. "I think it's neat you have a kid."

Dawson wondered what made her ask the question, but now that she thought about it, not once had Kurt tried to engage with Adam, or make any effort to include him in anything.

"So it would be okay for me to bring Alex along on a date?" She folded her arms over her chest.

"Uh...um...well, yeah, I guess so, if you wanted to."

Dawson could see the last thing Kurt wanted on a date was a tag-along child, not when he couldn't even attempt to know Adam's name. "Kurt, I appreciate the offer, and it was nice to see you again. But I'm a mother first and that always must be a priority in anything and everything I do. Anyone who cannot embrace that philosophy with me will not be able to be a regular part of my life. Do you understand?"

"Yeah, I get it." Kurt backed off, looking like she was handing him burning sticks of dynamite. "It's been real, Dawson. See you around."

After that, when Kurt showed up, she made it a point to leave soon afterward.

And finally, each night she would fall into bed, exhausted by the day, crying into her pillow, and wondering when Samuel would return. And what was going to happen when he did?

"What happens when you listen to a tea kettle whistle?"

"Huh?" Samuel looked up from scrolling through his phone. He glanced at the stove but didn't see a burner warming a kettle. He looked back at Evelyn. "Did you want a cup of tea?" His news feed could wait, and he started to get up.

"Sure, if you'd like to join me, set the water to boil."

It was Evelyn who taught him to appreciate a fine cup of tea and she refined his taste in good herbal blends. He scanned the flavors she had on the shelf, running a fingertip along as he read each box. "White, green, vanilla chai, oolong, hibiscus, ginger and mandarin, or valerian and bee balm?"

"Surprise me." She waved a hand at the stove and sat down. He dropped two mesh steeping balls into the cups and joined her. He crossed his arms and leaned on the table.

"Anything good?" she asked, inclining her head at the phone at his elbow.

"Nope. Just the same old news of late. Caught between two big holidays, we're at a lull."

She nodded. "That's what Mike says every year at this time."

The kettle whistled and Samuel poured the water. He arranged the cups, serving kettle and sweetener on Evelyn's silver service set and carried it to the table. For a moment they busied themselves with crafting the perfect cup of tea.

"Very nice. Now, what happens when you listen to a tea kettle whistle and ignore it?"

He considered that a moment. "Eventually the boiling water will evaporate, and the kettle will burn. If ignored long enough, it could be disastrous."

She reached across the space separating them, placing her hand on his arm. "Yes, and that's what is going on with you, Samuel."

He blinked. "I'm boiling or evaporating or becoming disastrous?"

"All of the above. You're ignoring the call of Cedar Falls. You have your mother waiting there."

"Maybe. She could have crawled back to Johnson County or wherever she came from."

She gave him a disapproving glare and continued. "You also have a charming lady friend with an adorable toddler who miss you."

"I don't know that she misses me. It'd be nice to think that, but I have no proof."

"And last, you have the clock ticking on a generous offer Mike made you for a business property that will not last for long. Someone is going to snatch that place in Dustin up if you procrastinate, not able to decide if you can stand to leave Cedar Falls, and Dawson, for good."

"Evelyn—"

"Samuel, your tea kettle is whistling loud and long." She wagged a finger at him. "You better figure out which burner to turn off, and soon, or you're going to be in a mess of trouble."

He chuckled, stood up and moved to her side. He bent, brushed her hair aside and gave her a kiss on the cheek. "Evelyn, you've always had the sweetest ways to kick my backside."

He grabbed his jacket and headed outside. The air was cold and crisp, brushing his skin like a bristled paintbrush. He looked up into the gray sky and smiled at the small flakes tumbling from the tree limbs. He swore he smelled Dawson's peach and lavender perfume in the fresh air.

"Magic in the snow." He stooped over and scooped up a handful of snow, weighing it in his hand. How many times had

Adam or Dawson mentioned that phrase? He saw frozen water droplets, insulation in an emergency, and a host of other practical applications and explanations. And they saw magic. Right now, he needed some magic.

He reached the end of the driveway and stood beside a big oak tree, just watching the snow tumble down. Eventually he heard Mike's truck.

Mike rolled to a stop and lowered his window. "Aren't you a sight, just standing around with your hands in your pockets, staring up." He chuckled. "What are you looking for?"

"Just some magic. You happen to have any laying around?"

Mike's smile got bigger. "Get in. I'll drive you up to the house."

He wasn't ready to return, but he climbed into the cab anyway. Mike turned down the radio and Samuel caught the disappearing strands of an opera song.

"I'll be leaving this afternoon, heading back to Cedar Falls," he said.

Mike nodded. "What made you decide to go now? Evie and I were hoping you'd stay till after New Year's."

Samuel chuckled. "Well, Evie just gave me a polite boot to the backside, effectively telling me I'm waiting too long while the kettle is boiling."

"She did?" Mike parked the truck and cut the ignition. He turned to Samuel, his expression serious. "Woman's darn intuitive. Which burner are you going to turn off?"

Samuel used to grit his teeth at their use of metaphors, and now he remembered why. He dragged a hand through his hair. "I don't know, but she's right. I need to do something." He fiddled with the window crank a moment. "I think I waited too long to say I loved her."

"Dawson? Or your mother?"

His head swiveled to Mike, who raised his hands. "Hey, legit question. You have a lot of kettles whistling."

"Can we just stop with the metaphors please? I get it."

Mike laughed. He placed his hand on Samuel's shoulder. The heavy weight felt warm and comforting. "Look, we've enjoyed having you back with us. You're welcome any time, don't wait for a holiday. But we know you have a life there, and people who count on you. As far as foster children go, you have made Evie and I the proudest. What you decide to do about Dawson—and your mother—is ultimately up to you. We have faith you will make the right choices. But, son, would you mind a small bit of advice?"

His throat suddenly tight, his chest swelling, Samuel nodded.

"You said you waited too long. No, that's not true. It's never too late unless you don't say it at all. Tell her what you're feeling in your heart, not what your logical, analytical mind is telling you. And as far as your mother goes, she put a lot of work into finding you. Would it hurt to give her the benefit of the doubt? Maybe she woke up one day and realized she'd lost you and she regrets it. Maybe she just wants your forgiveness. Or your friendship. Whatever she wants, and what you need, you won't find out until you talk to her with an open mind."

Tears pricked Samuel's eyes and he blinked rapidly. "You sure talk a lot," he said, his voice husky.

"I love you too. Drive safe. And call us when you get there."

Half an hour later he hugged them both again, thanked them for their hospitality and promised to call. He toyed with the radio stations until he found a nice jazz station. As the miles rolled by, he mulled their sage words of advice over. He made a couple pit stops along the way, including one spontaneous stop. By the time he reached Chapter Twenty-Five, it was late, and he had made up his mind on a couple of things.

The streetlights cast a welcoming yellow glow as he slowed

down through town. The red ribbons tied on each pole fluttered in the wind. Doors were graced with illuminated wreaths and lawns were decorated with animated angels and reindeer. Candles glowed in windows. The big tree in the center shined like a multi-hued star and assorted windows held lighted gingerbread and nutcracker characters, stars, and oversized snowflakes.

Hallmark. He eased out a weary breath. And home.

He parked and unlocked the door, suddenly eager to see Sampson. He missed that crazy cat. Tomorrow he'd call Barb and talk to her about adopting the feline.

He entered the dimmed store and moved toward the stairs, his bag in his hand. He stopped, his heart thudding at the human-sized shape slumped in the chair by the counter. In the dark, his eyes couldn't make out any distinguishing features. Then he caught a faint whiff of a familiar perfume. He couldn't be imagining it this time.

"Dawson?"

"Shh. Don't wake Adam." She rose out of the chair with a finger to her lips. She looked over to the front window and he followed her gaze to see little Adam spread out on a mat, sound asleep under a blanket.

"What are you guys doing here? It's late."

She yawned and pushed her hair out of the way. "I was waiting on dad to go to bed and then we'd go home. I guess we both fell asleep." She searched his face. "Are you mad?"

Mad? That she had to hide out here to wait for her dad to go to bed? Yes, he was mad, but not at her. "How have things been for you two?" Even in the dark he could see the sorrow on her face.

"Good and bad. He fights me on the medical stuff. Lots of tests and nothing conclusive yet, but the doctors feel something's off. Normally I can deal with it, but earlier today he jumped me about not taking down the tree yet. Mom's memory got dragged into it, I said a few bad things and left in a huff. I swore I wouldn't go back until he was in bed."

He blew out a breath. "And what about tomorrow?"

"By tomorrow he might forget all about it. If not, I'll take the stupid tree down if it makes him happy."

He looked around, his gaze lingering on Adam. "Look, I'm glad you're here. I was going to come out and talk to you in the morning. Why don't we go upstairs so we can talk above a whisper?"

Something flashed over her face, and he wondered what it was, as it faded just as quick. She nodded and stepped toward the stairs. He watched as the kittens tumbled out of their carrier and latched onto their legs. He snagged Sampson and cradled the beast to his chest. He noticed she did the same with the gray kitten for a moment before putting it back down with the third kitten.

Upstairs he turned on the lights and put the kettle on. "Would you like a cup of tea?"

She nodded again as she sat at the table, hands in her lap as she watched him.

He dropped his bag on the bed and sat down across from her.

CHAPTER 11

Dawson worked hard to keep from either wringing her hands or thumping them against her leg. Now that Samuel was back, she was terrified. Of what he might say next. He seemed upset about her and Adam dozing off in his bookstore. And now, as he prepared the tea, he held himself tight, from his jaw to his spine. Rigid emotions rolled off him like smoke.

"Did you have a nice trip out of town?" she asked when she couldn't stand the silence.

"Yes. I went back home to my last foster parents."

Sometimes going home was a good thing. And sometimes it wasn't. He poured the water and brought the cups, sugar, honey, and cream and spoons to the table. "Sorry, I don't have fancy tea service like my foster mom does. Please, help yourself."

She would have preferred cocoa, but the tea was warm, and it smelled good. Lavender and lemon. She only added a bit of honey and stirred. Samuel took a sip and pushed the cup aside.

"Dawson, I've had a lot of time to think and there's some things I need to share with you." He drew in a big breath.

Her heartrate doubled as she held her breath. Her chest

constricted and the sweetness of the tea turned to mud on her tongue. Still, she waited as he gathered both his thoughts and himself.

"I was wrong about a few things. Like when I told you to find another guy to be a male role model for Adam. I just spent the last few days around the best role model I ever knew. Mike is a fantastic man and his wife is a wonderful woman and anyone would be hard pressed to find better role models. And they have had a huge influence in my life, so I think I can be a decent male role model for Adam. That other guy you skated with might be fun, and that's why I suggested you settle for him. Because you deserve some fun. I can't give you much fun, but I'm willing to learn how. But I sure can give you steadfastness and faithfulness."

She opened her mouth to respond but he moved forward to place a finger against her lips. The touch created a lightning reaction from her lips, to her cheeks, to her throat, and quickly spread all over her body.

"And I think you and I had something wonderful going too. You don't know it, but you bring magic to the snow. You bring magic to everything. You have magic in your heart, and it glows like golden glitter or something and it just affects everything you touch, including my heart."

He dragged a hand through his hair. He caught her hands in his. His thumbs rubbed circles over her knuckles. Shivers slid over her.

"Dawson, I've lived without love for most of my years. I've loved briefly without life. I've learned to do one but never both. You make me want to have both life, and love, but only if I can have them with you. And Adam.

Her heart crushed and tears burned her eyes. "Samuel, I knew all along you were the perfect man for me and Adam. Kurt is fun and going down memory lane with him was nice. But he lacks maturity." She shook her head. "Adam doesn't like him much, but he loves you. That tells me all I need to know."

Samuel smiled and she smiled back, then sobered and asked, "What about your mother?"

"I was wrong and rude in how I dealt with her too. This isn't easy for me, but if she comes back, I'll be more open-minded and hear her out. I'm still not sure what I feel about her, but as much as I preached forgiveness to you about your dad, I would be a hypocrite if I didn't take a lesson for myself. Christmas is all about forgiveness, right."

"You've been busy."

He lifted a shoulder in a shrug. "Not really. Just thinking mostly. But I did stop and get you something on the way back. Hold on." He moved over to the bed, pushed Sampson gently out of the way, and shifted through his duffle bag. She watched, still amazed at the things he'd had to share. He returned and placed a small box in her palm. It was dark blue with a white satin ribbon. The name Infinity Jewelers was embossed in silver across the top.

Her pulse raced and looked into his eyes. "Is it an ugly sweater broach?"

He grinned. "Open it and see."

She opened the box to reveal a stunning silver band with a small, heart-shaped opal sparkling in the center. She slipped it on. "A perfect fit." She angled the stone at the light and the shimmering facets of blue, pink, and green shifted from soft iridescent to fiery shades of bolder colors. She gaped at it for a moment, speechless.

"Do you like it?"

"Yes, I do. Very much. For a man who says he doesn't give gifts, you have been quite generous."

"Call me old-fashioned, but that's a promise ring. One day I hope to ask your dad for his permission to marry you and I hope

Adam can be our ring bearer. But until that time comes, I want to promise to be your steady rock, Adam's role model, and be as large a part in your lives as you will allow me to. If you would wear that ring for everyone to see, I would be incredibly happy. Until such time I get on bended knee with an engagement ring."

Bless his heart, but he sounded nervous. She forced her attention away from the sparkling opal. "I love it, it's beautiful. I'd be honored to wear this as a promise from you." She giggled. "But the idea of you on bended knee does make my heart flutter."

He coughed and glanced at Sampson. "Good. There's a few more things I'd like to do, but they'll have to wait until tomorrow. I think we should contact Barb about adopting two of these kittens. I do feel bad about the third one though."

Dawson held up a hand. "The third kitten is what they call a tuxedo. Barb assures me people like tuxedos for their outgoing and fun personalities. Usually more so than tabbies and grays. She said she's already had two phone calls from people interested in her. We wanted to wait until you get back before having people come in to meet the kitten. Chances are, she would probably be leaving soon anyway."

He let out an audible sigh. "Good to know. The other thing is I'd like to head down to the tree lot and see if they have any trees left over. I tossed my little tree before I left, but maybe I can still find a nice one and decorate it with that cranberry and popcorn garland."

She grinned. "That is sweet of you. I rescued your tree and wreath and they are in the storage room. But if you put up a real tree this season, the residents will expect it from you every year."

He looked down for a moment. "Yeah, I know. Guess it won't kill me to put up a tree."

He stood up and took her hands, pulling her into his embrace. It felt so good to be held in his arms. She relaxed and inhaled his clean spicy scent. His voice rumbled at her ear.

"I also guess it won't kill me to rehang the wreath, and maybe a mistletoe."

Dawson smiled and hugged him tight. He inclined his head to hers and she eagerly sought his lips on hers. He tasted of herbal tea and sweet creamer. His rough beard scraped her chin. His hands moved to her waist as their kiss—and promise—deepened.

She had found permanent happiness for herself and her son. For now they would raise kittens, and she hoped someday they raised more children.

Eager to hear what's next for Ryan Jo Summers?

Join her mailing list!

www.ryanjosummers.com/contact.html

Don't miss out on your next favorite book!
Join the Satin Romance mailing list
www.satinromance.com/mail.html

THANK YOU FOR READING

❄

Did you enjoy this book?

We invite you to leave a review at your favorite book site, such
as Goodreads, Amazon, Barnes & Noble, etc.

DID YOU KNOW THAT LEAVING A REVIEW...

- Helps other readers find books they may enjoy.
- Gives you a chance to let your voice be heard.
- Gives authors recognition for their hard work.
- Doesn't have to be long. A sentence or two about why
  you liked the book will do.

WILD WHISPERS

CHAPTER ONE

Season Moriarty gripped the steering wheel, feeling herself tighten with tension. According to the sign she just passed, she was almost there. It felt like she'd been driving forever, but it was only an hour since she refueled and left Riverton. The sign she passed was one of the first indications of life beyond the patches of dried grass and bare trees. Their ghostly silhouettes did nothing to comfort her. Reflecting, she had to admit these western highways had a habit of appearing never-ending if one wasn't used to such wide-open spaces. She felt more at home in the rolling green grass of Kentucky.

At least the roads were in good condition considering the early January weather. She was thankful for the good fortune of avoiding severe storms during her long trek from Florida to Wyoming. Why hadn't she just taken a plane? At the time, the drive seemed like a good idea. Blowing out a shaky breath, she patted the steering wheel. Only two more miles to go and she would be there. Heritage Farms.

And possibly the start of her new future. Or at the very least, a job interview.

Seeing an advertisement last month for a head trainer at

Heritage Farms, famed birth place of some of the greatest record breakers of the turf, she'd written. Preparing her resume, credentials, and references all in a tidy little package, she sent it out into the postal world with a prayer and a kiss. She appreciated the old-fashioned charm of someone who still preferred snail mail paper over digital downloads and emails with pasted-in documents. Considering the reputation of Heritage Farms, and the elusive owner, she expected an old-fashioned gentleman.

The owner, Ty Masters, had written back, requesting she come for the weekend. Since there were a number of qualified applicants, he was offering everyone a free weekend vacation at the farm in exchange for an interview. One lucky applicant would end the vacation with a new job contract. Either way, Season surmised, just spending the weekend at Heritage Farms was quite an honor by itself. It was history and fame come to life.

Taking her mind off the fact she was quickly approaching her destination, Season thought about the reclusive owner of the farm. What she, or anyone else, knew about Mr. Masters would barely fill a bucket. He had been born to wealthy English parents. He was rumored to be the black sheep of the family, always seeming to have different ideas than anyone else. The fact that he preferred to live in the wide-open spaces of Wyoming and fly his racehorses to the tracks east and west supported this. Most all other racehorse farms were kept relatively close to the tracks themselves.

When Ty Masters' parents died, he took his share of the vast inheritance and came to America with one foundation stallion. With that single stallion, he worked hard and gradually built the world famous and respected Heritage Farms.

People seemed to know more about the incredible horses that came from the farm and their record-breaking feats than they did about the man who started it all. Every once in a while, he would allow a few snapshots of himself from within the winners' circle, hiding his face behind something and always refusing to comment. It was if he preferred remaining a mystery to the fans and keeping the spotlight on his horses instead. Season liked how he gave more credit to his jockey and horses. It showed he didn't possess an inflated ego like some racehorse owners she knew. A few acted like they had gone out and ran around the track themselves. Mr. Masters earned a bonus point in her opinion.

However, it struck her as odd that he would choose to name his farm Heritage when he clearly wanted nothing to do with his own. Rumors flying around the tracks say he left brothers and a wife in England.

Well, none of that mattered now, she decided as she turned her small pickup truck onto a dirt road labeled Heritage Way. The driveway? One step closer at least. All that mattered was she do well at this interview and get that job. She needed this job, so she had to do better than the other applicants. Absently she wondered who they were. Anyone she might know? The racing world could be a small world too.

Topping a small hill, Heritage Farms spilled into view, giving her the first look at history come alive. Driving past pastures closed in with white planked fences, they looked out of place in the wilds of Wyoming. Miles of white fences stretching across acres of green grass was what you expected to see on the horse farms in Florida, not way out here. Nonetheless, horses grazed lazily in the pastures, soaking up the late afternoon sunshine, not caring if it were Florida or Wyoming sunshine. It was all the same to a horse.

Stopping the truck, she looked them over carefully; a few raised their heads to peer curiously at her before resuming their grazing. She liked what she saw in their confirmation, and she stepped back on the gas, resuming her slow descent down the long, winding driveway.

Several white, crisp outbuildings scattered the landscape. An oval training track lay in the distance. Further to one side, she saw a sprawling white, two-level house. Stately pillars flanked the long balcony. A wistful sigh escaped her. It would be nice to live in such a lovely home.

Driving under the iron arch with a horse statue standing atop a circle, she grinned at the letters *HF* inside. She'd finally made it! She was here! Braking to a stop beside five other dusty and travel worn vehicles, she let out a pent-up breath. One hurdle successfully completed.

Stepping out, she leisurely stretched, sucking in a big lungful of cool mountain air and took in the views of the snowy mountains high in the distance. The air smelled fresh and clean. So different. So good. She bent over to touch her toes, then reached up over her head, and eased the kinks out. It felt good to stretch and feel her muscles expand. Twisting her torso each direction, she continued surveying her majestic surroundings.

It was beautiful here to say the least. Exhilaration chased away her road weariness.

"Very nice. May I see that again?"

A deep male voice behind her made her jump. Whirling, she spotted a tall man leaning causally against an equally tall chestnut horse. He stared at her, smug amusement lighting blue eyes. He towered over her five feet five inches. A well-worn, almost battered cowboy hat covered his head, but a few defiant locks of dusty blonde hair still managed to peek out from under it. A mustache sat under his nose, looking like a comfy caterpillar. Full lips curled up into a mocking grin.

A few soiled patches of straw clung to his faded denim jacket and his form-fitting blue jeans. If he were showered and in cleaner clothes, he might appear handsome. If he were not wearing that mocking smile. He had one of those familiar kind of faces, like she had seen him somewhere before. Nothing came immediately to mind though. It was doubtful. He had most likely never left the Wyoming area in his life.

"That was the best thing I have seen all day," he drawled slowly. "Care to repeat it?"

A male chauvinist. Suddenly, she felt no amount of soap could ever make this man appear handsome. In her line of work, male chauvinists were an occupational hazard. Still, they always made her skin crawl.

"Sorry, only one to a customer and that was for the horse," she said, mustering as much patience and charm as possible. "Could you please tell me where the trainer's interviews are being held?"

The mocking smile instantly vanished like a wisp of smoke. The man ducked his head, his hat shading his eyes. "Inside the house, after supper," he murmured. Pulling the horse's lead shank, he quickly headed for one of the barns, seemingly not able to get away from her quick enough now.

Shrugging, Season wondered what got into him. Well, whatever it was, at least he was gone now. Good riddance. She always got along well with the stable hands, but if she got this job he might be the exception. She grabbed her duffel bags from the truck, and headed up the flagstone path leading to the elegant house.

Sensing someone was watching her, she glanced over her shoulder. The parking yard was empty. The blond man with the chestnut was gone. Somewhere a horse snorted. Quiet blanketed the area.

"All right, Season, get a grip," she told herself softly. "You made it. You're here now. Don't lose it just because you ran into a chauvinistic jerk right away. You can handle this."

Finishing her pep talk, she mounted the stone steps to the

brown wooden door. Knocking, she wondered if the illustrious Mr. Masters would personally greet her. Just in case, she put on the brightest, best smile she could, her breath held, shoulders straight, and ready for anything.

Within a few minutes the door swung open and a pimply faced teen-age boy stood there.

"You seriously lost or something?" he asked, clearly surprised to see her. He popped a bubble with his gum, chewing noisily.

"No. I'm here to interview for the trainer's position." Rattled, Season worked to recover. Did Mr. Masters have a teen-age son? She couldn't make the image work in her mind. It did not go with the reputation he made of himself. No one ever spoke of a child—an heir to the mighty Heritage legacy.

The boy's face dropped. "The trainer's position?" he repeated, as if he hadn't heard right. "Well, the rest are over in the library room I guess." He jerked a thumb behind him as he motioned her in and then started walking past her, back outside.

"Wait! Who are you?" she spun and called out quickly.

"I'm Ernie. I deliver Mr. Masters' weekly groceries," he said, waving his hand behind him and leaving her standing at the foyer of the house.

Hoping it was okay to traipse around the house, looking for the library, she wondered why the host hadn't yet put in an appearance. And the delivery boy answered the door? How odd.

Following the sounds of male voices, she came to a huge room, lined wall to wall with books. A giant stone fireplace dominated one wall, with a fire cheerily snapping. Cleverly placed chairs invited people to sit and relax. The crackling fire filled the room with the scent of pine, mixing with the smell of old books. Five men, all middle-aged, sat around, smoking and joking, telling stories and resting.

Glancing at them, she did not recognize any. All dressed the same, in faded western shirts, blue jeans and cowboy hats, they instantly reminded Season of the stable hand out in the yard. How quaint. Dropping her duffel bags, she loudly cleared her throat, announcing her presence.

"You guys all here for the interviews too?" she asked cheerfully when they looked up.

"You a horse trainer?" one asked boldly, drawing from his cigarette, doubt written on the deep lines of his face.

"Yes, of course." Season stepped into the room, her friendly smile fading as she noticed their collective looks of surprise. Much the same as the teen-age boy at the door.

"What did I say?" she asked any of them, feeling a chill slithering up her spine. Whatever was going on around here, she was starting not to like it much at all. And where was the missing host, Mr. Masters? The inviting fire and pine scent of the room faded away, replaced by the startled and suspicious glares from the men. She needed somewhere else to go and wait for Masters.

Hearing sounds coming from another room, she followed the noise, hoping the next person she encountered would be more helpful, or be her weekend host. Hopefully he wouldn't be upset with her exploring around the house.

At the end of the hall, she stepped into a kitchen, so huge it looked like the cook could feed an army. Shiny clean and modern, it was out of place with the rustic decor she'd noticed so far. A long shiny counter top stretched from end to end, two ovens were stacked by the twin stoves and a jumbo fridge and freezer sat along another wall. Three bar stools lined one side of the long counter. An industrial sized coffee machine and several cups rested on one end. A small table and three more chairs sat nestled near the coffee machine. Fresh fruit sat in a bowl on the table and another on the counter.

A heavy set, burly man with a white apron tied daintily around his wide waist was putting groceries away. He was, without exception, the largest man she had ever seen. Seemingly unbalanced, his small, bald head sat upon a fat, short neck and broad shoulders.

Clearing her throat again, she crossed the kitchen's threshold. The man turned around slowly, a chewed up, unlit cigar dangling from his mouth. Small, dark eyes checked her over, surprised flickering in them.

"Yeah?" he snarled irritably, the noise ending in something of a grunt.

Oh Mercy, they just kept getting stranger and stranger. Convinced she'd never make it to the interview anyway, she pasted on a pale smile. "I'm Season Moriarty, and I'm here for the trainer's interview." This time she was more prepared for the same look of surprise that crossed his pudgy face.

Recovering quickly, he pulled out his cigar, stuck his mammoth hand out to her, smiled broadly and introducing himself as Moose, cook of Heritage Farms.

"Pleased to meet you, Ms. Moriarty," he said, taking his gigantic hand and dwarfing hers, giving it a solid pump. A grateful sigh of relief escaped Season as she met his friendly grin.

Moose took her around the lower level of the house, showing her the room she would use for the weekend, the study where Mr. Masters would conduct interviews, and added that supper was served at six. Rounding out the tour he added that Mr. Masters would begin interviews promptly at seven and did not like to be kept waiting.

Supper was an uncomfortable affair. With only three bar stools or three chairs to choose from, Season was stuck at the small table with the other men staring curiously at her. She ignored the hushed murmurs until she'd finished her meal and had enough of the men. Marching into the library, she picked the most comfortable chair, near the snapping fire. The Grandfather clock assured her she still had plenty of time before seven and she'd just bet the men would reassemble back in the library.

Shortly after the men strolled in, lighting cigars and pouring drinks from the bar, she rose. She could finish her waiting time by making sure she was totally polished. Selecting a not-so-faded pair of blue jeans and an ivory and peach checkered sweater, she surveyed herself in the full-length mirror. Nice. Both professional and western looking at the same time without either look being too much. Removing all traces of makeup, she completed the professional look by pulling her unruly brown curls into a single thick braid trailing down her back.

Five minutes before seven, she congregated with the other applicants outside the study door. Smoke and travel dust still clung to them, making her glad she took the extra few minutes for a fast shower. Five times she heard a deep masculine voice coming from behind the heavy oak door, calling out a name and nothing more. Five times one of the men entered, disappearing into the depths of the dark room beyond. Each one returned approximately twenty minutes later, looking shell shocked and worn.

Like a mighty clap of thunder, Season's name was the last one called. Drawing an uneven breath, she closed her eyes for a moment, pulling from within herself, and then strolled into the room.

It was dark inside, largely due to the dark paneled walls, dark carpeting and heavy drapery. It was a man's room. It was a giant of a room. A true primeval man cave. The fire blazing in the stone fireplace did nothing to dispel the dim lighting. Suddenly she was eager to meet the man.

"Close the door," the ominous voice ordered.

Doing so, she turned back, stopping dead as her eyes adjusted to the low light and she recognized the man behind the desk. She felt her mouth hanging open, first in surprise, then disbelief and horror. No, it couldn't be.

"If you leave your mouth open too long, a bug will fly in," the voice warned harshly. "Who the devil are you?"

"Season Moriarty." The words tumbled from her tongue as dread filled her, churning in her stomach. Only barely did she acknowledge the heavy English accent.

Ty Masters, the world-famous racer and breeder, was the very same male chauvinist with the chestnut horse she'd met earlier in the yard.

His cowboy hat was off now, lying on the corner of the tidy desk. A thick, clean unruly heap of dusty blonde curls covered his head. Gone were the dirty clothes. He smelled fresh and clean and extremely male and wearing a blue checkered flannel shirt with the top two buttons left undone, showing off a chest lightly peppered with curly hair. She had no doubts he would be wearing hip hugging jeans and boots behind that massive desk. What startled her more was that he actually could be handsome after all. The blue checkered shirt brought out the blue of his eyes.

"That's impossible!" he snarled, dismissing her with an impatient wave. "I have an interview with Season Moriarty for a horse trainer's position. I have no time for bloody jokes, woman. Be gone."

"I am Season Moriarty," she repeated tartly, sensing his anger. He must have thought one of the other men brought her along as a companion. "I have an interview with you. You wrote me back in Florida, asking me to come here for the weekend and to give me an interview," she paused, emphasizing her next few words as though speaking to a dim-witted child. "A job as chief racehorse trainer."

Coolly, he appraised her like a yearling colt at an auction. Leaning back a little in his chair, lifting the two front legs, he took his time. One blond eyebrow lifted as a sardonic grin crept over his face. His eyes, now freed from the obstruction of the hat's brim, were the bluest shade Season had ever seen. Deep blue like the bottomless lake or the clearest sky after a storm.

Forcing herself not to bend from his steady glare, she reeled in her temper. He was the boss; she had to play by his rules if she wanted the job. Pasting a bittersweet smile on her lips, she waited until his inspection was done. Would he get up to check her teeth next? She was beginning to wonder.

"You are Season Moriarty?" he finally spoke, his voice and eyes daring her somehow.

Nodding in curt confirmation, she gladly proved him wrong, "Yes, I am."

"Season," he muttered, bringing the chair back down, shaking his head. "How was I supposed to know Season would end up being a woman," he said to no one in general. "All future advertisements will need to specify photos be included with applications."

Okay, she would overlook how sexist that sounded, and continue to fight for this job. Leaning back a little, she intended to fight hard. "It is a feminine name," Season countered. Yes, a little unusual perhaps, but not worth the attention it seemed to be getting at the moment. What difference did her gender make? She'd been a trainer for several years.

"It sounds like a man's name. As in son of the seas or something," he said, giving her a dark look of accusation.

She started to feel a ball of worry forming in her stomach. Just what was he driving at?

"Sorry to prove you wrong, but Season is my name, has always been my name and has nothing to do with sons or seas. And you can obviously see I am a woman." She hesitated briefly, a light dawning in her mind, making her stomach do a sick little roll. "What exactly does my name have to do with this interview?"

"Everything!" he snapped. Grabbing some papers, he shuffled them around. "Now, I'm very busy so let's just end this and—"

Season blinked in astonishment. He was dismissing her? "Are you saying I'm not qualified solely because I am female?" she demanded of him, feeling her temper rising. Not caring about making a professional impression anymore, she stepped up close to the desk, daring him to look away from her.

"You said it, not me," Ty Masters murmured, staring directly into her eyes, unflinching.

Now she understood why everyone was so puzzled as to her presence. It all made sense now. Why hadn't she picked up on it quicker? Fury, hot and raw, rose up within her, heating her like lava. She stood ramrod straight, using every ounce of self-control not to slap him. She blinked, chasing the red away that swam before her. She could probably claim sexual harassment, but she wanted this job. Dammit, she deserved this job.

Slapping her hands down flat on the desk instead, scattering papers, she leveled her stare into his cool blue pools, noticing with some satisfaction a tiny tick begin working in his jaw.

"My name and my gender are of no concern to you or at this interview," she spoke clearly and distinctly. "My abilities and credentials, however, are." Her gaze fell on a sheet of paper. Her reference page. "Now, if you will be so kind as to review my resume, you will see my qualifications are superior and my references are top notch. They adequately prove I'm capable of doing the job you are asking."

Willing it to happen, she held her breath, concentrating, waiting until he did as she ordered. He was going to look at her application if it killed her. And him.

Suddenly powerless, unable to stop himself, Ty felt himself grabbing the papers and seeing the words before his eyes. He really didn't need to, he already knew what they said. One thing had been clear from the very moment he received the application package; Season Moriarty was the best person for the position.

Both father and grandfather were world renowned horse trainers. Surely they had passed along some family secrets for gaining speed from a horse. Season's experience and past records were more than adequate. Everything he was looking for in a trainer was right here in black and white. He had already intended on hiring this person if the interview went half as good as the application looked. But he never dreamed Season Moriarty would turn out to be a woman!

It wasn't that he didn't like women. He liked them a lot. Just not working with his horses or living on his place. He knew from past experiences that women on his ranch always equaled disaster, trouble he didn't need. Men got into fights over each other's girlfriends, men and women fought over endless things, and it usually ended with the woman leaving and the men all mad at each other. It created friction, distrust, and bad work habits whenever the men had women around. And likewise, prohibiting women to be on the ranch encouraged life to operate smooth and harmoniously, which pleased both Ty, the men, and his horses.

Logically, he had reached the only reasonable explanation: women did not belong on a racehorse ranch. Especially this woman. From the second he saw her turn into the driveway, park and start easing out kinks, his warning lights started flashing and screeching in his mind. Her jeans hugged her long legs, giving the impression she was muscular beneath that medium frame. Her shirt stretched over her lovely bust and the sun shone on her brown hair, burning it to an auburn that matched the chestnut mare he had been leading. At the time, he'd assumed she was a traveling companion of one of the applicants here to watch the horses run for the weekend. Eyeing her now, he realized how terrible an assumption he had made.

He had liked her hair better when it was loose, all wavy and curly, making his fingers itch to touch it, play with it, twirling some around his fingertips. She looked more professional now. Her green eyes, green as the Emerald Isle her family hailed from, had been soft and friendly before, now they were hard, blazing into him, like blazing lights of fire. And making him feel more than a little uncomfortable. Quite an unusual experience.

Wait a minute. Suddenly he wondered why he was the one feeling uncomfortable here. He was the one in control. He was the master. People followed his orders without question. His word was law. Always.

So why did he even care that she was furious? Why did he suddenly feel like a naughty schoolboy? Why was he even continuing this interview? He would give the job to one of the men outside.

So why didn't he?

"Do I have the job or not?" she demanded, her patience just about spent, her green gaze never wavering from his cool glare.

Inwardly, he sighed, feeling something deep inside him collapsing. Realizing he had somehow lost total control of the situation, he also saw he was about to break his number one rule. And worse yet, he was completely unable to stop himself. What just happened? What had she done to him?

"The trainer is to reside here," he heard himself say, the words coming out by themselves. "That person is expected to fly with the horses to the tracks, stay with them for the duration of their final training and race schedule."

"Okay," Season said evenly, eyes boring deeply into his, until he suspected she might crawl into his lap. The thought—and images—both frightened and thrilled him. Shaking his head, he cleared his throat before continuing.

"Everybody is expected to do their share. The trainer is in charge of training, obviously, and to oversee the studs for breeding. Their opinion is wanted for selected breeding partners. Of the horses," he added, swallowing a hard lump and clearing his throat again. "But that person may also be called upon to help feed the stock or do whatever else is required." His eyes lit up dangerously. "Even I have been known to muck out a stall or two," he challenged, taking back a little bit of control from this situation.

"Fine," she agreed crisply. "I can muck stalls with the best of them. I've been mucking stalls since I could barely lift the fork. I have been brushing and grooming since I needed a bucket to reach their backs."

More images popped into his mind, of a brown-haired wisp of a girl standing on an upturned bucket to brush a horse's broad back, or heaving mightily at a pitchfork to muck a pony's stall. That lump in his throat slid south and settled in the pit of his stomach, churning and making a mess of Moose's fine dinner. How could he still manage to convince her not to take the position?

"We are currently racing three horses. One three-year-old colt and a three-year-old filly. I hope to have another two-year-old colt ready for his first start in a few months." He paused, and then added, "Do you believe you can handle all this?" Here was where she could back out gracefully and make an exit easier for both of them. He nearly closed his eyes in prayer as he waited for her response, feeling as though his entire life depended on her answer.

❄

Meeting his challenging gaze Season sensed the currents of electricity coming from him. She also sensed the questions burning in his mind. Giving in and hiring her was costing him a lot, more than he would ever reveal.

"Of course," she said sweetly, flashing a smile, taking a small step away. Was it her imagination or did he sink a little behind that massive desk? Feeling his surprise, she felt a brief thrill of victory. It took a bit of effort but now she had a job!

"You might as well come meet your new charges," he said, not looking, or sounding, overly thrilled. Standing up, he waited for her to move to the door first. "Do I need to remind you these animals are worth thousands and millions of dollars? They are not cart hags," he warned softly.

"Of course not. I have trained a few racehorses before," she reminded him.

"You alone are solely responsible for their health, their happiness and," he paused, "their performance on the tracks." Shouldering past her, he spoke briefly to the men in the library and then wordlessly lead the way outside. Quietly, Season followed her new boss into one of the white barns she'd seen earlier.

"I shall introduce you to our foundation stallion," Ty announced, pride heavy in his voice. He escorted her to the last stall in the row of about twenty. It was the largest stall, sturdy and well-constructed, as was the entire barn. A black head peered over as Ty whispered softly and Season felt a chill creeping up her spine as she approached.

She automatically knew who this creature was. Here was the king of Heritage Farms. Black Warrior. With utmost reverence, she cautiously approached his stall to look him over.

He was a full eighteen hands high plus a little more, huge, jet black and meaner than a cornered wildcat. Looking closer, she noticed the streamlined body, wide nostrils and well-developed shoulders all great racehorses needed. She felt the fire burning in his soul, the fire of pure hatred. This horse, quickly approaching the ripe age of thirty-two was evil, mean and totally unpredictable. But Season knew this was also the horse Ty Masters had gambled his inheritance and life on. This was the one thing he brought from England and gambled everything on this single animal's speed and competitive spirit. Looking at Heritage Farms now, clearly it had been a good gamble.

"His dame was destroyed when he was just a weanling," Ty offered, gazing affectionately at the old stallion. "Folks said she was a killer. Funny thing is folks said the same thing about him and he never killed anyone."

"Not for lack of trying from what I've heard," Season pointed out. The horse's evil deeds were legendary around the tracks. It seemed Ty Masters was the only person who could handle the huge horse with immunity. "I'll safely say he's dangerous."

"He needs a gentle voice and a firm hand," Ty argued. "In the right hands, he is as gentle as a pet lion." Ty's mouth quirked slightly. That was the most polite way to describe Black Warrior.

"This way." Motioning for her to follow, they left the dimness of the barn, stepping out into the cool Wyoming dusk. Ty headed for some distant fence, Season having to take two steps to match one of his giant swinging strides.

Ty slammed to a halt at the gate of a white fence, whistling sharply. Scanning the dark field, Season saw nothing but the outlined silhouette of some trees. Then she heard the echoing beat of pounding hooves and a smile flashed over Ty's face.

Following his gaze to the horizon, she watched a large black horse galloping into sight from the night cover. Sliding to a stop before them, he blew air from his nostrils, tossing his head and whinnying.

"This is our main racer, Sky Hunter." Ty reached out,

affectionately patting the horse's glossy neck. "He is sired by Black Warrior."

If Black Warrior was king, here was the young prince. He was every bit as large as his mighty sire, coal black with four white socks and a striking white blaze racing down his face. He lightly tossed his mane, prancing sideways, unsure what to make of Season. He snorted and blew her direction a few times, looking to Ty for reassurance.

Season saw the same unpredictable wild look in his eyes as she'd noticed in his sire's back in the barn. She reached out to pat him, drawing back when he laced his ears flat, pretending to nip her. Snorting, he pranced away, ears back and head shaking.

"He is no pet," Ty pointed out. "He is powerful and needs to be handled just right." As if to prove his own immunity, he reached a hand out and waited calmly.

Soon Sky Hunter returned, stretched his neck out, sniffing loudly. Taking a step closer, he stomped his foot once, sampling Ty's upturned palm, looking for goodies. Within a mere minute, Ty rubbed his hand along the horse's white blaze, sliding Season a leveled look.

"See, it is all in the handling."

"I'm also new to him. He undoubtedly has known you since he was foaled." Was he implying she wasn't capable of physically handling a large and powerful horse? She'd surprised other men before and she was sure Mr. Masters was going to be in for a surprise soon too. "I will have him eating out of my hand before long."

Sky Hunter snorted once, and as if to prove her wrong, reached out to nip her.

Instinctively, she jumped back, feeling her face grow warm. Glad for the pale moonlight around them, she watched as Sky Hunter curled his lips back in what looked to be a horsey laugh, twist and take off across the field, blending into the night with only his hoof beats echoing behind him.

"It appears our main star feels differently," Ty said slowly, folding his arms along the fence rail.

"Clearly you and Sky Hunter share the same opinions. If you ask me, it's the waste of a perfectly good horse."

Ty blinked in stunned silence.

Season wished she could take the words back, and knew Master's surprise was because no one dared speak to him like that. Except she just had. And he did not immediately bellow out 'You're fired', so she drew in a deep breath and pressed on before the shock on his face was gone. "I assume there are other horses to view?"

"Of course." Galvanized, he strode off in the direction of another barn, leaving her trotting to keep up.

They toured the entire farm by ten o' clock. Season saw the breeding barn, the mare barn, the foaling barn, the weanling barn. She inspected the training track and other points of interest. She saw the airplane hangar where Ty housed the plane for the horses and the adjoining runway.

She met Richmond, the youngster she was to school for his first break in the spring. He was a high stepping blood bay colt. Lacking the cruel spirit of Black Warrior and Sky Hunter, he slowly sniffed her over, finally deciding she was alright. She also met Winter's Dawn, a nice chestnut filly, sired by Black Warrior too. Ty held high hopes for her as a racer. She liked the track, having raced twice and placed well. Ty stressed the right training could coax the last bit of speed out of her. The desire was there, he said, she just needed the skills.

The last horse she met was a stable pony named Doodlebug, a delightful mixture of Welsh and Shetland pony. He had the honor of being Sky Hunter's travel buddy. Barely over twelve hands and covered in white and gray patches, Doodlebug took an immediate liking to Season, sidling up against her and begging for a scratch.

"I see you finally found someone you can properly handle," Ty pointed out, watching the pony make cozy with Season. "I'm afraid Sky Hunter will not be so easy to make friends with. Doodlebug is a friend with everyone he sees." He said the words as if they left a bad taste in his mouth.

Season was struck with the feeling Ty Master had few real, trustworthy friendships. He seemed like a man who could be friendly on the outside, to a point, but managed effectively to keep all people at arm's length. At least he gave her the strong impression he did not want her too close. But she suspected it extended to more people than just her. A sadness filled her at the thought of anyone wanting to be alone.

Measuring her words carefully, Season met his visual stare. "Actually, Doodlebug is the smarter one. He plans ahead to the day he will need someone to lean on." She entwined her fingers into the pony's mane, waiting for his response. He was starting to remind her of a powder keg. If she were not careful, she wouldn't have to worry about having the job.

He forced his gaze away from her, steadily looking out toward the door, as if considering bolting for the exit. *Do I make you that uncomfortable, Mr. Masters?* She nearly asked the question but stopped herself, searching for a better one.

"Don't you ever need somebody?" she asked lightly, still scratching under the pony's mane.

"I try not to," he bit out, stalking away, leaving her alone in the dark with the pony noisily searching her pockets for more treats.

Well! She blew out a breath. She had a challenging new job, a beautiful place to live, and a new boss. And, unless she was mistaken, the battle lines were clearly drawn.

It was unusually warm for Wyoming and the pale moonlight shown bright, cutting through the trees with alabaster rays. Watching Ty's backside as he strode angrily away, Season felt her nerves stringing out like a worn guitar. Knowing no sleep would come to her any time soon, she decided to explore her new home instead. She could use the time alone in the moonlight.

The air was quiet and cool, only a steady breeze blowing across the snowcapped fields, fed by the colder air flowing down from the snowy peaks surrounding the farm. Night birds called to her, beckoning her down past the barns and into the distant fields, away from humanity and horses. Brushing the snow from a rock, she sat down. This space was quiet, serene and tranquil. Just what she needed.

Spreading her arms wide, she closed her eyes, chanting softly. The night winds spoke to her, whispering, filling her with soothing emotions and gentle thoughts, erasing the earlier strains. Her chanting growing faster and louder, she lifted her arms wider and higher, reaching up toward the shining moon. She felt whole, connected, invigorated. As if she were the only person in the world.

Purchase Wild Whispers wherever books are sold online!

ABOUT THE AUTHOR

Ryan Jo Summers is an author who writes across the genres. She pens romance novels blending elements of Inspirational, suspense, mystery, paranormal and time travel in any combination. She covers non-fiction as well as fictional short stories and poetry.

In her spare time, she likes to hang out with her pets, go to the nearby forest and river or gather with friends. She enjoys chess, Mah Jongg, word-find puzzles, and houseplants. She also likes to cook, creating new recipes from old favorites. If she has any time left over, she paints ceramics and acrylics on canvas. She makes her home in a century-old cottage in the beautiful mountains of Western North Carolina.

Visit Ryan Jo at her website to sign up for updates on her writing!

Website: www.ryanjosummers.com
Blog: summersrye.wordpress.com
Facebook: www.facebook.com/RyanJoSummersAuthor